Steamed

**Center Point
Large Print**

**This Large Print Book carries the
Seal of Approval of N.A.V.H.**

Steamed

Jessica Conant-Park
& Susan Conant

CENTER POINT PUBLISHING
THORNDIKE, MAINE

This Center Point Large Print edition
is published in the year 2006 by arrangement with
The Berkley Publishing Group, a division of
Penguin Group (USA) Inc.

Copyright © 2006 by Susan Conant and Jessica Conant-Park.

The text of this Large Print edition is unabridged. In other
aspects, this book may vary from the original edition. Printed in
Thailand. Set in 16-point Times New Roman type.

ISBN 1-58547-788-5

Library of Congress Cataloging-in-Publication Data

Conant-Park, Jessica.
    Steamed / Jessica Conant-Park & Susan Conant.--Center Point large print ed.
    p. cm. -- (A Gourmet girls mystery)
    ISBN 1-58547-788-5 (lib. bdg. : alk. paper)
    1. Women graduate students--Fiction. 2. Cooks--Fiction. 3. Boston (Mass.)--Fiction.
4. Large type books. I. Conant, Susan, 1946- II. Title.

PS3603.O525S74 2006b
813'.6--dc22

                                                                    2006001850

To my personal chef—and husband—Bill, and the best thing he ever helped to cook up, our son, Nicholas.

—Jessica

To my husband, Carter, and the best thing *he* ever helped to cook up, our daughter, Jessica.

—Susan

Acknowledgments

For generous help throughout the writing of this book, we are grateful to Alexa Lewis and Lillian Sober-Ain. We also want to thank our agent, Deborah Schneider, and our editor, Natalee Rosenstein, for their enthusiasm and support for our mother-daughter project.

For their appearances herein, many thanks to everyone at Eagles' Deli, especially Stein and Robert.

ONE

the cushions, gripping a bottle of Jack Daniel's.

Higher education in Boston had officially begun for
the year.

On Saturday morning I woke up at eight, poured a
nasty cup of coffee that had automatically brewed
itself at 5:00 a.m. instead of the programmed time of
8:00 a.m., and plopped myself at my kitchen table to
do some early morning people watching out the
window. I sipped my coffee-sludge and peered down
at the street. My hope was to catch sight of some miserable soul ambling home after a night of drinking or
to witness a minor car accident followed by entertaining screaming and swearing. The good thing about
my neighborhood in Brighton, Massachusetts, was the
excellent opportunity it afforded me to spy on my
neighbors from the safety of my apartment.

Just yesterday I'd enjoyed a good fifteen minutes of
bantering among three college kids attempting to
move a massive seventies-style couch through their
building's small entryway, a space that was clearly too
narrow to accommodate the gigantic sofa. After much
debating and tilting of the couch at varying angles, the
group made one final and admirably collegiate
attempt to move the beast into the apartment. The
effort, which involved bungee cords and ropes, was
aimed at hauling the monstrosity up the side of the
building and through a window. This misguided, if
entertaining, plan failed. I later saw the couch on the
curb with a pleading note written on cardboard, Please
Take Me Away, and one of the students passed out on

9

the cushions, gripping a bottle of Jack Daniel's. Higher education in Boston had officially begun for the year.

Unfortunately, there was no activity this morning. Most of my college neighbors were sleeping it off on this Labor Day weekend, but since I was about to start my graduate studies, I felt obliged to behave like an adult and not spend most of the term in a drunken state while pretending to attend class and do schoolwork. I glanced through my *Welcome to Boston City Graduate School of Social Work* folder with the pointless abbreviation BCGSSW scrawled over every enthusiastic page. "Welcome, Chloe Carter," the first letter began. There followed a tediously detailed breakdown of this Tuesday's orientation, which ran from 8:15 a.m. to 4:00 p.m. Right, like I was going to make it through an entire day of what would turn out to be a team of bright-eyed social work doctoral students leading mobs of us through soul-baring "trust falls" and, as the brochure promised, opportunities to "share our personal stories," especially those that would lead us to "develop social work skills based on an understanding of the impact and influence of socioeconomic, biochemical, familial, and racial factors on mental health and social policy."

The welcome packet went on to assure me that I'd be given the chance to explore my own racist attitudes and the contributions I had made to the downfall of our society. The hour and a half allotted to lunch was supposed to afford me the chance to socialize and thus to begin developing relationships with my fellow students. And most of all, as luck would have it, I was informed that I would be learning to take many "proactive" approaches in my work over the next two years. Quick learner that I am, I immediately embarked on my very first act of proactivity by vowing never, ever to utter the word *proactive* aloud—and damn the consequences, which would probably include getting kicked out of social work school for my blatant failure to demonstrate fluency in the language of political correctness. Many students, I read, were eager participants in coalitions and committees that sent representatives to legislative meetings and protests at the State House. I could pretty much guarantee that I'd do whatever I could to avoid any sort of participation in any of those horrible-sounding groups. As liberal and feminist as I was in many ways, I was not someone who enjoyed engaging in overt displays of my political views.

The letter ended with a "personal" invitation from the president of the school to drop by his office any old time to discuss how my year was progressing. I considered dropping by his office to say that after reading the welcome packet, I was not all that interested in attending BCGSSW. In fact, I was doing so only to get my inheritance from my late and loony Uncle Alan, whose will contained the following moronic clause: "If Chloe Carter wants her inheritance, she must complete a master's degree program in any field this fine young lady selects." The will granted me a moderate monthly stipend during my years of graduate school hell—my term, not the will's—and a lump sum should I actually manage to graduate. When I'd read through the packet, it became clear that social work was a less than ideal choice for me. But I had always enjoyed my undergraduate studies in psychology, and social work wasn't that far off. And it was only two years of school. So, when Uncle Alan died last winter and I was forced to pick something to pretend to study for a few years, I did minimal research into choices, decided I liked helping people, and impulsively applied to this program.

Now here I was, faced with phrases like "social policy," "victims of a capitalist society," and "disenfranchised youth." Not that these weren't important issues; I just didn't want to be trained as some militant avenger of world evil. I'd simply have to avoid courses that focused on anything cosmic, global, or political. But when I examined the class schedule I'd been sent, I found it jammed with required classes, including Global Perspectives on Social Welfare, Peace, and Justice; and U.S. Public Policy Through the Eyes of the Social Worker. As far as I was concerned, the word *eyes* did not belong in a course title—except maybe in Ophthalmology and Therapy? At least I'd gotten into Psychopathology and Deviant Behavior, a course that should be full of juicy details about personality disorders and behavioral problems—I loved that stuff.

So I continued to drink my thick and bitter coffee

and plan my day. I definitely had to do laundry and dishes, but my Saturday was otherwise pretty free. I hoped to meet up tonight with my downstairs neighbor, Noah Bishop. It is a bad idea to date a neighbor, but it is really a bad idea to date someone who lives in your building, especially when you aren't even dating but engaging in some sort of weird, undefined (I hesitate to say) relationship that is mostly built around occasional sex. So, of course, that's what I'd been doing with Noah. And since we lived in an old house converted into condos, the floors creaked and all the tenants could hear who was coming and going, and when and with whom. Noah and I had agreed that we'd be up front if we were sleeping with other people. Well, truth be told, *I* had said that we would be up front, and Noah had made a vague remark about not wanting a relationship now or some such stupid thing that men say so that they don't have to limit their carousing. But desperate for any hint of that boyfriend feeling, I let slide his comments about the need for freedom and not wanting to be exclusive. In other words, I managed not to hear what he was saying. He clearly wasn't long-term material, but since no one else had come along in quite a while and since there was the convenience of only having to walk down a flight of stairs for a thrill, I went ahead and ignored all the monumental warnings that this was an idiotic pursuit. I'd just enjoy a little fling with no regard for the inevitability of disaster.

And Noah was enjoying a fling, too. Just not one

with me. Or not *only* with me, as indicated by the damned bleach blonde in a tight red tank top who was making her way out of our building. Following her was a shirtless Noah. He walked her across the street to her white BMW and planted a quick kiss on her lips as she started the car. I glanced down at my poor little silver Saturn Ion coupe, which I'd been so proud of leasing a few weeks before. Next to her luxury car, it now seemed pathetic. The lovers exchanged a few parting words, inaudible to me, and that sleazy Noah swaggered back toward our house. The pair of shorts he'd tossed on after his fun fest didn't do much to cover his morning glee. Bastard! He knew I lived upstairs. He knew I could see the street from my condo. I was seething. And mortified and ashamed. According to our undefined and open agreement, Noah had been allowed to do whatever he wanted with whatever tacky woman he wanted. It just hadn't seemed to be a real possibility. Why had he needed that twit last night when I'd been right upstairs watching the Discovery Channel until midnight? God, I'd been so dumb. So stupid. I just didn't realize that men existed outside the FOX network who actually behaved in this stereotypical *Playboy* fashion. And now *I* was the stereotype of the girl who thinks she has enticed a reluctant guy into monogamy.

I felt sick to my stomach as I debated the question of who was the bigger dope, Noah or I? I claimed the honor for myself. Idiot Suave downstairs had been the honest one; like some clever lawyer, he'd made the statements required to retain his legal right to go off skirt-chasing whenever he so desired. Jerk! I, on the other hand, had made a poor attempt to convince myself that I didn't care what Noah did when he wasn't with me. I mean, I'd gone to college, for Christ's sake; I wasn't naive. Or was I? I was in the sense that I hadn't counted on Noah's fooling around with anyone else. And I'd missed the possibility that he'd bring someone back to our building and, in essence, parade his female captive in front of me. Unfortunately for me, and probably for eighty or a hundred other women, the hitch was that he was pretty hot.

I'd first met Noah last spring, a few weeks after he'd moved into his second-floor condo. I'd been out on my deck (okay, fire escape) watering my plants when my cat, Gato, had managed to push open the screen door and jet down the steps. I'd made a feeble effort to follow but knew it was a fruitless pursuit. When Gato escaped, he typically waited until sundown to return. Since I was on the second-floor landing and still clutching my watering can, I decided to water the one droopy and unidentifiable plant the new neighbor had placed on the railing. I'd caught only a glimpse of him from my window as he'd stood supervising his movers, but he'd looked attractive and, from my bird's-eye view, I could see that he wasn't balding or gray haired, and was thus more suitable for me than for AARP. So I was watering Noah's plant, as a good neighbor should, when his screen door opened and that sexy mouth of his appeared and said, "I didn't know a gardening service came with the condo fees."

"This isn't really gardening," I'd replied. "This is called 'neighborly watering to prevent death' and is free of charge."

That was the beginning of my spiral into sexual idiocy. The verbal flirtations soon progressed into physical flirtations, a touch here and there, until the night we rented *Daredevil*. As Ben Affleck began his ludicrous transformation into his superhero persona, Noah and I started a foolish liaison that would end with the bleach blonde and her BMW. With his dark hair and green eyes and the muscled body that he showed off by always wearing as few clothes as possible, Noah provided compelling relief from the dry spell I'd been going through. I'm a sucker for a good-looking guy, but who isn't? Although charming and flirtatious, he had a style that I was pretty sure he'd copied from prime-time television shows. All in all, although Noah was an undesirable boyfriend, he was a sexy guy. And he lived a flight down from me.

And we did have fun. We cooked romantic dinners together. Well, truth be told, I would make chicken simmered with fresh vegetables, wine, and herbs, and Noah would add a tablespoon of butter to the rice pilaf mix and ask the names of the strange ingredients I'd used. "That's called *thyme,*" I'd explain. "This is a *mango.*" Food savvy he was not. Although he usually ate whatever I cooked, he exhibited minimal gastronomic satisfaction with my meals. But the illusion of

16

romantic dinners was there, I suppose. It was for me.

We went to the movies and walked to local wine shops to pick out bottles with the most artistic labels we could find—activities usually reserved for couples actually *dating.* So, although Noah *said* he didn't want a girlfriend, he acted as if maybe I'd be the exception to that rule. And maybe he was protecting himself because he'd had his poor heart broken so many times before. And I bought that crap, by which I mean his phony charm and my rationalizations.

I can see why I fell. Take the time we went to the grand opening of the Trader Joe's grocery store up the street from our place. ("Our place" always sounded as if we actually lived together.) The store was packed with fabulous frozen health-conscious meals, gourmet sauces and chutneys, aromatic coffees, and miniature bamboo plants. Noah and I browsed the aisles together, but we got into separate lines for the registers. In retrospect, I realize that Noah was so uncommitted to me that he didn't even want us to be seen as a couple waiting in line together. Then there was the time I cajoled him into coming with me to my parents' house to pick up an air conditioner. When my father innocently suggested that we all have dinner together, I believe Noah momentarily stopped breathing.

But back to Trader Joe's.

"Noah," I called over to him, "look what I found! Frozen gyoza!" This to a person who couldn't tell Japanese dumplings from Chef Boyardee ravioli and would have preferred the taste of the latter.

17

Noah looked innocently around at the customers in his line and then turned those green eyes on me. "Ma'am? You found some purchases you like? You've had a nice shopping experience?"

"Look," I continued, "and a bag of dried papaya!"

"I'm not sure who she is, but I'm glad she's so enthusiastic about this store," he stage-whispered to the elderly woman ahead of him.

"Noah, stop it!" I laughed. "Don't pretend you don't know me!"

We developed a small audience, smiling at the playfulness of the young, happy couple. And so it continued for a few moments, Noah pretending I was some lunatic shopper raving about her finds, and me insisting to those around us that he did, in fact, know me and that, no, I didn't typically shout about the joys of white-chocolate-covered pretzels to strangers. But it was fun and flirtatious and felt good, as if two weeks into our affair we were safe and secure enough to play around like this. I totally overlooked the significant feature of the episode, which was the boring barrenness of Noah's shopping cart. One bunch of bananas and a box of cereal? I should have run.

I hadn't. I was now facing the consequences, which, on this Saturday morning, consisted of shame, guilt, anger, embarrassment, and feelings of such inadequacy that I felt a desperate, impulsive desire to bleach my red hair to white blonde, begin regular tanning sessions at our local QuickTan, and trade my Saturn up for a BMW I couldn't possibly afford. But I decided I must stick to the rule of not doing anything drastic when in distress. I didn't want to leave my apartment because Noah might see me, and I didn't want to stay in my apartment because Noah might stop by. *I will never sleep with any neighbors, I will never sleep with any neighbors,* I repeated to myself. *I am not going to cry, and I am not going to care!*

But I did impulsively call up my friend Daniel.

"Chloe, it's too early," he mumbled in an I'm-still-asleep voice. "Call me back later."

"It's an emergency!" I pleaded.

"Nobody has emergencies at eight thirty on Saturday morning. Go away."

"No, listen! I need your help."

Daniel had had a serious girlfriend for over a year, but after explaining this morning's events, I demanded that he come over and make out with me in front of the condo building. We'd slept together before, so I didn't see the harm in a little kissing. Actually, we were each other's backup person in case of a dry spell. In fact, I'd probably slept with Daniel more than with anyone else—meaning little sleep and rarely a bed. The front entryway to his apartment building, a parking garage at two a.m., and an empty football field? Yes. A bed? No. And as much as we liked having sex, we never got it together to actually get *involved.* But somehow we had managed to stay friends. And right now I wanted him to be a good friend and help me out of this humiliating situation with Noah.

"I'm not getting out of bed to come make out with you. The guy sounds like a prick. And, besides, I can't. What about Shelly? I don't think she'd exactly be thrilled."

"Just explain it to her! She'll understand!" I practically screamed at him. "It's not real kissing. It's helping-out-your-friend kissing. *Revenge kissing,* we'll call it. And maybe a little groping, like I've been having another man on the side the whole time?"

Daniel gave a simultaneous sigh and laugh. "I'm sorry, Chloe. I'd help you if I could, but I can't."

"I'd do it for you!" I slammed down the phone, furious, flopped on my bed, and pictured Noah's face as he looked out his window and saw me entwined in a passionate frenzy with a mystery man. He'd probably just nod with approval, the jerk.

I called my sister, Heather, who didn't hear a word I said because her three-year-old, Walker, and her two-month-old, Lucy, were both wailing. In the background, her husband, Ben, was saying something about orange-colored poop. Over the family noise, she did seem to understand who was calling and shouted that she'd call me back.

Heather is only two years older than I am, but at twenty-seven, she already had her life totally together. Married at twenty-three to the wonderful Ben Piper, an architect, she was happily settled in wealthy Brookline in a four-bedroom house I completely envied. Hard not to hate her sometimes.

My best girlfriend, Adrianne Zane, who has insisted

on being called Adrianna since *The Sopranos* first aired, didn't even pick up her phone. Thanks to voice mail, screams for help wouldn't boom out of an answering machine and wake her up. I left a message, anyhow. I said that Noah had had sex with a blonde with bad roots and tawdry fashion sense.

Adrianna is an independent hairstylist who works for herself. In private, she likes to say that she is willing to do almost anything nonsexual for money. She'll do hair, clothes, and makeup. She'll liquor up a terrified bride who refuses to walk down the aisle without a dirty martini in her system. Unfortunately for me, she sleeps until noon most days, so I was left to stew about my love life alone.

I was lonely. And pissed off. It had been seventeen months since I'd had a *real* boyfriend, a *real* relationship that didn't involve "arrangements" and "mutual understandings." What really annoyed me was that I didn't *need* a boyfriend to feel fulfilled. I liked my alone time. I could watch videos without snuggling with a guy on the couch. I was a self-reliant woman. I just wanted *somebody* in my life. I was fighting back tears. What was wrong with me that I couldn't find a normal boyfriend? I wandered in and out of my bedroom and looked around at my disheveled apartment. Even if I got my act together today and cleaned up the mountainous piles of laundry strewn across the bedroom floor, there would still be the matter of the damn non-dishwasher-safe pans molding in the sink—the dumb pans I'd stupidly bought thinking, *Of course, I won't mind a few extra high-quality pans to scrub.* Well, no wonder no one wanted to be with me. Every guy out there probably sensed that I was a huge slob with a schizophrenic decorating sense. I eyed my walls with growing embarrassment.

In a moment of inspiration after watching some cable do-it-yourself show, I had taped off a series of lines on my bedroom walls and halfheartedly started to paint alternating stripes of Tiffany blue and homestead yellow. In my rush to create a dramatic transformation, I had failed to level the lines, which now angled crookedly across the room. Also, when I had started to remove the tape from the wall, bits of plaster had ripped off, leaving a real disaster behind. I'd left the remaining tape in place in the hope of creating the impression of a composition in progress with artistic results to come. I *had* to stop watching those home improvement shows.

I hauled myself toward the bathroom to take a shower. En route, I passed through the neon-red living room. What had I been thinking? Neon red! I had to get out of the house. Even if it meant the risk of running into Evil Noah, I had to get out. But first, I needed to handle my mortification by getting the best revenge; I was going to look *good.* And so began a long shower, complete with ginger-rosemary salt scrub, grapefruit shampoo, banana conditioner, and green-tea bath splash. I shaved every traditionally shaveable part of my body. After a careful application of three smoothing, shining, rejuvenating hair products, I spent forty-five minutes with a blow dryer and a straightening iron until I had coiffed my shoulder-length hair into what I hoped was a go-to-hell style. I did use my styling time to consider why a so-called feminist like me was doing all this grooming and to wonder whether salt scrubs were banned at social work school. Did slathering myself in girly products mean I supported sexist thinking? I had no idea, but I did know that the early fall weather made this a good day for tight black pants, a padded bra, and a fitted sweater. Call it the new feminism.

I was off to Home Depot to correct my painting mis-judgments. I would clean up my apartment, decorate with style, and charge into social work school with a passionate drive to save the world. And, most impor-tant, I would show Noah what he was missing out on.

TWO

Sashaying out of my apartment, down the stairs, out the door, and past the Evil Bachelor's window, I sported what I hoped was a look of confidence and sophistication. There was no indication that Noah saw me—fortunately, since I caught my high-heeled boot on the bottom step and crashed into the peonies. Brushing the dirt off my pants, I thanked God that I was wearing black and continued to strut to the car. On the off chance that Noah was peeking out his window and eyeing me with regret, I gave a great hair flip and slid into the seat. I peeled out of our driveway and sped away, presumably off on an adventure of my own.

The driver of a black Lexus SUV honked at me for daring to pull into his lane to make a right turn into the Home Depot parking lot. God forbid he let one car get in front of him! It's amazing that Boston drivers ever reach their destinations alive; this is a city where changing lanes means a near-fatal accident. And who needs a luxury SUV? A sedan is insufficient to cart kids from private school to private lessons to the ultra-private mansions tucked away in Weston, Lincoln, and Wellesley Hills? But maybe I just had it in for expensive cars this morning.

All dolled up for paint shopping, I left the car, grabbed the first massive shopping cart I saw, and wheeled my way into the hallowed halls of the do-it-yourself wonderland. And I would do it myself, I thought pathetically. All alone, with no companion to work with me, to reach the high spots on the walls, or to finish the inevitable third coat all my projects required. *Don't cry in the store!* I ordered myself.

Coming out into the world was beginning to seem like a mistake. Had I really thought that Noah would see me from his window and rush down the stairs to admit that he was a fool and that I was the right girl for him? No. I knew better. But I wanted *someone* to rush after me, someone to realize I was fall-in-love-get-married-have-children-live-happily-ever-after mate-rial. Yes, I was going to be a big hit with the radical feminists at social work school.

I pushed the cart as fast as I could to the Oops paint section. My favorite part of this store was the steel cart with shelves full of returned cans of paint. Gallons were five dollars, quarts only a buck. I refused to pay full price for paint I was doomed to paint over the next month. On some days, the choices were so unappealing that it was easy to understand why buyers had brought the colors back. I always felt sorry for the returned cans, as if the unwanted colors had been hoping for a purpose, longing for the opportunity to change a room's atmosphere. How hurtful to have an unappreciative buyer slop a sample patch on the wall and exclaim, "Ugh! What a revolting shade of violet!" And the poor paint would cry, "But you picked me! I was chosen! I was just what you wanted!" So I went on empathic rescue missions to the steel cart to save some of the unwanted. Hm . . . maybe I *was* cut out for social work after all.

I looked at the lids of all the cans, each lid with a dab of the paint color and a small neon orange splotch sprayed on to indicate the "Oops" status of the reject. Lots of beiges, browns, and other earth colors today. Perfect. I felt suddenly inspired, and my spirits even lifted some. I would clear off all the bold, disarming hues and designs from my walls to create a solid, clean feel. Simplify, get back to basics, and tone it all down. Clean, organized living was just what I needed to begin the fall. I collected a rich brown, a few coffee shades, and a yellowish color with a sandy texture to it that I hoped would add a brushed-stone effect to the entryway. I gathered up brushes and a heap of plastic paint trays so I wouldn't have to go to the basement and scrounge through piles of supplies that I hadn't cleaned properly. Best to start fresh.

I went to one of the self-checkout aisles and started to scan my items. The register's computerized female voice began to scold me in loud tones for failing to bag my last scanned item. When I set a gallon of Navajo brown back down on the counter, the computer woman went into convulsions and began asking how I could have been so dumb. Didn't I even know how to bag items? And what was wrong with me that I couldn't stop myself from sleeping with a narcissistic pig like Noah? Well, not that last part, but she did rail on at me until a lanky male teen with a ponytail and an orange vest ran over to me to recite informative facts about the self-checkout process. He fixed my purchasing errors and finished the scanning for me.

"And the money goes in here." He pointed to the slot.

By the time I got to the car, my cheeks were streaked with tears. I barely managed to slam the door before I broke into full-blown sobbing. I was so ashamed, not about the paint-buying incident, but about the embarrassment I felt at my latest romantic disaster. I let myself cry for the next twenty-five minutes, but had no tissues and had to blow my nose on a paper bag from Eagles' Deli. I wiped my face with my hands and checked my appearance in the rearview mirror. The reflection sent me into a fresh bout of wailing. Why had I left my apartment, and how was I going to get back in looking like this? My pale skin was red from crying, my eyes were puffy, my makeup was shot. What if Noah saw me and knew he was the source of my misery? How humiliating would that be? I called Adrianna again from my cell phone but still got her voice mail, so I just hung up. I fixed myself up the best I could, started the engine, and drove out of the parking lot toward home.

I peeled into my parking spot at the condo and prayed not to run into the guy with the wandering body parts. I unloaded my purchases and tried to slink inconspicuously to the house. Fortunately, Noah wasn't around. At a guess, he was still languishing in his apartment, savoring the memory of the previous night.

But Harmony was outside on the lawn.

Harmony lived on the first floor of our building and annoyed the hell out of me. She weighed next to nothing but had bought herself enormous silicone breasts that threw her off balance, thus creating the impression she was on the verge of toppling over at any minute. Harmony's involvement in a car accident a few years back had netted her a good-size settlement that had paid for her massive boobies. The bosomy funding source was no secret; she shared it with everyone she met, usually within a few minutes.

Her asinine banter always drove me completely bonkers. I was still irritated with her from the previous winter, when she complained at one of our monthly condo meetings about the poor job I'd done of shoveling the walkways around the house. In theory, all the tenants were supposed to take turns shoveling snow. The January condo meeting turned into a massive fight about who had actually met the obligation and who had not.

Harmony was loudly relating an encounter she'd had with a car salesman that afternoon. As she needlessly pointed to her breasts, she said, "'I'm a big girl,' I says to him. 'And I need a lotta seat room,' but he just wants to show me this little compact thing, and I keep sayin', 'I'm too busty for that little thing,' and he keeps tellin' me to move the seat back, but I keep tellin' him I can't reach the little bar unda the seat 'cause of the girls up here, and then—"

At that point, Tyler, an acupuncturist on the first floor, was so desperate to shut her up that he shot to his feet and spat out, "So, there seems to be a dispute about the shoveling?"

Harmony responded by delivering a speech about how dissatisfied she'd been with the path I'd shoveled after the twenty-four-inch snowfall we'd endured the week before. My path was way too narrow for her, she maintained. *Did her breasts need more room?* I wondered. I snarled that the path had been perfectly acceptable and that at least I'd waited until the snow had stopped before I'd shoveled. I went on to remind everyone of the time Harmony had shoveled only the first three inches of what had turned into a foot-and-a-half blizzard and had claimed she'd met her shoveling obligations. At the end of a long and irritating discussion, the group agreed that all the tenants would like a wider path next time, so Tyler requested that I add, say, another ten inches to the width of my paths. Easy for him to say. He hired some man named Sergio to do his manual labor.

So my crummy mood held fast this Saturday morning when I saw Harmony, who was standing over a hot Weber grill. She wore what looked like a teeny nightgown with a pattern of miniature flowers but was presumably a dress. As she flipped super-size meat patties, balls of sweat dripped down her face, hit the coals, and sizzled. She and her breasts turned to me as I approached the house. She tilted her head and, with a look of concern, asked how I was doing.

"Fine," I replied hesitantly.

Harmony pursed her lips and gave me the thumbs-up sign. "Hang in there. There's otha' fish in the sea." Sympathy and sisterhood! Harmony must have seen Blondie leaving this morning, too. I felt worse than ever.

Having failed to shrivel up and perish, I nodded halfheartedly, started up the fire escape steps, rushed past Noah's door, and finally reached the security of my apartment.

"Bastard," I said for the hundredth time that day.

Gato greeted me as I tumbled into the living room with my painting supplies. He quickly brushed up against my leg before rubbing the gallon of honeyed

29

pecan with his long body and letting out an overly affectionate purr. Gato couldn't even tell the difference between human beings and paint cans—no wonder my mother described him as "socially challenged." His rubbing and purring meant either that he was in love with my new colors or that he was hungry. I assumed the latter. In the kitchen, I filled his dish with Iams, grabbed the phone, and checked my voice mail. Nothing. Just me and my paint and my socially challenged cat. I stroked Gato while he devoured his meal and then gave him a final pat.

I had another shot at brewing a pot of Peet's coffee and was rewarded with billows of steam surging from the appliance and dark paste seeping out the bottom. I poured a gross cup, changed into torn sweatpants, and decided that if Noah showed up, I wouldn't answer the door. I threw on a Patty Griffin CD, cranked the volume, taped off the trim in the living room, loaded the paint tray with primer, and started rolling. To cover the red, I'd have to put on a good two coats of primer before I could even begin to create my tranquil room.

My apartment was small: bedroom, living room, kitchen, and bathroom all joined by a small hallway with a large linen closet. The garish paint and unfinished projects made the place seem cramped. I was convinced that my new design plan would remedy everything. By the third time Patty had sung "Blue Sky," I had put on two coats of primer. I was just about to start the first earth tone when the phone rang.

My sister, Heather, had finally called back. I rattled off my woeful Noah story in expectation of sisterly outrage.

Instead of agreeing that I'd been terribly wronged, Heather said, "Well, what did you expect, you dummy?"

"Did you not hear the words *tank top* and *swagger?*" I demanded.

"Oh, Chloe, get over it." She covered the phone and yelled, "Walker, pull your pants down *before* you start to pee! When is he going to stop doing that? Look, Chloe, I'm sorry that things are bad for you right now. I keep telling you to use Back Bay Dates. That's how Ben and I met, in case you've forgotten. I didn't meet my husband in college the way everyone says you're supposed to, so I used modern technology. That way you can weed out all the bad ones and match up with someone who shares your interests, wants a relation-ship, and all the other things you're missing with these bozos you keep dredging up from God knows where."

Heather raised her voice and practically shrieked with glee, "In fact, this is a perfect idea! You can marry your Internet date and both the Carter sisters will be written up in the paper, and we'll be, like, spokeswomen for Back Bay Dates, sharing our love stories with the public, encouraging people to take charge of their dating lives. It's a very logical approach to finding the perfect mate. Walker is tan-gled up in his pants! I gotta go, call me later!" And she hung up.

There was no way I was going online to meet some serial-killer date. Those Web sites were even worse than the horrible restaurants that hosted "speed dating." I knew all about speed dating. My old college roommate, Elise Jackson, tried it when she was heart-broken about the end of her calamitous six-month marriage. She prepared by memorizing a short speech outlining her background, her interests, and the top five reasons she was an excellent candidate for further dates. Clad in a professional-looking suit from J. Crew, her hair in a bob, Elise marched off to a round of speed dating prepared to make an eloquent presen-tation and snag a dream husband. She spent approxi-mately six minutes with each man there, and each time she swapped tables she used up all the allotted time by rattling off the same speech. As each man looked at her with glassy-eyed boredom, she started to panic and began to perspire profusely. By the time she reached her final date, she'd become such a wet, stut-tering disaster that she flung her speech away, yanked off her sweat-soaked blazer, downed the rest of her date's Heineken, and begged him to take her out of there. To her surprise, he agreed. He introduced him-self as Teddy and took her for drinks at Rialto. There he confessed that he'd made a mockery of himself by passing out "cheat sheets" to the women: his romantic résumé, including all his contact numbers, printed on four-by-six cards. He said the ultimate humiliation had come when a severe-looking brunette had taken out a red pen and begun correcting his notes. "See where you've written, 'Adventurous and ready for anything'? You should really give an *example* of what you've done that's adventurous so your dates know what you mean by that." Elise and Teddy laughed their way back to her place and spent the night giggling about Miss Editor and how lucky they were to have found each other.

Teddy and Elise are now married and domestically settled in a suburb of Chicago. I hate Elise.

But it still seemed so unromantic to me, the notion of people speeding to present themselves to one another and then racing to evaluate amorous possibilities on the basis of minimal profile information—not at all the way I pictured meeting my future spouse. I was sure that if I tried this increasingly popular method, either I'd end up talking to a bunch of dopes who were dying for my number, or I'd spend the evening swooning over men so far out of my league that I'd leave feeling inadequate and depressed. Just because Elise and Heather had found great matches through contemporary means didn't mean I was cut out for it.

I stood peering into the fridge in the hope of finding comfort food. Perhaps there was something to be said for taking control of one's love life, I thought. I mean, meeting a man in some random place like the supermarket or a bar didn't necessarily mean that fate had somehow planned the encounter and didn't guarantee that you and the guy would be even vaguely compatible. Television and movies had tainted my perspective on how couples can actually meet; my fairy-tale idea of romance was the result of too many hours of seeing actors, beautified by makeup artists, stylists, and personal trainers, collide with destiny, which had been equally beautified by set designers, lighting experts, and production crews. Lies, lies, lies! Besides, hadn't I just dated the ultimate caricature of big-screen sex appeal and charisma, Noah? And look where that had gotten me. Well, speed dating was out. But I did contemplate Heather's Back Bay Dates. A rational, logical approach was what I needed.

THREE

By six o'clock that evening I had finished the first coat of Oops paint in the living room. Each wall was a different neutral, earthy tone. I'd cleaned up some of the clutter but had left the furniture in the middle of the floor. Although peace and calm had yet to fill the space, I'd done enough for one day. I'd been listening for signs of Noah downstairs. Except for some blasting of Jimmy Buffet, I hadn't heard anything. It was a miserable feeling, both yearning for and hating him.

I warmed up my favorite junk food for dinner, a frozen puff-pastry pie filled with spinach and feta, and took a huge slice to my bedroom. I positioned myself cozily in bed and ate my million-calorie dinner while I watched a rerun marathon of *Queer Eye for the Straight Guy*. Except for the homosexual thing, that

Kyan would make a wonderful boyfriend. I almost cried as he gently and sensitively convinced a straight man to remove his horrendous toupee and reveal his bald head to his family. Even when the cast returned for their second season with terrible new hairdos, I forgave them because they had accomplished their mission of correcting the wrongs, fashion and otherwise, of straight men everywhere.

I'd have given my entire supply of beautifying lotions and potions to have had the forethought to stock my fridge with pastries from the North End. The only other cheer-up food I had were some chocolate-covered Oreos, which, although not Italian delicacies, did momentarily take the edge off my heartache. By ten o'clock, when another newly made-over straight guy had shared his new look with family and friends, I was exhausted. I shut the television off, lay down to go to sleep, and promptly developed a horrible case of insomnia.

I'd gone through bouts of it before. It used to afflict me almost every Sunday before school or work. I'd be awake until four or five in the morning, tossing with nerves and anxiety, sweating, crying from exhaustion. I'd count the few hours I had left to sleep and worry about how I'd function the next day. Tonight, my mind raced with the fear that I'd live the rest of my life in my zany-colored condo above Noah, alone with my socially challenged cat and an unreliable coffeemaker.

My heart started pounding, and I grew more and more frustrated with myself. Why couldn't I sleep?

Anxiety flooded my brain, memories of mistakes I'd made and fears of mistakes I would undoubtedly make. I remembered the embarrassment I'd felt at the age of seven when my mother had caught me stealing a Snickers bar from a convenience store. I thought of the time in tenth grade when I'd failed a pop quiz in French class, where I usually got As. My teacher had written *"Mauvais!"* with an accompanying frowning face at the top of my paper. Even the checkout incident at Home Depot!

Then my brain started rehashing memories of relationships and rejections. Like, there was the day I had finally broken up with Sean. He had loved me so intensely, and for whatever reason, I just hadn't loved him back enough. I had broken up with him three times in the two years we had dated, each time getting back together with him because I hadn't been able to tolerate the pain of being apart, the anguish I had caused him, and the unhappiness I had caused myself.

We had made plans to move in together, and after avoiding apartment hunting for weeks, I'd gone to see a therapist friend of mine, Debby.

"Look," she'd pointed out, "Sean has become more like a brother to you than a boyfriend. And you don't sleep with your brother." She'd paused. "At least you're not supposed to."

Deciding that I didn't want a life of brotherly love, I called Sean and, in cowardly fashion, ended things on the phone. I hadn't wanted the burden of seeing his face and watching his heart break.

I pulled the pillow down tightly over my ears, as if I could block out the memory of his angry words. "You're not doing this to me over the phone. I'm coming over," Sean had said in a panic. He had raced over to my place, and I hadn't even had the decency to look at him. Instead, for the twenty minutes he'd been there, I'd kept my face buried in my hands, but I hadn't been able to stop crying and shaking because I was tearing him apart. I forget most of his words, but I remember hearing him pace across my floor. I'd just kept telling him how sorry I was. He'd punched the wall, walked to me, kissed me on the forehead, and said, "I love you." Then he'd left quickly, and I'd sobbed on the couch for two hours.

Maybe I should have stayed with Sean, who'd loved me so much, who'd been such a great guy, who'd wanted to marry me and live happily ever after. Why I hadn't loved him that way, too, I just didn't know. I replayed the scenario in my head until I couldn't stand it any longer. When I finally sat up and looked at the clock, it was one in the morning. I tossed myself back down on the bed and spent the next two hours in an insomniac search for comfort: smoothing the sheets, adjusting the pillows, trying to relax and clear my head of everything negative. At three, I gave up, turned on the lights, and went to the computer.

And visited the Back Bay Dates Web site.

Fatigue made me feel as if I'd been chugging cheap beer; it loosened my inhibitions and nudged me in directions I wouldn't otherwise have turned. Opening the Web page, I could see why people used Back Bay Dates. The site wasn't filled with idiotic photos of happy couples strolling along a beach flanked by a fabulous sunset. There were no flashing hearts, no bridal bouquets bouncing across the page, no promises of perfect love, no matrimonial guarantees.

On the contrary, everything was professional and streamlined. All right, I did have to fork over $39.95 for the perks of membership, but would I want to date someone who was too cheap to invest so little in a future with me? Of course not. I was worth the money. I was weeding out cheapskates by joining this fee-for-service site rather than one of the free-for-all-freaks sites. So I punched in my credit card number and silently thanked dead Uncle Alan for funding my foray into modern dating. After debating user names for twenty minutes and deciding that there were no cool user names, I settled for GourmetGirl.

I answered approximately three hundred questions regarding my leisure activities, basic physical attributes, and hopes for a partner's qualities. I struggled over the first thirty questions as I debated the pros and cons of each response. I mean, if I said, "Yes, I am spontaneous and enjoy flying by the seat of my pants," would I attract a chaotic and untrustworthy man with no sense of commitment? Or would I meet a man who would surprise me with a midnight flight to Rome to dine al fresco at his favorite hidden jewel of a restaurant on pasta made by a cute little old Italian lady who would proclaim us a match made in *par-*

adiso? I eventually gave up wrestling with my responses and just clicked my mouse on the multiple-choice answer that seemed most me. I then previewed my profile, posted myself in Women Seeking Men, and set up my Back Bay Dates mailbox. Members could browse one another's profiles, even search by various categories, and if interested, e-mail the person at a BBD mailbox, all anonymously. I could always back out of this lunacy by ignoring my mailbox or canceling my account.

I had nothing to lose by reading profiles. I checked out dozens of men and discovered that BBD was not the cyber meat market I had imagined. Most of the profiles read like mine: they described relatively normal people looking for love. Some of the men had even included pictures, often images that eliminated some sweet-sounding guys. Even though I was becoming a politically correct and open-minded social work student, I still wanted a hottie.

I finally chose three profiles, none for any particularly good reason except maybe the lack of self-descriptions such as, "I enjoy extreme skateboarding and body piercing for pleasure." I sent each man a BBD "postcard," which was the site's way of letting someone know you were interested in a profile. I had a nasty case of buyer's remorse after I hit Send, but was so tired that the twinge of doubt didn't keep me awake.

I woke at ten on Sunday morning to the smell of burning coffee, welcome reassurance that some things in life were dependable. I cracked my front door, listened in the hall for signs of Noah, and then rushed down the stairs to the front hall and stole his *New York Times*—the least he owed me. I sat at the kitchen table and tentatively looked out my window. No blondes today, I was relieved to note. I sipped my coffee, devoured an egg bagel with lox spread, and started on the *Times* crossword puzzle.

Somewhere around 28-Across, I was struck by the realization that I'd done something hideous. Oh God! Back Bay Dates. What could I have been thinking? I was not supposed to do anything drastic in my post-breakup state of mind, and there I had gone ahead and joined a freaking dating service. I leaped to the computer and found the site. What was my user name? This was worse than waking up to a wretched hangover and remembering you've spent the previous night dancing on a bar counter to "Oh, What a Night" with your skirt yanked up way too high and your bra straps hanging down your arms. I looked around my desk and saw *GourmetGirl* and my password, NoCheapThrills, scrawled on a sheet of paper.

I logged in, and, yes, I had indeed posted myself on Back Bay Dates. Shit. Maybe I could delete my information before anything horrendous happened. I navigated around the page and was just about to cancel my account when I noticed that one message was waiting for me.

No, no, no! I'd been so bleary eyed last night I couldn't even remember whom I'd written to or what

I'd said. I clicked on my mailbox and was terrified to see a message from someone called DinnerDude who had apparently read my message that morning. I groaned and shut my eyes in the superstitious hope that the message would evaporate. I opened my eyes.

Damn. DinnerDude's message was still there. He thought our foodie user names were pretty funny, a comment that completely ticked me off since I couldn't stand people who referred to themselves as *foodies*. He'd read in my profile that I was a "culinary whore," a phrase he thought was hysterical. I couldn't have written *that,* could I? The ill-chosen term implied that plied with the right risotto, I might just rip off my clothes and sprawl across the dinnerware to show my gratitude. My prospective date went on to write that he was thinking of investing in a new restaurant, Essence, and was going there this evening to check it out again and to speak with the owner and the chef. Because I was so into food, would I like to meet him there tonight?

Suddenly, the man sounded interesting! And he apparently had money to fling about in investments. Perhaps what had doomed my previous romantic escapades had been food incompatibility! My relationship failures hadn't been failures at all, but Mother Nature's way of preventing the propagation of culinarily challenged people, natural selection aimed at eliminating poor palates from the gene pool. All along, I'd been meant for a man who shared my love of wonderful food. This DinnerDude had great possibilities. We could become the new hot Boston couple who invested together in zillions of spectacular restaurants and were written up in *Boston Magazine* as the premiere patrons of local eateries. With unusual confidence and positive thinking, I wrote an e-mail agreeing to meet DinnerDude at Essence. I then sent Heather a message saying she ought to start organizing my wedding.

The day planned itself. I had to clean myself up and find something sexy and yet appropriate to wear to dinner. My face was puffy from all of yesterday's crying and late-night computer activities, and I generally looked pretty disgusting. I called Adrianna and left another pleading message, this time yelling incoherently about e-mail and restaurant dates. Okay, what would my fashionable friend tell me to do first? The solution leaped out at me: free makeover, of course!

I tossed on jeans and a fitted V-neck T-shirt, raced down the fire escape, didn't even glance at Noah's window, hopped in the Saturn, and sped down Route 9 to the Chestnut Hill Mall and charged toward the Lancôme counter.

A woman named Dana greeted me and listened while I explained yesterday's mess in excruciating detail, ending with the heinous reality that I would have to see Noah the Jerk again, and probably soon, and that under no circumstances was he to be allowed to witness me looking so gross. And that I had this blind date tonight and better look damn good. Forty-five minutes later, I left the mall with a bag full of gorgeous products and words of encouragement from Dana.

I arrived home to find a gigantic bag outside my side door. I'd never left anything at Noah's, so it couldn't be the traditional returning of items belonging to an ex. I read the card taped to the bag: "Chloe, I'm not sure what is going on, but I can tell you're having a wild weekend. Sorry I haven't been able to call. I'm working the rest of today, but we'll talk tomorrow. Thought you might need something special to wear . . . for an Internet date?!? Love, Adrianna."

I took the bag inside, ripped it open, and pulled out the ultimate beautiful dress: straight cut, midcalf length, low across the chest, with thin straps over the shoulders. This stunner was made of some luxuriously silky material in a deep periwinkle blue. I looked at the label sewn in the back and smiled. Adrianna, it read. I knew she'd been slaving over this dress for weeks now: I'd suffered being stuck with pins the numerous times she'd had me model it for her. Ade had been working on a few designs that she hoped to sell to her posh hair clientele, and I'd been secretly coveting this creation during all those fitting sessions. The dress was perfect for the restaurant tonight— fancy but not too formal, sexy but not slutty. She'd even given me matching heels that tied around the ankle, and a pair of sheer nylons. I loved my best friend. I called her cell phone, poured out praise for the dress and thanks for her generosity, and said we'd talk the next day.

I checked my Back Bay Dates mailbox and found a note from my mystery man to confirm our plans for tonight and to tell me his name, which was Eric. The service had advised against sharing any identifying information until we were comfortable, and it said to meet in a public place. Eric didn't give a last name but did go on to write that he had blond hair, was six feet tall, and would meet me at our table, which would be reserved under his first name. I wrote back that my name was Chloe and that I was five-five, had red hair, and looked forward to meeting him.

I puttered around the house for the rest of the afternoon: tidying and organizing, moving furniture, and paving the way for a new life of order and simplicity. Any woman who cleans her house before a date has the secret hope that the man she's going out with will return with her to her spotless abode. According to some women, though, if you prepare for intimate encounters by shaving your legs, cleaning the apartment, and buying condoms, then absolutely nothing will happen; to guarantee a hot night of passion, you need hairy legs, a messy house, and faith in the rhythm method. Screw that. Clean-shaven neat freaks on the pill have sex, too. But my messy, half-painted walls might even things out in my favor. God, I'd love to have someone's car parked behind mine all night. That would stick it to Noah. Not that I was in the habit of one-night stands with strange men. Still, I could make a sacrifice this one time if it meant causing Noah any unpleasantness whatsoever.

A full two and a half hours before I was to meet Eric, I began my preparations. I yanked down all my hair supplies for a repeat of yesterday's marathon styling session and then hopped in the shower to scrub and douse myself with all my products. I even shaved about seven times. Clean and buffed, I turned off the faucet and wrapped my hair in a towel.

I have never understood the policy on applying lotion after a shower. On the one hand, you're supposed to apply lotion to damp skin *immediately* after showering, and on the other hand, you're forbidden to apply lotion after shaving because it can irritate the skin. Risking irritation, I slathered on gobs of Sweet Pea Lotion and even rubbed a little in places that a first date theoretically shouldn't get near. When my hair was finally flatironed and the front clipped back, I dove into the Lancôme bag, spread my glorious cosmetics across the sink, and followed Dana's application instructions precisely.

Finally, the blue dress and matching shoes. Since I'd been the model for the dress, it fit perfectly and showed off all the right places. I did look pretty good, I had to admit. I sauntered out the back door and down the stairs, off to meet this blond Adonis named Eric who would whisk me off in a romantic whirlwind.

I ran smack into Noah, who was outside watering his puny little plants.

"Hey, gorgeous." He flashed a hungry smile at me. "Where are you going all dressed up?" As though I could possibly be dolled up for any reason other than to please him. The nerve. I paused on the landing and with a great sense of superiority announced, "First of all, it's none of your concern. And second, I really don't want anything to do with you."

As I stepped past him, he looked at me in some confusion. One of his harem not drooling over him? "All right . . ." he said slowly, drawing out the words to give himself time to regain his composure. He smiled flirtatiously, as though I were joking.

"Noah, I'm not an imbecile," I said calmly. "I started my day yesterday by looking out my window to see a blonde tart emerging from your apartment." Why did I say *tart?* Who says that? What am I all of a sudden, British?

But Noah's face fell. Caught.

"Christ, Noah, do you think I don't have feelings, that it wouldn't be weird for me? Did you forget that I live upstairs?" I asked cooly.

"Chloe, I'm sorry you saw that, but I did tell you I didn't want a girlfriend, and you seemed to be okay with that. I guess I should've known you'd get hurt." Pig.

Before he could elaborate on his supposed sympathy for my wounded feelings, I cut him off and nailed him with a lecture on considerate behavior. "You know, I don't care what you said to me. You don't get to feel okay about behaving badly because of a technicality. I know you said all the necessary things, but you also *acted* like you were dating me, like you were interested in me. I don't care so much about *you* in particular. What I care about is how little respect you've shown for me. I mean, honestly, it's just rude to parade other women around in front of me. I take responsibility for my part in setting myself up for something like this, but you need to take responsibility, too. You've been all cuddly and cute with me, which, in the *human world,* indicates interest and a certain level of caring. You have an obligation to be careful with people, and you didn't do that."

"I'm sorry you see it that way, Chloe," was his lame response.

"I'm sorry it *is* that way." Feeling pretty damn smart, I pivoted sharply and strutted sexily down the steps. Unfortunately, I managed to weaken my first-class moralizing when I reached my car, looked up to see Noah back at work on his plants, and shouted moronically, "You're no Tom Hanks, you know!"

"Are you sure you—?" started Noah, and I could see he was trying not to laugh.

Dammit, I meant to say Tom Cruise. Although, now that I thought about it, Tom Cruise had turned into a raving lunatic. I'd spent my formative years with Tom Cruise behaving like a normal, gorgeous celebrity and still couldn't wrap my brain around the new nutjob he'd become.

"Yes," I stammered. "Tom Hanks. A man known for his upstanding morality and loyalty. He's been with the same woman for years. Mr. Cruise, on the other hand, ditched his wife, ran off with Penelope, and had a Scientology-laced manic phase in which he jumped on

Oprah's couch and hooked up with Katie Holmes after seeing her supposed *work* on *Dawson's Creek*! Mr. Tom Hanks is a well-behaved citizen with ethics. And you, Noah Bishop, are no Tom Hanks!" Hoping I'd recovered, I ended with, "And I'm going on a date!"

I opened the car door.

"You watch *Oprah*?" he called down after me.

"Shut up!"

I replayed my talk with Noah on the way to Essence. All in all, not disastrous, minus the severely fouled up Tom Hanks part.

I reached the South End and by the grace of some parking angel managed to find a space. Because it was Labor Day weekend, half of Boston was on the Cape, but I chose to see the parking availability as a good omen. If so, it foretold only short-term luck. What's more, the good luck was strictly mine and certainly not my blind date's.

FOUR

Even from the outside, Essence was a beautiful restaurant. Large windows faced the street. Through them, I could see the glimmer of candlelight flickering on the walls. A menu was encased in glass next to the front door. I snuck a quick peek and glimpsed the words Baby Artichoke and Shallot Ragout, enough to send me flying into the entryway. If Eric turned out to be a big loser, I would still get a scrumptious meal out of this night.

48

I was surprisingly relaxed as I told the hostess I was meeting someone named Eric. My usual first-date nerves were nonexistent, probably because I felt I had nothing to lose. The anonymity provided by Internet dating meant that if I chose, I'd have an easy way never to see this man again; I'd just cancel my Back Bay Dates account and vanish. The hostess introduced herself as Joelle. She was in her thirties, with short, curly dark hair. She had the look of a mom, a combination of warmth, huggability, and an air of parental authority you didn't mess with. In other words, she struck me as a person to whom I could run screaming if this date sucked.

I followed Joelle to the back of the long restaurant. The walls were deep burgundy, and a long panel of ivory velvet hung from each window. The tables were covered in simple white linen with coordinating dishware, and tealight candles added a romantic glow to the cozy dining spots. Dark wood flooring led the way to an open kitchen at the far end of the restaurant. Joelle took me straight to the high-backed stools at a counter that separated the kitchen from the dining area. She gestured to the man seated there and said, "Mr. Rafferty?"

"Ah, you must be Chloe," Eric said as he swiveled around in his chair. "I'm Eric Rafferty, your fellow food afficionado for the evening."

Hm, not immediately drop-dead gorgeous, but not monstrous either. Eric was as tall as he'd said, about six feet, with neatly trimmed dirty-blond curls and wire-rimmed glasses that framed brown eyes. His features were, well, normal—nothing distinctive, but nothing alarming either. No huge nose or enormous ears protruding from the side of his head. But no smoldering eyes or sensuous mouth. Hardly the blond hunk I'd conjured. I quickly reminded myself that storybook love-at-first-sight attraction was purely fictional and that I'd better stop judging him and my potential attraction to him until the night was over.

"I *am* Chloe, and it's very nice to meet you." I smiled at him.

When Eric stood up, I put my hand out to shake his. Unfortunately, Eric leaned over to put his hands on my shoulders and kiss my cheek, and my outstretched hand slipped inside his jacket to rub against his waist. *Even though I have now inadvertently fondled my date, I will not die of embarrassment,* I assured myself. Mercifully, Eric appeared as flustered as I was and chose to ignore our fouled-up greeting. He pulled out a stool for me next to his and then repositioned himself in his seat.

"Well, I hope you'll share your opinions with me about my potential investment tonight." He waved his hand around the room. The hostess, Joelle, reappeared with a bottle of wine and held it out for Eric's inspection. "Ah, Joelle, thank you," Eric said. "I ordered us a bottle of sauvignon blanc. I hope that white's okay with you?"

"Absolutely," I replied. "I'm not much of a red wine drinker, so that's perfect."

Eric intently examined the bottle and nodded his approval. Joelle poured a bit into Eric's glass, and I tried to avoid cringing as he staged a display of swirling, sniffing, and tasting. There was a long pause as Joelle and I silently awaited his judgment. I felt for Joelle, who had to humor customers who'd taken wine-tasting courses and now viewed themselves as amateur sommeliers.

Eric peered seriously off into space as he presumably garnered the effect of the wine on all his senses. I prayed to God he wasn't planning to spit it out. Mercifully, he finally issued the opinion that the wine was fit for consumption. The hostess and I both sighed with relief. I smiled apologetically at her, and she gave me a knowing smile back. She filled our glasses and rushed off to seat a group of diners waiting by the entrance.

"Joelle does a nice job. Excellent hostess, as you could see. I like that in a restaurant. The hostess is the first person you have contact with when you go out to eat, and that encounter really sets the stage for the caliber of establishment," Eric explained to me.

"I suppose you have to get a good feel for all aspects of a business if you're considering investing?" I asked him. So far I was not into what struck me as Eric's pretentious analysis, but if he was going to be dropping a bundle of money into this place, research and judgment were necessary. But pretension? Was it necessary, too?

"Of course. Timothy Rock, the owner, will come

over, I'm sure. And we'll talk with the chef, too. His name's Garrett, and he does nice work. I used to eat at Magellan all the time, Tim's old restaurant. Now *that* place will blow you away."

Magellan was way out of my price range, but I'd read countless mouthwatering reviews in the papers and on the Internet. If things went well tonight with Eric, maybe I'd actually get a chance to eat there myself! Just the thought of a meal at the famous Magellan brought out the flirt in me. Smiling, I leaned in close to Eric. "So, you know Tim from dining at Magellan? Is that how you became a potential investor at Essence? I didn't know Magellan had even changed hands."

Eric took a slow drink of his wine before answering. "Yeah, I love Magellan. Great place for business dinners, and I took clients there all the time, so I got to know Tim pretty well. He was always out on the dining floor, talking to guests and making sure they had everything they needed. I mean, usually when you go out to eat, you don't see the owners that much. Or maybe you do when the place first opens, but Magellan had been open for a few years, and Tim and his wife, Madeline, they owned the place together, and those two were always in the dining room, meeting people, talking. If you ate there once, they'd remember you when you came back, and that's part of the reason Magellan has done so well. People like to feel important, that they're 'in' with a restaurant, you know?"

I nodded. One person who clearly loved to feel important was Eric himself.

He continued. "Tim and Maddie never left things up to the general manager. They were at the restaurant every night. Probably one of the reasons they got divorced—too much time together working and not enough time away from the restaurant." Eric took off his jacket and gestured for Joelle, who immediately swooped over, took his coat away, and left us with menus.

The menus were presented in leather-bound folders, suitable covers for the delectable descriptions inside. I looked at the appetizers, but just after drooling over Roasted Portobello Mushroom and Arugula with Stilton-Pink Peppercorn Vinaigrette, I was inter-rupted by Eric, who resumed his monologue. "And, actually, I was such a good customer there that I ended up partying with the staff after hours. I became friendly with Tim, and when he opened Essence, he called me to invest. Partying there was also how I hooked up with my ex-girlfriend, Veronica. She does the books for Magellan, and now she works here at Essence, too."

Oh, great, we've been here fifteen minutes, and he's already talking about his ex. Probably hung up on her, and this is his way of letting me know he's not totally available. Well, if he'd shut up, maybe we could get to eat, which is half the point of being here.

"So," I said, trying to change the subject, "I've never sat so close to a kitchen like this before. It's fun to be able to watch the chef work. I can't wait to taste the food." I took a gulp from my wineglass and surveyed the busy scene in front of me. Our counter curved gently around the kitchen to offer a clear view of the stoves and the prep counter. The chef, who wore the usual white coat, was rattling a pan over a hot flame. In front of us, a cook was mincing herbs with a gigantic knife.

But back to the menu. The appetizers all looked amazing: Steamed Countneck Clams and Nauset Mussels in a Spicy Orange Bouillon, Vegetable Spring Rolls with Spicy Strawberry Sauce and Black Vinegar Reduction . . . Oh, choosing would be impossible! Glancing ahead, I studied the entrées: Seared Trout with Purple Potato Puree; Caramelized Pineapple and a Lemon-Thyme Essence; Grilled Filet with Fingerling Potatoes, Lobster and Artichoke Hash, and Cognac Sauce. Good God, I'd died and gone to culinary heaven! I kept reading in spite of Eric's background commentary: "Ah, the pork is a new dish . . . Oh, good, the prawns were taken off. Not my favorite. What else? Oh, dammit, where's the guinea fowl? And the venison? I thought that would be on by now. They must be saving my favorites for the fall menu," Eric rambled.

I'd just about narrowed my choice of entrée to the Osso Buco with Sweet Potato Polenta and Roasted Root Vegetables or the Roasted Half Chicken with Warm Potato Salad and Roasted Corn Salsa when Eric snapped his fingers to summon the server to take our order. "Cassie? We're ready."

"Oh, sorry. I haven't quite decided," I apologized. I glanced up at Cassie and was horrified at how attractive she was. Shouldn't the ugly servers be sent to take care of couples on a first date? With the way my love life had been going, I didn't need nearby competition. Worse than just being hot in a *Playboy* centerfold kind of way, she was way too *cute:* gorgeous tanned skin, black hair that looked *naturally straight,* and beautiful dark eyes. Well, if things didn't work out with Eric, maybe I'd ask her out . . . no, no, I hadn't given up on men yet.

Eric shook his head while smiling at me. "Don't worry. I'll take care of things. I just had menus brought over to see how they read from a customer's point of view." Funny, since he hadn't asked me for my supposedly valuable input. He looked over at the waitress. "Cassie, why don't you have Garrett cook us up something special? Anything he wants. But no clams. And no cilantro. I'm tired of cilantro all over everything." A bad sign. I love clams *and* cilantro. And his manners! My mother would have had an aneurism. But at least he hadn't sat gawking at Cassie and her killer cleavage.

"Of course, Mr. Rafferty. I'm sure Garrett will prepare something wonderful for you two." She flashed a perfect, toothy smile, whisked the menu out of my hands, and dashed off into the kitchen to speak to the chef. I had wanted to order off the delectable menu and again felt embarrassed by Eric's request for special treatment. But having the executive chef create

55

something on his own? How many times would I get that treat?

"Oh, great! Here comes Timothy." Eric looked over me and waved.

Timothy appeared and stood between us. He was attractive, probably in his early forties, with dark hair and only a little gray just beginning to show on the sides. He was dressed in a pair of khakis and a long-sleeved navy pullover. His dark brown eyes looked exhausted, but even fatigue couldn't hide the obvious excitement he felt about Essence.

"Eric! What do you think? The place is doing okay tonight, huh? In about half an hour, we've got another few parties coming in. Things are picking up, I think. And this is Chloe? I've heard so much about you. It's wonderful to have you here tonight. And you must convince this fine man that investing in Essence will be the best move he's ever made."

How has he heard so much about me? I wondered. *And why does he think I have any influence over Eric and his money?*

"Nice to meet you, too," I said. "This is a beautiful restaurant you have. I can't wait to try the food."

"Yeah, Tim, what happened to the lobster dish you told me about? I was hoping to see that on the menu tonight," Eric told Tim.

"Well, another reason to invest, my friend. I've been keeping the food costs down. Everything has just been so expensive. When Maddie and I opened Magellan, she took care of most of the financial arrangements and left the creative and staffing parts up to me. I didn't realize how tough this would be. So, for now, I've asked Garrett to try to stick with chicken, pork, salmon . . . ingredients that can make us a good profit. I'd like to get in venison and halibut, and I'd love some Kobe beef. Garrett's good, though—he can dress up the lower-cost food and come up with solid dishes on our budget. But he needs some pricier ingredients to work with to make the menu spectacular. Fresh morels, foie gras, that sort of stuff. We've got a few high-priced items thrown in, like the filet with the lobster hash. Got to have a filet—there are always people who have to have *steak.* Chefs get so damn tired of making it, so I let Garrett splurge on that—spruce it up and make it a unique dish."

"That looked wonderful," I spoke up. "I was thinking about ordering it, but Eric is having the chef do something for us." I paused. "I hope that's all right?"

"Excellent. I'm glad you went ahead and asked. Actually, I've already arranged for Garrett to give you a tasting. I've brought in a few more ingredients for him to play with tonight so you can see what the menu could look like if we had another investor to increase our budget." Tim winked at me and patted Eric's shoulder. "But Garrett's coming along. This is his first *executive* chef gig, and he's struggling a bit, but I think he's going to work out. I begged Maddie to let me take Josh from Magellan, but there was no way she was parting with him. Not that I blame her. I wouldn't

57

have parted with him either. Josh Driscoll is unreal. I don't know how we were lucky enough to find him. But she let him help Garrett with the menu, which has been great. And she let me take Magellan's hostess, Joelle, and one of the waiters, Ian, so that's helped me out a ton. And even Veronica to do the books here, too."

Just then, a tall flame leaped from the grill, and Tim, Eric, and I reflexively leaned away from the heat.

Chef Garrett started yelling at no one in particular. "Dammit! Who turned the heat up? Where are my apps? Move it, move it!" He rubbed his eyes and continued working over the now-subdued grill, sweat visible on his forehead and neck.

Eric just shook his head and smiled and called over to Garrett, "You okay?"

"Yeah, just my damn eyebrows again. Third time this week I've singed 'em. Might as well just shave them off and get it over with," he answered. Garrett shook a saucepan, violently mixing its contents and sending an aromatic cloud our way. He turned around to face us. "Hey, Eric! Sorry, I've been so crazed tonight, I didn't even see you at my counter. Hope I haven't scared you off from joining forces?" Garrett reached out to shake Eric's hand.

"No way, kid. Things are looking good to me." Eric pumped Garrett's hand. "Just gotta taste your dishes tonight, though, to make sure! I can't pass up a free meal," Eric snickered.

"Don't worry," Tim assured him. "If you get on

board with Essence, every meal here'll be on the house, of course." A look of concern cut across his face.

"Hey, I'm just kidding. I know you'll take care of me," Eric said. "Oh, Garrett, this is Chloe. She's the one you're really going to have to impress."

"Well, then, Chloe. What'll it be?" Garrett asked. "Any special requests?"

I was momentarily distracted by the chef's charred eyebrows but managed to regain my composure enough to say that I was sure anything he made would be outstanding.

He clapped his hands together and announced that he was off to work on our mystery dinner—our chef's tasting—which would be five courses, each a sample of what he could do.

"I'm up for anything," I replied excitedly.

Garrett left to work some magic, I hoped, and I turned to Eric. The sights and aromas of the kitchen, as well as the fun of meeting the owner and the chef, had changed my mind about Eric's harping about his insider knowledge. Now I wanted to hear the secrets of the restaurant world.

Instead, I got a boring lecture on Eric's business (something incomprehensible about financial planning) and a monologue about his professional success, which, he emphasized, had afforded him the opportunity to drive a Land Rover and invest in Essence. Eric took my hand in his. "It is *so* wonderful to have you here with me tonight. The beautiful Chloe, here helping me with one of the biggest decisions of my life. I couldn't ask for a more perfect companion on this special evening." Inappropriate though the words were on a first date, and a blind one at that, they would have sounded touching if Eric had been looking at me instead of over my shoulder as he spoke. Not big on eye contact, this guy.

I slid my hand from his and drained what was left of my wine. "So, a chef's tasting should be fun, huh?" What was he looking at? I turned around to see a couple at a nearby table who were having an acrimonious discussion with their waiter.

"I'm going to help out here, my dear. Ian seems to have gotten himself in another jam," Eric announced as he leaped up and rushed to the other diners' table.

Good God, he was irritating. This wasn't his restaurant, and whatever was going on over there was none of his business. The meal had better be outstanding. The romance wasn't going to be. Maybe I'd go to Adrianna's after dinner and spend the night there—so Noah would see that I hadn't come home.

Eric's undistinguished build began to look lumpy, his skin pasty, as if his looks were morphing before my eyes from mediocre to outright unattractive. And was that a nose hair I'd seen peeking from his left nostril? Oh, help me. For now, I'd just get through the dinner. So I refilled my wineglass and spun around on my stool to get a good view of the dispute.

"What seems to be the trouble here, my friends?" Eric had assumed an air of affable authority.

The diners, who I assumed were husband and wife, must quite reasonably have mistaken Eric for an owner or manager, because they launched into a complaint about their bill. The man, well-dressed and probably in his late fifties, spoke impatiently. "There seems to be a mistake here. We've been charged for some sort of 'miscellaneous item,' whatever that means, which we did not order. With the amount of money we're spending here, I'd expect our bill to be correct."

The waiter, Ian, began apologizing profusely. "Sir, I'm terribly sorry for this error. This is obviously a cashier's mistake, and I'll correct the problem immediately."

"Maybe while Ian is fixing your check, you'd like some dessert? On the house, of course." Eric smiled genially at the two guests. For a free dessert, I'd happily ignore a cashier's goof that was being corrected.

The woman smiled politely and addressed Ian. "It's not a problem, but dessert would be nice, thank you." She shot a look at her husband that said he'd better shut up or dessert would be all he'd get that night. "Honey, just let it go. It's just a little mistake," she assured her husband.

"Excellent, folks. I'm glad I could help here. Now let's get you those desserts," Eric said. He gripped Ian's arm and led him past me, toward the kitchen. "You'd better be careful. Remember what we talked about," Eric growled angrily as he flashed Ian a quick but ominous look. Ian nodded with understanding and rushed off to order the appeasing desserts.

My date returned to his seat beside me, suddenly relaxed and exuding composure and cheer that somehow felt false. "Just a small misunderstanding about their bill. Happens all the time at restaurants. You should always check your bill. Remember that." Eric winked at me.

Freak, freak, freak!

Cassie set two plates down in front of us. "Here's your first course. Garrett has made you lobster and Brie wontons with papaya-mint dipping sauce. Can I bring you anything else right now?"

"Double vodka," Eric directed her.

I wasn't sure that even lobster could compensate for my date's behavior, but when I took my first taste, I knew I was wrong. I'd put up with anything for this. Two crisp wonton skins, perfectly browned, held rich bites of lobster meat floating in melted Brie. I decided that I could survive on these for the rest of my life. Easily.

"This is what I'm talking about!" Eric nodded, his mouth full of food.

"Amazing," I agreed. "These are phenomenal. I could eat a plateful!"

"You want some more? I'll get Garrett to make as many as you want," Eric offered, looking into the kitchen.

"No, no!" I shook my head in protest. "I want to save room for the other courses." *And keep you from embarrassing me yet again.*

"All right. So, we like dish number one, then? I guess Essence will need my money to get lobster on the regular menu, though. What do you think?"

"So far, I vote for investing, even if it's just to save these wontons from extinction," I said.

When the next course arrived, Cassie announced, "Mr. Rafferty, Garrett knows your favorite. Venison carpaccio with blackberry glaze, cranberry vinaigrette, eight-year-old Gouda, and arugula."

Wow! Another winner. Eric and I actually smiled at each other while we silently devoured our carpaccio. Possibly by accident, he made eye contact. But really, how could you not connect with someone, at least a little, when relishing such an amazing dish?

"A woman who eats venison. I like that," Eric said.

Unfortunately, the rest of our dishes were not nearly so fabulous as our first few courses. The Pan-fried Oysters with Fennel-Fenugreek Aioli contained oysters that were simultaneously soggy and chewy. The Foie Gras Ravioli with Sweet Corn and Black Truffle Bouillon did not live up to its enticing name. Eric frowned as he pushed his tongue around in his mouth in a disgusting display of tasting. "I'm disappointed in this. The foie gras is dried out, and the bouillon is flavorless. A totally forgettable dish."

Our final course, called Grilled Ahi Tuna with Sweet Rice, Mustard Greens, and Hoisin Sauce, was just as unpleasant as the ravioli; the tuna was overcooked, the rice gummy, and the greens bitter. I started to wonder why such delicious-sounding dishes were so disappointing. Eric pronounced the tuna *dégousse,* which, he informed me, was French for "disgusting." (French for disgusting is *dégoûtant,* as I didn't point out.) Although I agreed with Eric's assessments, I couldn't stop picturing him as a child critiquing his birthday cake: *Well, Mommy, the overall presentation was nice, but the cake was too dense, and the frosting too sweet for my liking. And the Big Bird candles were gaudy.* In the case of Essence, I thought his criticism was justified. I didn't know whether I'd sink money into this place, which clearly had kinks to be worked out. The quality of the food, for example. Rather a large kink.

Poor Garrett. I saw him in the kitchen, sweating and running back and forth from oven to counter, shouting at staff members, sometimes in English, sometimes in Spanish, struggling desperately to succeed. Although this was my first inside look at a restaurant kitchen, even I could tell by watching the manic pursuits of the entire kitchen staff that things were out of control. Eric was watching Garrett as well.

"He seems pretty harried," I remarked.

"Yeah, well, kitchens are always wild. But I'm worried, considering that it isn't even that busy tonight and Garrett looks overwhelmed. That just can't happen," Eric said, shaking his head in disappointment. "The other meals I've had here have been much better."

"Well, if this is his first executive chef job, he must still be learning a lot. Maybe he'll get better?" I asked hopefully.

"I don't know. The lobster and venison were so damn good, but he's losing it as the night goes on. I mean, look at him. He's a wreck. There's a big difference between being a great chef and being able to stay a great chef all night—especially on a busy night." Eric pointed to the kitchen just in time to catch sight of Garrett grabbing a smoking frying pan that was emitting a vile stench. "It's a gamble. He might learn quickly and become one of the best chefs around. Or this job might be too much for him. And I guess I'm concerned that Timothy put someone like Garrett in this position. Tim's got a lot riding on the success of this place, so he should've found someone with more experience. There are some great menu ideas here, but they're not coming out right."

"Well, the staff seems solid, and Timothy obviously has great experience. From Magellan. Why is Essence having such a tough time? Just because of Garrett?"

"No, probably not just Garrett. It could be a staffing issue. It's a good staff, but there's always the usual conflict. The front of the house—the hostess, the waitstaff and bartenders, the managers—and the back of the house—the chef and his crew—have to be able to work well together. And that's rare. See, the waitstaff can make quite a bit of money on the right night and at the right restaurant, because they get tips. And, frankly, half the time they don't care about the food all that much because they just want their money. They're not in this business because they appreciate good food." Eric finished his drink quickly and thumped the glass on the table before continuing.

"But the chefs and the line cooks hardly make any money. Those guys, or at least the executive chef and executive sous chef, cook because they love food and they love to cook. For them, it's an art. So when they bust their asses to prepare and plate a dish perfectly, they get outraged when the server doesn't pick it up on time. Either the food gets left out getting cold, or it sits under a heat lamp getting dry. Then the chef gets criticized for making lousy food, when it was the server who pretty much ruined the dish. Or the servers will blame the chef. They'll claim they had to wait so long for their orders that they got backed up and had to leave the food sitting out. And sometimes the chef just screws up a dish. I don't know the specifics about the staff here, but I'd guess there must be some problems."

If the food had been even moderately good, I'd have kept eating while Eric talked. As it was, I just listened. My lack of participation obviously didn't bother Eric at all; if he'd been alone at the table instead of with me, he'd probably have delivered the same soliloquy. If he'd looked significantly adorable, I'd at least have been able to sit back and stare at physical perfection. Unfair as it was, hot guys could get away with boring, useless attitudes. But those who looked like Eric? Well, his bland looks and mousy hair were doing nothing for me.

"To top it off," he went on, mainly to himself, "a lot of restaurant owners, who are concerned about their own financial success, can get angry with the executive chef. See, the chef orders the food for the restaurant. But if business is down, then the food costs get too high because the restaurant isn't taking in as much money, and they end up throwing out expensive ingredients, thereby losing money. The chef gets blamed for high food costs and an empty restaurant, when the fact that business is down might not have anything to do with the quality of the chef's food. A bad economy, poor advertising by the owners, that kind of thing. I mean, let's face it. There are plenty of very successful restaurants in Boston that serve crummy food, but the restaurants have been so hyped up and blitzed all over the media with the right spin that nobody even cares."

Eric didn't seem to get the idea that a two-person conversation is supposed to be like tennis: back and forth. Instead of sending the ball to my side of the court, he just kept hitting it against the backboard.

"So," he persisted, "people in this restaurant business are always blaming somebody for something. Tim is a great guy, though, and I think he knows when to assign blame and when not to. But no matter who gets blamed, most nights the whole staff will end up staying out together until the bars close. It's a crazy world."

Although I realized that Eric was by no means my soul mate, and not even second-date material, and although I was pretty sick of having him monopolize the conversation, I was interested in some of what he had to say about the restaurant world. I knew a lot

67

about food and eating, but except for what I'd read in *Boston Magazine*, I didn't know much about the business itself. After Cassie had cleared our plates, Eric evidently remembered that I, too, possessed the power of speech, and we discussed the pros and cons of investing in Essence. I almost started to enjoy the conversation. I noticed, however, that not once during the evening had he asked anything about me. He knew my name and knew I liked eating, and that information alone was evidently enough to make him comfortable in sharing his thoughts on possible financial transactions. Keeping the discussion away from anything that might further identify me was fine. After tolerating his self-important and dictatorial attitude all evening, I'd be content to fade away with my belly full and with Eric unable to contact me again.

Note to self: Cancel Back Bay Dates account immediately upon completion of date!

Eric's cell phone rang. He glared at the Caller ID and picked up. "Hello? I told you not call me," Eric hollered into the receiver.

God, having lacked the decency to turn off the phone during our date, he went ahead and answered it? And screamed! Oh, what did I care? Dessert would probably be good. I had been eyeing the house speciality, honey-lavender crème brûlée, which I knew would have been made in advance. The sugared top would be seared with a torch just before serving, and even in his befuddled state Garrett probably wouldn't mess that up.

"Phil, if I were you, I'd take care of it." Eric signaled to me that he was leaving to finish the call somewhere else. He headed toward a corridor at the back of the restaurant.

Cassie brought me a cappuccino, which was delicious. Nothing can kill a good meal like a finale of bad coffee. I can never understand why some places serve *the worst* coffee. How hard can it be to buy a good bean and brew a pot? Okay, myself not included. But if I owned a restaurant, I'd buy a coffeemaker that worked.

When I'd finished the cappuccino, Eric still hadn't returned, and I was itching for the crème brûlée. Unfortunately for me, my mother's training prevented me from ordering while Eric was gone. I looked into the kitchen to see whether Eric had invited himself into the heart of the restaurant to pester poor Garrett. I didn't see my date and practically threw my hands up in exasperation at the evening's events. Two cappuccinos later, I said to hell with manners and ordered dessert from Cassie.

"Have you seen Eric?" I asked her. "He left to finish a call on his cell phone and hasn't come back."

She shook her head but promised to look for him. She wasn't worried that he'd skipped out; as a guest of the restaurant, he'd hardly have run off to avoid paying a nonexistent bill. I wasn't worried, either; I was annoyed and insulted. If my date could disappear, I decided, I could do exactly the same thing. It could take me a long, long time to touch up my makeup and fuss with my hair; it could take me long enough for Eric to return to the table, find me gone, and sit there all alone wondering where I was. My crème brûlée would have to wait.

Essence was not, of course, the sort of restaurant with large, garish signs pointing to the restrooms. Looking around, I couldn't find so much as a small, tasteful arrow and had to ask Cassie for directions. "Down that little corridor at the back," she said. "Ladies is the first door on your left. If someone's in there, use the men's room. Everyone does. It's the next door."

After making my way around a few tables, I entered the narrow corridor, which led to a door prominently marked Exit. The first door on the left showed a stylish sketch of a figure with long hair and a skirt. The door was locked. I took Cassie's advice and pushed open the second door, the one with a matching sketch of a debonair figure in a coat and tails. Although the door was unlocked, the men's room was occupied.

Sprawled on his stomach on the slate floor was a tall man with curly dirty-blond hair. His legs were bent awkwardly, and one arm was stretched out at a painful-looking angle. The man, however, was beyond pain. His head lay in a pool of blood. The blood led away from the blond curls and toward two objects that lay on the tile. One was a mobile phone. The other was a knife with a black handle and a long, thin, curved, and bloody blade.

I had found Eric.

FIVE

I stood under the fluorescent lights in the men's room for a good two or three minutes while I tried to take in what I was looking at. I couldn't look away from the repulsive wound in Eric's neck. The skin was split open, the cut long and somehow clean despite the bright red, glistening blood. I could feel my heart pound and my whole body shiver, but I just couldn't move. It felt impossible that Eric, who had just been critiquing food and yelling on his cell phone, was lying here on the floor, dead. I suppose I should have dropped down to the tiles to begin some sort of life-saving attempt. As it was, I was frozen, in part, I suspect, because no one could have survived that dreadful wound. Also, the thought of stepping into the pool of blood churned my full stomach.

I had visions from the first-aid class I'd taken when I was working as a toddler teacher in a day care center. I knew we had covered CPR, but the only thing I could remember was what to do if a child had the misfortune to get a pencil stuck in an eye. I remembered that one should *not* try to pull the pencil out of the eyeball, but rather should tape a Dixie cup over the protruding object. I had raised a question: since most pencils are much taller than Dixie cups, shouldn't we stockpile some tall, latte-style cups for such occurences? There had been a memorable photograph of some poor child model forced to demonstrate what a Dixie cup taped over the eye looked like, a photo that had sent my fellow teachers and me into gales of laughter. Not helpful here.

I also remembered that should one happen upon a compound fracture in which a bone is sticking out of the body, one should *not* attempt to push the bone back in place. The banned maneuver had struck me as the grossest possible thing ever, and I was sure that if I were to find myself faced with a bone sticking out of a body, the *last thing* I would do would be to try to push it back in place. Still, if Eric had fallen victim to a sharp stick in the eye and a compound fracture, I might possibly have been of some assistance.

Eric's cell phone started to ring, and the electronic rendition of Guns N' Roses' "Paradise City" jerked me out of my daze. What a lame song to set your ringer to. This disgraceful thought made me realize that I had to do *something,* and since vomiting on what I assumed was a crime scene would not be helpful, I figured I would pass off the problem to somebody else. Before I could instruct my legs to get moving, the restroom door opened, and Timothy burst in.

"Oh, Jesus." Timothy, in a show of gallant behavior far exceeding my reminiscences of first-aid photos, practically fell onto Eric's body and cupped his hand over the bleeding slice in Eric's neck while yelling, "Oh God! Oh God!" Timothy pulled off his expensive navy shirt and pressed it to Eric's neck. "Chloe, don't look! Get out of here! Go!" he shouted at me.

My feet finally decided to work. I hurried out of the

men's room, came to a halt, and found myself staring numbly at the bustling restaurant, which was full of diners and waitstaff. Looking toward the kitchen, I saw Garrett hacking away at a piece of red meat. I stared at the huge cleaver blade as Garrett repeatedly whacked someone's dinner.

I've heard people say that when you faint, your vision narrows, like a black circle enlarging to constrict your field of view. Truth. The last thing I clearly saw was the chef's cleaver cracking through a bone.

"Chloe? You okay? Come on, wake up." I opened my eyes to see a shirtless Timothy peering at me with great concern.

There I was, sprawled out on the floor with a group of restaurant patrons murmuring pitying comments like, "The poor thing!" and "She just absolutely collapsed!"

When I tried to sit up, Timothy immediately pushed me back down. In my dazed state, I somehow noticed that he'd washed his hands and wasn't going to leave a bloody print on my arm.

"No, don't sit up," he instructed me. "Just lie still and don't move." Ordering a perfectly healthy woman to remain motionless after a minor fainting incident? What kind of stupid first-aid class had he taken?

First aid! Oh, Christ, when I'd fallen, I'd probably given myself a revolting compound fracture! I looked down. All my limbs were intact. "Seriously, I'm fine. Just let me get up," I assured the crowd. I rose from the floor and walked to a nearby table, where I sat down and tried to assume an air of normality. Oh God, poor Eric! Then I asked a question so stupid that I can't believe it left my mouth. "Tim, is Eric okay?" What did I expect to hear? That really, aside from the knife wound that had practically severed his head from his body, he was in great shape?

"Chloe, I'm so sorry . . ." Timothy's voice trailed off. "Eric is dead. The police and the ambulance should be here any second."

How odd: an ambulance for a dead person. I mean, the EMTs weren't miraculously going to revive a cadaver. Shouldn't EMTs devote themselves to tasks that had a chance of success, such as taping cups over eyes? Although my thoughts felt logical, I must have looked woozy. Timothy went to fetch me a glass of water and instructed Cassie to sit with me, presumably to make sure I didn't keel over again. It's a good thing that Cassie became a waitress instead of a nurse. She did nothing except smile politely as we sat uncomfortably together and listened to the sirens approach the restaurant. I looked out the window to see what I guessed to be about six hundred emergency vehicles pull up outside.

The scene that followed could have been staged for some prime-time cop show. Official-looking people took over the premises, as I imagined the restaurant would now be called, and no one was allowed to leave. After pushing the crowd away from the men's room, the police sealed off the corridor to the restrooms with neon yellow streamers printed with Do

Not Cross. Cassie and I watched as cops and EMTs rushed around. And firefighters. Why were they here? Not to hose down the bloody tiles. To put out Garrett's flames?

Looking around, I wondered about all the guests and what they'd do and should do in this freakish situation. Should they keep eating their dinners? Some were doing just that. Would they have to pay for their meals? Should they leave big tips to console the wait-staff? After this ordeal, would they leave no tips at all?

Garrett and his crew had apparently stopped cooking when news of Eric's death had reached them. They'd left the kitchen to cluster behind the bar, where they were talking amongst themselves.

A charred smell wafted our way. "Cassie, I think something is burning in the kitchen," I said flatly.

Cassie yelled to Garrett, who bolted across the room to the kitchen to scrape up the remains of what looked like a trout that had seared itself to the cooktop.

All of my television watching helped me to identify the medical examiner, a tall woman with a severe face and an air of authority. She entered through the front door and immediately barked orders at the men trying to do their jobs. She was escorted to the back corridor by one of the police officers and disappeared into the men's room. I bet *she* never fainted.

Clad in a white chef's coat, Timothy returned with my water. "God, I'm so sorry, Chloe. You must be devastated about Eric. I can't imagine how you must be feeling. I know you weren't together that long, but I know you two had a strong connection. Eric just adored you. He did." Tim shook his head and actually had tears in his eyes. This man truly thought he was comforting a brokenhearted girlfriend. It seemed callous not to play along. What was I going to say? *I'm in shock from seeing the gory body of a murder victim. Eric has nothing to do with it!*

Actually, I was in shock. If I'd been myself, I'd probably have poured out the whole story to Tim. Instead, I decided to play it as if I were so grief-stricken that I was unable to discuss my overwhelming feelings for Eric. "I just can't believe this is happening," I said truthfully. "Have the police said anything to you yet? Do they know who did this to Eric?"

"No, nothing yet. The detective—his name's Hurley—needs to talk to everyone here tonight and get their information so he can contact them later. And obviously he said he wants to talk to you, since you found Eric. Actually, let me go see if he's ready for you. The sooner you talk to him, the sooner you can get out of here. You must want to go home more than anything." He stood up and rubbed my back briefly before he took off in search of the detective.

The strange thing was that I didn't feel a desperate need to flee—or wouldn't have, except for the sorrowful glances everybody kept casting my way. Since the consensus seemed to be that I had just lost the love of my life in a grisly crime, the whole restaurant seemed to be staring at me. I didn't like being the center of attention, especially under false pretenses, but I have to admit that this kind of real-life high drama was new and intriguing to me, mainly because I grew up in the safe, uneventful suburb of Newton. The biggest crime ever to occur there was the discovery of a massage parlor that offered quite a bit more than massages. The establishment was shockingly located above a pediatrician's office. One female so-called masseuse was quoted as saying that she charged one hundred dollars for her *services* "unless they think that's too high." But the news that really alarmed Newtonites was the discovery that *not only* was this place servicing its clients sexually but— gasp—some of the employees *didn't even have their massage licenses!* The only competition for that story was the exhilarating debate over whether or not Newton schools should become peanut-free zones to protect children with allergies. One mother was interviewed and insisted that her child's diet *required* him to have peanut butter for lunch. In typical Newton fashion, her child's need for peanut butter was greater than another child's need to avoid anaphylaxis. So the commotion in the restaurant was totally new to me, and once the initial physical shock of finding the body had mostly passed, and even after I began to appreciate how horrible Eric's death was, my forensic curiosity outweighed my nonexistent relationship with the deceased.

Timothy returned with a skinny man in his late forties or so with incredibly mussed-up black hair. "Hey there, Chloe," Tim said somberly. "This is Detective Scott Hurley. He's got to ask you about tonight. I told him how distraught you are, but he says it can't wait. Are you going to be okay talking to him?"

"I think I'll be fine. But thank you for your concern," I told Tim, who then left with Cassie.

Detective Hurley looked exhausted, as if he'd been working nonstop all day or maybe even all week. He seated himself across from me at the table, ran his hands through his hair, and looked right at me. "Ma'am, I'm very sorry for your loss. You're the girlfriend, huh? And you found the body?" he asked, jumping right to the point. "Name?" he continued, pulling a pen from behind his ear.

"Eric Rafferty," I answered.

"Not the victim's name. Your name." He glared at me.

"Oh, sorry. I'm Chloe Carter," I answered. He took my address and phone number, and asked me to describe my relationship with the victim.

I leaned in conspiratorially. "Well, to be honest, I didn't have a relationship with him. I just met Eric tonight. We were on a blind date. Well, an Internet date. I met him through Back Bay Dates, one of those online dating services, and this was our first date."

"You're not his girlfriend? Timothy and a couple of the waitstaff here said you two were pretty involved. Said you'd only been together less than a month, but that things were hot and heavy."

"No, I'm definitely not Eric's girlfriend. Wasn't. I just saw him for the first time tonight. Maybe he'd been dating someone else. You know, he did say that he used to go out with the woman who does the books for Essence and for Timothy's old restaurant, Magellan. Veronica, he said her name was. I think that's right."

"Last name?"

"Sorry, I don't know. You'll have to ask Timothy. I don't know much about Eric, except that he was thinking about investing in Essence. He wanted to eat here tonight to check it out again. He said he used to eat at Magellan a lot, and so he knew Timothy through there. I don't even know exactly what he does, well, *did,* for a living. Something to do with financial planning and having clients."

The detective leaned back in his chair and adjusted his wrinkled gray suit. "So I don't suppose you'd have any idea why your date is dead in the restaurant's restroom, then, huh?" He actually smiled a little.

I shook my head apologetically.

"Since I'm assuming this man didn't slit his own throat, we're treating this as a homicide. And I've got to find out everything I can about what went on tonight. So, tell me exactly how you met him. About this Internet dating thing. And take me through everything that happened tonight." Hurley sighed as if expecting my description of my time with Eric to be as boring as it actually—and, in retrospect, sadly—had been.

79

I ran through the events of the past day. Hurley asked questions. In particular, he wanted to hear about ex-boyfriends of mine. Trying not to portray myself as a total idiot, I reluctantly told him the whole story about Noah and concluded by saying, "Noah is sort of a jerk. You know, one of those fear-of-commitment guys? Definitely a mistake on my part. But if you think he had anything to do with this, you're totally wrong. I guarantee you that there is no possibility that Noah would ever be jealous that I was going on a date."

"All right, give me his last name, address, and phone number." The detective had a pen and notebook ready. Oh, great, like I really needed the police questioning Noah about Eric's murder! Now Noah would definitely know that my date had been a miserable failure. And be totally pissed at me for siccing the police on him.

"No, no, please don't talk to him! He didn't even know where I was going tonight," I pleaded.

"We just have to cover all the bases here."

I reluctantly reeled off Noah's info.

"Now, you also said Eric got a phone call. He had an argument on the phone. Do you know who he was talking to? Or what they were arguing about?"

I shook my head. "I have no idea. Just someone named Phil. Can't you trace the call? And it wasn't exactly an argument. It sounded more like Eric was irritated with whomever he was talking to. Like he'd already had the same conversation before. He just said something like, 'I told you to take care of it.' And that's when he left to finish the call. And that was the last time I saw him. Well, saw him alive. His phone was on the floor next to him in the men's room. And it rang while I was in there."

"Let's go back to just before you left for the ladies' room. See if you can tell me who you saw."

"Just people at their tables. And Garrett. The chef. And Cassie. Our waitress. She showed me where the restrooms were," I said.

"So you didn't see Timothy or any other staff members?" the detective questioned me.

"I don't know. Um, well, no, not that I remember."

"Okay, and this waiter? Ian? What exactly did Eric say to him when he was walking away with him?" The detective leaned over the table and looked right at me.

"Um, I think he said, 'Remember what we talked about.' That's all I heard. Eric didn't say anything about it when he came back to our table. I don't know what he meant. But it was a statement. A reminder. Not a question."

Detective Hurley asked me to point out the couple who had had the dispute with Ian, but they were nowhere in sight. "They must have left soon after that," I said. "They were getting dessert, so they must have left while Eric and I were still eating."

"All right. That should do it for now. I'll get in touch if I have any more questions for you, but you might as well get home. And, hey. Chloe? I'm sorry you had to find his body. It's not pleasant stuff. I've been doing this job for almost twenty years, and it's not easy."

"Thank you," I said. "Um, can I ask you a question?"

He nodded.

"Well, when I found Eric, I didn't do anything. I mean, do you think . . . was there anything I could've done? What if, you know, he was still alive?" I started to tear up.

"No. From what I know, there wasn't a thing you could've done. Except contaminate the crime scene. That's what Timothy did, trying to help. Did more harm than good."

"I saw the knife. In there. It was a strange knife. With that curved handle?" Now I could feel a few tears run down my cheeks. My disbelief and shock were wearing off, and I was scared and confused.

Without saying anything about the knife, Detective Hurley reached over and patted my hand. "Here's my card, Chloe. Call me if you think of anything else. Now, why don't you go home and get some rest."

So I left Essence without saying good-bye to anyone.

SIX

I slept deeply that Sunday night, almost as if my blind date's murder had put me in a protective coma. I woke up late on Monday morning and flicked on the television only to be bombarded with news updates detailing Eric Rafferty's murder. Tim Rock appeared on an interview. Looking haggard, he kept repeating that he was so sorry this had happened and that the entire staff sent their condolences to Eric's friends and family.

I'd left a message for Adrianna the night before, and when the phone rang at eleven that morning, caller ID informed me that she was getting back to me. Finally. I picked up the phone and started crying.

"I'm coming over," she promised. "Just hold on. I'll pick up supplies and be there soon."

For once, I was glad that she worked unusual hours and could drop everything to rescue me. While I waited for her, I made a pitiful attempt to continue painting my living room but found myself too distracted to get anything done. An hour after we'd talked, Ade burst into my apartment, her arms full of bags that she dropped to the floor when she saw me frozen on the couch clutching a dripping paint roller, my leftover mascara smeared down my face and paint splatters everywhere.

I looked up at my best friend, stunning as always. Today's outfit consisted of shiny lavender pants, a sleeveless ivory top, and strappy sandals. By comparison with her usual wild style, the look was tame. Adrianna was seriously beautiful: piles of blonde hair, chocolate brown eyes, perfect skin, knockout body. Most women would hate her, and, in fact, she was not very popular among other females. I'd never been threatened by her good looks or her assertive, even aggressive, nature. One of the few women in her life, I couldn't have been more grateful for her friendship.

"Chloe! This isn't worth ruining your wood floors over." Adrianna eyed me and my apartment and pronounced us both filthy. "Time to get you two fixed up. Listen, I don't know what to say about last night. We'll get to that later. We'll take things in chronological order. So that means the Noah situation first." She wrapped an arm around my shoulders. "It sucks, and it's embarrassing. He may be hot and sexy and charming, but he's an insensitive, egomaniacal ass. And you already know all that, and you knew he wasn't good for you, but he was there and charmed you into bed, and you made the same mistake we all have. So cry it all out today. Then you can tell me what the hell happened last night." She stood up and carried a huge box of pastries to the kitchen. "I brought over every season of *Alias* on DVD, so we'll gorge ourselves on Thai food and the pastries I brought over from Mike's in the North End. Let's finish painting and clean this disaster area up," she called from inside the fridge. "Oh, and I'm staying over tonight." I smiled to myself. I wasn't alone.

At 6:30 that evening, Adrianna and I had finished up the living room. She'd patiently tolerated my diatribe on the woes of my involvement with Noah, and she'd repeatedly shaken her head in disbelief as I'd described everything about my evening with Eric, including the meal, his pretensions, and, of course, his murder.

After the painting, we sat on the couch together. "Come on," Adrianna said, "it's not like you had any relationship with this guy. I mean, it must have been exceedingly disturbing and revolting to see a bloody body, but you can't actually be *sad*, right? This date with Eric was only supposed to be a retaliation for Noah's philandering. It's not like you gave a shit about him."

Adrianna is always practical, sometimes to the point of seeming coldhearted. Objectively, I suppose, she was right. But I *did* feel sad. "Ade, the thing is, though, you didn't see Eric's dead body on the floor. You didn't see all the blood. It's not like on TV. It smells, and it's just awful looking. Somebody died last night, and it doesn't matter, in a way, who it was. I feel sad about that, and I feel sorry for myself that I had to see what I did. Is that selfish? And maybe I got what I deserved for my stupid attempt at revenge, but as annoying as Eric was, he didn't deserve what he got. I mean, being annoying and pretentious didn't mean he should die. Because if it did, Noah should be dead, too."

"Not such a rotten idea," Adrianna responded. "But you're right. I'm a bitch. Forget I said any of that. You can feel whatever you want to feel. It must have been terrible. I've never seen a dead body, so I don't know what it was like." She leaned over to give me a hug.

"You know, even though I was there, in a way, I don't even know what it was like, either. God, Ade, his throat was cut open! And . . . well, what if it was my fault? If I hadn't gone on that stupid Web site, and we hadn't made this date, maybe Eric wouldn't have been at the restaurant and would still be alive and doling out his preposterous culinary observations! And why did everyone think Eric and I were practically on the verge of marriage? How could he have been talking about me when he only found me on the Internet yesterday?"

Adrianna lit some scented candles—she believes in aromatherapy—and, amid the smell of wild strawberries, she tried to reassure me. "Chloe, you don't know why Eric was killed. If it was random violence, that's not your fault. Look, we live in a big city, and the reality is that people get murdered, and if it's some psycho out there, then I'm glad you weren't hurt. But if this Eric was a target, someone wanted him dead for whatever reason, and you just happened to be there."

"You're right. But I still feel terrible. This whole thing is confusing and upsetting, and I wish to God I'd never met Eric!" I fell to pieces for a few minutes while my good friend rubbed my back and fetched me tissues. The image of a lunatic out there randomly killing people in restaurant restrooms didn't reassure me. In a gruesomely comforting way, I preferred to think that Eric in particular had been the intended victim.

When I pulled myself together, Adrianna took my head in her hands and asked, "Okay, you done? Stop feeling sorry for yourself. You've cried enough to flood this place." Adrianna got up and went over to grab her purse, which she'd left on a chair. "Now, for one of this evening's activities . . . ta dah!" She whipped around to show me a box of hair dye.

"Why are we dying my hair?" I demanded.

"We're not dying yours," she responded. "We're dying mine. I don't know how to fix the Eric problem. But I do know something about friendship. I'm too blonde, and you're in no state to be socializing with blondes right now. In an act of solidarity, I'm going brunette. Or more precisely, I'm going Walnut Shine."

"Oh, Ade! I don't hate *all* blondes now. Just Noah's blonde tramp. You have gorgeous hair." She did have excellent hair: a thick, silky mane of magnificent locks that curled softly the way you see in all those shampoo commercials. She regularly colored her hair at home and had at least four different blonde shades streaked through her tresses. How her hair stayed healthy, I had no idea. Mine was full of split ends and frizz no matter how many times I conditioned, hot-oiled, or trimmed it.

"Yes, yes, Chloe, I know there are many lovely, friendly blondes out in the world, but right now we're going to hate all of them! Get me a towel, and help me get this glop in my hair. And get the menu for Bangkok Bistro. We need major takeout tonight."

After we'd ordered half the menu to be delivered, we holed up in my bathroom, Adrianna seated backward on the toilet, half-naked, with a towel wrapped around her shoulders.

"I can't believe you're trusting me with this," I murmured as I massaged the brown dye through her hair.

"It's just hair," she replied, a comment I thought was

pretty generous, considering that hair was her profession.

As I worked on her new look, I found that instead of wanting to complain about my nightmarish love life, I just wanted to be quiet. I didn't even want to think about Noah or my year and a half of infrequent and unsuccessful dating or the bloody mess I'd seen on the men's room floor. I just wanted a night with my best friend.

After washing Adrianna's hair in the tub and declaring her new walnut shade a victory for scorned women everywhere, we sat in front of the TV. I had showered and scrubbed the paint out of my own hair and was comfortably wearing my sushi-print pajamas with my hair twisted elegantly on top of my head, thanks to significant tugging and pulling from Adrianna.

Having not eaten all day, I was so famished that when the deliveryman arrived with our Thai food, I practically tackled him. The day of fasting was unlike me. I typically spent a good portion of each day thinking about what I was going to have for my next meal. Whenever I was depressed, I usually had a few hours when I didn't want anything to do with food, but when my bad mood even hinted at lifting, I craved food. And not just food, but gourmet food. I was all about soothing trips to Whole Foods or dinner at *Boston Magazine*'s review of the month. When I'd ended my last serious relationship, I'd ransacked my shelves of cookbooks and selected Charlie Trotter's

Rack of Lamb with Vegetable Ragoût, Mustard Spätzle, and Mustard and Thyme Reduction as my medicine. Instead of slaving over homemade spätzle, I'd substituted store-bought gnocchi, but I'd figured that under the circumstances, Mr. Trotter would forgive me for cheating.

We opened pad thai (no peanuts), tod mun, chicken curry, warm beef salad, and white rice. The smells were spicy, salty, and sweet. I inhaled the aromas and felt a cozy, healing comfort wash over me. While Sydney Bristow continued to kick some serious ass, we polished off the delectable chocolate mousse cake Adrianna had brought and washed it down with tall glasses of milk. The last time Adrianna had broken up with a boyfriend, the highlights of the evening had included, from what we could both remember, drowning our (her) woes in apple martinis, getting kicked out of the Purple Rose bar, and vomiting in my bathtub late into the night. The hangovers we'd both had the next day led to the resolution that future heartaches were to be dealt with sober.

And sober we were when late that night we both crashed in my bed together. I was exhausted from my emotional-roller-coaster day, and Adrianna had to get up early to do yet another final hair run-through for a bride-to-be. Ade pulled the comforter up to her chin. "I keep telling her to wait until a few days before the wedding to decide, since she keeps changing her mind about what she wants. One day it's up, the next it's down," Adrianna complained.

89

We giggled and chatted like kids having a sleepover until we were both silent and falling asleep. I rolled on my side and pulled a pillow on top of my head, a habit that always left me in a state of potential suffocation but was my favorite way to sleep. It felt nice to have a warm body in my bed, even if it was just Adrianna. Better her than Noah. Or Eric, obviously.

I slept dream-free and woke up cozy and warm and still satisfied from the delicious Thai food. It was only 6:45 a.m., but I could hear Adrianna in the shower preparing for her bridal nightmare. I snuggled in my comforter and remembered when my food-love connection had first begun, namely, during a family trip to Europe when I was thirteen. When my now-beloved parents, Bethany and Jack, had packed us up, the last thing Heather and I had looked forward to was vacationing with our parents, and we'd especially resented the expectation that we girls actually *learn* something. I'd devoted the first part of the vacation to devouring *Gone with the Wind* and delectable food. While Scarlett pursued her precious Ashley, I munched on buttery baguettes smeared with a triple-cream Brie and air-dried beef, the perfect love story and perfect food. I'd taken breaks from the Civil War (truces, I guess) for meals with my family. When I finished *Gone with the Wind*, I started *The Great Gatsby*. While our parents toured the Louvre and Notre Dame, my sister and I sat on benches in the Paris sun enjoying spinach-filled crepes and cones of exotic sorbet. I embedded myself in the world of Gatsby's all-night parties, lavish food, and romantic quests, and looked up occasionally to join Heather in gazing with vague longing at beautiful French boys. (At that point, my graphic knowledge about boys came from the one pornographic picture my classmate Elliot had shown me.) So, my pursuit of the perfect blend of romance and food dated to that summer, when I basked in literary love and bombarded my senses with new tastes and smells. Especially since then, good food had always meant love or the hope of love: Scarlett, Ashley, Rhett, Gatsby, Daisy, French boys, and surprisingly good times with my family. It had meant weddings and holidays. Until now, it had never, ever meant death. Never before.

Adrianna interrupted my reminiscing when she entered the bedroom looking intolerably glamorous in a black spaghetti-strap sundress. "How can you look like that this early in the morning? Or ever, for that matter?" I demanded.

"Oh, shut up!" She waved away my words and handed me a steaming cup of perfect coffee that she'd somehow extracted from my defective coffeemaker. No wonder I was the only woman friend she had. No one else could tolerate her perfection.

"I'll walk you out." Holding the coffee cup, I hauled myself out of bed, walked her out the side door to the fire escape, and sat down in the one rickety chair I had managed to squeeze onto the little landing. I was just about to say my good-byes and thank-yous to Adrianna when I heard footsteps coming up the stairs. Noah.

This was how my life worked. Faced with an ex, I was dressed in silly pajamas, and my hair was a mess. Meanwhile, my gorgeous friend stood beside me in all her glamorous glory with Noah flagrantly ogling her, black dress and all.

"What do *you* want?" demanded Adrianna, who stood beside me in more ways than one.

"Hi, Adrianna." Noah leaned flirtatiously against the railing. "You look good." Oh, I hate him! "So, Chloe, I see you've moved on nicely. A little switch for you, but you've got good taste."

I jumped in before Ade socked him. "Noah, what do you want?"

His flirty expression vanished as he turned to me with irritation. "Well, I didn't realize you were mad enough to throw the police at me." My stomach dropped. "Some detective came by asking me questions about where I was Sunday night around dinnertime and after. I explained that I'd had company here and therefore couldn't have *murdered* your date." I bet he'd been with that horrid blonde woman again. "Why the hell would you even have *mentioned* me to the police?" he continued. Boy, he was mad. Good.

"Well," I said as casually as I could manage, "Detective Hurley asked me some questions, and somehow your name came up. I mean, they *are* the police. They have to be thorough." I grinned smugly at him.

"Yeah, well this detective started asking me all about paint. Whether I'd painted anything lately, if my office had been painted, and on and on. And I was more than happy to inform him that the person who does all the painting around here is *you!* I told him all he had to do was go upstairs and look at your apartment."

"I have no idea what you're talking about or why he'd ask you about paint. But apparently you've survived your brush with the law, so just relax, Noah," I fired back.

"Well, now that you've had your little revenge, you can leave me out of your police conversations," he said as he turned and headed back downstairs—but only after giving Adrianna the once-over again. "It was nice seeing you."

Adrianna took a step forward as though she was going to leap after him and clobber the jerk. I grabbed her hand but couldn't stop her from yelling, "Don't you even *look* at me, you big, dirty male slut!"

"Stop, Ade!" I said, laughing. "You're the one who said it's not worth it."

"Oh God! He is so annoying. In fact"—she paused dramatically—"I found Noah threatening and potentially violent just now! He very well could have murdered Eric."

"Don't be idiotic. *You* may have been threatening and potentially violent just now, but Noah wasn't. Of course he didn't murder Eric. He has no motive whatsoever. He obviously doesn't give a damn about me and apparently had his hands full with Tank-Top Woman at the time of the murder."

"Fine," she conceded. "He didn't murder Eric. But I

don't know what you were thinking hooking up with him."

I shook my head at my own idiocy. "I have no idea either. I really don't."

After Adrianna left, I sat in the sunshine on my makeshift balcony and finished my coffee. The phone rang twice, but I let voice mail pick up. The third call finally got me out of my chair. "Yes," I answered irritably.

"Chloe? It's Detective Hurley here. From the other night."

"Of, course. Hi." Like I knew thousands of detectives all over Boston. I bet that damn Noah had tried to incriminate me in Eric's murder. Why did I have to paint everything? Hurley was probably calling to say he was on his way over to arrest me. Wait. Wouldn't he just show up with handcuffs?

"Listen, I'm just calling to check in. To see if you remembered anything else from Sunday." He sounded tired, and I had a suspicion that his hair was as wild and uncombed as when I'd met him. He struck me as a chronically chaotic-looking person.

"Honestly, not really. Um . . . I think I told you everything I could think of."

"Can we just go over who you saw at the restaurant again? Tell me all the staff members you can remember seeing."

I listed off everyone I'd met: Joelle, Tim, Garrett, Cassie, Ian, and the kitchen staff I'd seen but hadn't actually met.

"So only one chef? Or one person in a chef's coat?" Hurley asked.

"Well, I don't know. I know Garrett was wearing one, obviously, but I think the other guys in the kitchen were wearing them, too. Only theirs weren't as nice. You know, cheaper looking. But I wasn't paying much attention, to be honest with you. Does that help?" I felt like a lousy witness. If I'd known these sorts of details were going to become important, I'd have studied everyone there.

The detective continued. "Okay, now about the phone call Eric had. Could you go over that again?"

Again, I had nothing to offer this earnest detective—except a slight concern about Noah's casting suspicion on me with his paint comment. "Um, listen. My neighbor, Noah, just stopped by. He said you came over and were asking him about paint? Was there paint in the men's room? On that knife? I didn't see any on Eric's body at all. Or on Eric, for that matter. Before. And Noah said he told you that I paint all the time. In fact, I was painting last weekend. Calm, brown tones. I was trying to tidy up my place. Give it a little bit of a Zen feel, you know. But I took a shower before I saw Eric, of course. I hope you don't think I did anything wrong." I was blathering on in what increasingly felt like the manner of a murderer trying to convince the police of her innocence.

"No, you're not a suspect at this time. But I can't comment on the investigation." Sounded like some phrase he learned in detective school. But at least I was off the hook. He continued asking me about other people I'd seen that night, and I did my best to describe everything and everyone I could remember. None of it seemed helpful, and I was pretty sure that none of my information was going to blow this case wide open, as detectives and reporters said in second-rate TV shows.

Detective Hurley released a loud sigh. "Okay, Chloe. Look, please call me if you think of anything at all that you remember. Even if it seems unimportant, okay?"

Although I doubted that I'd recall any crucial clues, I assured him that I'd call if I thought of anything new. I hung up, convinced that would be my last contact with the murder investigation.

SEVEN

I'd just finished my shower when the phone rang again. I wrapped a towel around myself, grabbed the phone, and stared at the caller ID. Rafferty, P. What? Did I even want to answer this?

"Hello?"

"Is this Chloe?" a shrill female voice asked.

"Um, yes. Who is this?"

"Oh, Chloe, this is Eric's mother, Sheryl Rafferty." She muffled a sob. "I spoke with Timothy Rock yesterday. I got your last name." She stopped for a second and added, "From him. And found your number in the phone book." She started crying harder.

"Oh, Mrs. Rafferty, I am so sorry about Eric. I just can't imagine how devastated you must be." Why was she calling me? What in the world was I supposed to tell this woman? *Your son was dreadful and pompous during the two hours I knew him, and then I found him with his throat slit on a men's room floor?*

"Well, dear," she managed to continue, "Eric's father and I knew he'd been dating." She paused. "Dating someone serious. Well, not someone *serious*. Or not necessarily a serious person, that is. Dating *seriously*. There. And Timothy told us who you were. I know you must be just as heartbroken as we are. His parents. He was our only child, you know. I had the understanding . . . well, I may have misunderstood. Well, no, I didn't. I had the sense that this may have turned into a more permanent relationship. Cut short by Eric's death. But it's consoling to know that after all, he found great love. During his life." As opposed to after his demise? Although the bereaved Mrs. Rafferty claimed to be consoled by the thought of her son in love, this notion sent her into another loud gale of moaning.

I couldn't blame her, obviously, for her tears, and I attributed her evident confusion to grief. Losing a child must be unimaginably painful. No wonder Mrs. Rafferty sounded so fragmented. I had to do whatever I could to comfort her and decided that a nod-and-smile-and-agree-with-everything attitude would be the kindest approach. And very social workish. "This must be awful for you. Please let me know if I can do anything for you," I said in my best soothe-the-grieving-mother voice.

"Well, actually, Chloe, I want your advice. About the funeral. I'm sure you want to be involved. So I thought I'd let you know that Madeline Rock . . . Do you know her? From Magellan, it's called. It's a restaurant. She offered me her executive chef, a Josh something-or-other, and his staff to do the food. Catering. For the gathering at our home after the funeral. Now, Eric was a fan of Timothy's. But what do you know about this Madeline? What do I tell her? Of course, Eric is my only child, and I adored him to pieces . . . such a precious and wonderful son, but truthfully, Eric and I did not have the closest relationship in terms of day-to-day life. Or else we would have met you by now, of course. So, I'm not sure what he would want."

Okay, I'd hardly known Eric, but I did know that he had loved food and loved the whole restaurant business, and had seemed quite fond of Magellan. Furthermore, I felt certain that Eric wouldn't have refused the offer of free food. Who was I to talk? But why was his mother soliciting my advice, anyway? What ulterior motive could Madeline Rock possibly have that should arouse suspicion and require a consultation with me? The notion of a gourmet-catered funeral was a little odd, but it always struck me as peculiar that death was customarily surrounded by tons of food. When someone died, were the surviving loved ones hit with sudden cravings for casseroles and fruit salads? Still, after a death, visitors expected to be fed and, more than that, fed well. When our neighbor Ray died, my mother was highly irritated at the pathetic spread served at the family's house. Mourners were offered tea and crustless minisandwiches. "Protestant sandwiches," my mother had declared, by which she meant skimpy offerings. "This isn't tea with the Queen of England, for God's sake. They could spring for something more filling."

"I'm sure Eric would have been thrilled with that idea," I told his mother. "He was just praising Magellan's chef the other night. Eric was quite food oriented, as you know. He took me to Essence to see what I thought about his investing there. He talked a lot about the quality of the food at Magellan, and he was hoping Essence would reach that status. So, he'd want you to accept Madeline's offer. I can't think of a more fitting way to remember Eric and celebrate his life."

"Oh, thank you. I knew Eric's girlfriend would have the answer. Now, my husband, uh, Eric's father is here. He'd like to speak to you. We'll see you on Saturday at the funeral home. Ten a.m." Mrs. Rafferty gave me the name and address, which I reluctantly wrote down. Having resigned myself to attending the funeral of my supposed beloved, I hoped that there wouldn't be an open casket. Ugh. I'd already seen the poor man dead once. That had been enough.

"Okay, here's Phil," she said as she passed the phone to her husband.

"Chloe? Phil Rafferty here." Eric's father had a loud, gruff voice and shouted his words through the phone lines. "You must be quite shook up. Awful situation for all of us, but we'll get through it together. Listen, I'm a bit concerned about Veronica. Has she been bothering you?"

"Veronica? Um, I don't know much . . ." I started. In fact, what I knew about Veronica was almost nothing. I remembered that she was the bookkeeper at Essence and Magellan, and that was about it.

"That ex-girlfriend of Eric's is a pain in the neck. Couldn't get over him when they broke up. Has she been bothering you? Trying to break you up? I'm convinced that girl will show up at the funeral and steal your thunder, so to speak." Bookkeeper Veronica was welcome to play the bereaved girlfriend. Someone should, maybe, and I was going to have a pretty hard time acting forlorn.

"No, no. I haven't heard anything from her at all. No trouble whatsoever," I said truthfully. "Listen, Mr. Rafferty, Eric and I didn't know each other that well," I began slowly.

Ignoring what I'd just said, Mr. Rafferty replied, "Eric's mother and I know how special you were to him. You're part of this. We'll all grieve together," he assured me. Lucky me.

"Well, I need to get going, actually. I have school today. Orientation. I should probably run."

"You're so strong. So strong," Phil repeated. "I can't believe how well you're holding up. Looking forward

100

to finally meeting you on Saturday. Better late than never, I guess, huh?"

Relieved to have that unusual call over, I hung up. I couldn't believe I had to go to this funeral. And what was I going to wear? Every black dress I owned was more appropriate for doing tequila shots than for honoring the dead.

But today I had that damn social work school orientation. Who decided we needed orientation at eight fifteen in the morning? And what the hell were we going to do until four that afternoon? I figured that all the men there would probably be gay, so I didn't bother dressing up. Jeans, T-shirt, and Keds. Yes, Keds had been over with for years, but I didn't care. Cheap, easy, went with everything. Hair in ponytail. I grabbed a light jacket and was good to go.

I took a notebook and a pen, and drove the few miles to school only to discover that Tuesday's orientation sucked as much as I thought it would. I spent two hours in an auditorium listening to a series of progressively more boring speakers. The dean of the school made the mandatory welcome speech, which was about as scintillating as his welcome letter had been. The head of the library tried to present a virtual tour of the library's many state-of-the-art features, but her computer kept freezing, and we were left to gaze at a close-up of the book-drop slot.

At noon we broke up for lunch and were presumably expected to mingle and discuss our life's dreams of saving the oppressed. As I hid in a corner, I looked around and noticed that everyone else was much more dressed up than I was; the others were treating this event as a foray into the professional world of suits and ties. Earnest students were gathered in groups, probably to share their hopes for the year's academic pursuits. I felt so much like a wallflower at a high school dance that I wished I'd brought along a flask of peppermint schnapps—in high school, at least, it would've made me the most popular kid there.

We'd been handed massive notebooks full of graduate school information. Mine included my schedule of classes, which ran Wednesday through Friday, and the contact information for my "field placement," social work speak for *internship*. I'd forgotten about that. Monday and Tuesday were designated "field placement" days on which we were thrown into the trenches and expected to put into use the skills we were learning in the classroom. I'd been given a placement at the Boston Organization Against Sexual and Other Harassment in the Workplace and was to call Naomi Campbell (I swear that was her name) before Monday. Why was everything social work related required to have the longest possible title? And it was in downtown Boston, which probably meant I'd have to take the T, since parking downtown was either impossible or too expensive to do on a regular basis.

I spent the hour from one to two seated with three other students in my advisor's office. His name was Dick Dickers, and I passed that hour wondering what kind of parents do that to a kid. So his name was probably Richard, and Rick Dickers wasn't much better than Dick Dickers, but with a last name like that, the kind thing to do would have been to avoid anything that sounded remotely like Dickers. There were millions of names out there for parents to choose from: James Dickers, Adam Dickers, William Dickers . . . although Willy Dickers would probably have sent gradeschoolers into whoops of laughter. I was sure he'd been called Dicky Dickers by children throughout the public school system. Parents should name their children responsibly. Like, if my parents had had a son, they clearly couldn't have named him James, a choice that would have resulted in a baby Jimmy Carter crawling around. But poor Dick Dickers had been doomed to a life of students being too distracted by his name to hear any of the important information he had to impart regarding his availability as an advisor to overworked social workers. As I was leaning against the back of the hard wooden chair in Mr. Dickers's office and not listening to what he was saying, it occurred to me that when it came to naming babies, the parents of the United States had collectively lost their minds and didn't want to find them. In particular, no one wanted advice on what to name a child, as my sister Heather could attest. When she was pregnant with her first child, her friend Ruth had rejected every name Heather had come up with because it had reminded her of some celebrity. Donald had made Ruth think of Donald Trump, Theodore had led to Ted Kaczynski, and she'd even gone from Jennifer to Gennifer Flowers. When Heather and Ben had finally decided on the name Walker, Ruth had immediately said, "Oh, like *Walker, Texas Ranger*?" Heather had been totally fed up by then and had shouted back angrily, "Yes, EXACTLY like *Walker, Texas Ranger*!" Ruth was not consulted or informed about baby number two's name until after the birth certificate had been signed.

I made a minor attempt to focus on Mr. Dickers until eventually my ill-named advisor wound up his spiel on future course selection and started clamoring about plagiarism and its consequences. When he finally wrapped up his warnings, my school chums and I shuffled out of his cramped office.

From two to four that afternoon, I was supposed to attend the Peer-to-Peer Networking Social, which as far as I could tell was yet *another* opportunity to socialize, this time with advanced graduate students who'd share their wisdom with us newbies. I was irked enough at having to be here in the first place to bag the social. My plan for the next two years was to go to class and go directly home, and there was no way I was hoping to network with serious academic types who'd try to suck me into joining repulsive-sounding clubs such as, incredibly, something called the Social Work Student Class Spirit Committee. As I scampered out of school, I was already dreading the classes I had coming up over the next three days.

Correctly so. The following day I discovered that the main similarity between my social work classes and the classes I'd had in college was that the first day pretty much consisted of being handed piles of papers with monster-sized syllabi and listening to professors regale the students with proclamations about impending workloads. My Social Policy course was taught by a frizzy-haired guy in his late sixties, Professor Harmon, who handed us each a forty-page list of required reading. According to his plan, I was to read approximately six thousand pages from nineteen different sources each day. And should I find myself thirsty for even more social policy information, I could jump from the required to the recommended list. I would also be writing a ten-page midterm paper and a twenty-five-page final paper. Then Mr. Slave Driver told us to go buy our books and sent us on our way. That's just a sample. The rest of my classes that week were equally horrifying.

The good news was that I had morning classes only; my afternoons were free. I waited until after the week's final boring lecture on Friday morning to go buy my books. The cramped bookstore was overflowing with students, and I had to shove my way through to the back to reach the social work section. I started pulling books off the shelves, and by the time I'd filled my little basket, I realized that there was no way I could carry all these books, never mind do all the reading. I was going to have no life whatsoever. I started to panic. What had I done? I was going to flunk out of school. And embarrass my dead uncle. I stood staring at my book list in disbelief. The basket was full, my arms were aching, and I had the books for only two of my classes.

"Honey, you don't need to buy all those books, you know." I turned to my left to see a six-foot bald guy in a tight yellow T-shirt. On his face was an expression of genuine pity. His gold ear clips and blue-tinted sunglasses were making me guess gay—but I'd been wrong before. He reached over and grabbed the papers out of my hands. "Okay, now who do you have for General Practice? Oh, Wolfmann. So, you only need these two textbooks, and, well, maybe this paperback here." My savior reached into my basket and put back seven books for me. "I'm Doug Kingsley. I'm a doctoral student here. Thank God I found you, or you'd probably go home and put a bullet through your head thinking you'd have to spend the rest of your life trying to read all this crap."

"Hi, I'm Chloe. Thank you so much. I was beginning to think I'd need a truck to get all these books back home."

"Yeah, they like to scare all the first-year students by throwing the syllabus at you the first day and telling you all the reading you supposedly have to do. Don't worry, it's not that bad. Nobody does all the assigned reading. You'll figure out what you have to read and what you don't." Doctoral Doug finished helping me select what to buy and what to toss back on the shelves. "And I probably just saved you six thousand dollars in book costs, so you'll have to buy me a mochaccino sometime." Definitely gay. Damn.

106

"I'll buy you any caffeinated beverage of your choice. Thank you so much for your help. I am totally lost here."

Doug wrote down his phone number for me and said to call him if I needed anything. He'd gone home after his first day of classes and wept like a baby, he said, so the least he could do was prevent that from happening to another student.

I lugged my books home from school, checked my voice mail, and listened to a message from Heather, who demanded to know all the torrid details of my romantic Back Bay date and asked why hadn't I called her all week, and so on. I decided to call her later. The last thing I felt like doing was telling my horror story one more time. I also had a message from my parents to announce their return from Bar Harbor, Maine, and to invite me to stop by. That would have to wait, too. I called my new supervisor, Naomi, to check in about my internship. I mean field placement.

"Boston Organization Against Sexual and Other Harassment in the Workplace. This is Naomi, how can I help you?"

Oh God, please don't make me answer the phone there. I explained who I was and asked about starting next week.

"Excellent," Naomi said enthusiastically. "I'm glad you called. I was actually wondering if you could pop by this afternoon so I can show you around and get you set up for Monday. I have to go to a coalition rally at the State House early next week, so if I could get you situated before then, that would be great."

I groaned silently but agreed to come in at two and decided I'd park in one of those expensive parking garages. I'd thought that the school misery was over for the week, but now I had to go downtown and deal with this organization with the ridiculous name. This whole graduate school business was really going to interfere with my socializing and my television watching. What's more, since I should make a decent impression on my new boss, I'd now have to change into something other than jeans.

Totally annoyed, I threw on a good shirt and some decent footwear before driving downtown. I parked in a garage and found the address Naomi had given me, an office building right in the heart of Downtown Crossing. I made my way up three flights of stairs (the elevator was broken) and found Suite 412. When I entered, I instantly realized it was no suite, at least as I understood the word. To me, *suite* conjured up the image of luxurious rooms at the top of the Ritz with beautiful views, room service, and a minibar. What I saw before me were two rooms separated by a dilapidated door that stood open. Industrial gray carpet covered the floors, and one tiny window in the second room provided a view of a concrete wall. The only furniture in the first room were two cafeteria-style tables and some metal filing cabinets overflowing with papers.

"Hello?" I called into the apparently empty rooms.

"Chloe?" A woman popped her head out from the

far room. She walked toward me. I smiled weakly. Far from looking like an international supermodel, this Naomi Campbell had ghostly pale skin and medium-brown hair that fell to her knees and was plaited in tiny braids with multicolored beads adorning the ends. She couldn't have been much older than I was, but she was dressed in bland, hippyish clothing, her outfit completed with, ugh, Birkenstock sandals. I'd gone to a radical leftist, politically activist, politically correct college, and I thought I'd escaped when I graduated. And what was up with her hair? I silently christened her Braids.

Braids eagerly reached to shake my hand. "Well, let's get started. As you can see, we've got tight quarters here, but we make the best of it. I'm going to clear a space for you at one of these tables, so you can have a workstation for yourself."

Great.

"Come into my office, and I'll fill you in on the organization."

I followed Naomi into her dinky office and listened to horror stories of women who'd been harassed at their workplaces. My job was to answer hotline calls from women who were dealing with creeps at work and needed help in fending off the jerks. Then there'd be a lot of "outreach" work, as Braids called it. As far as I could tell, outreach work meant calling random companies I would select from the Yellow Pages and offering to present sexual harassment workshops.

"Now, even if they say no at first, you should always

109

make a follow-up call," Naomi instructed. "Every organization is required to have a sexual harassment policy, but not many places know how to educate their employees properly."

"So you want me to harass them about their harassment policy?" I suggested. My new boss glared at me. I couldn't blame her for feeling disappointed in the quality of student she'd been assigned. "Um, who else will I be working with?" I asked.

"Well, we have some volunteers who come in sometimes during the week to help out. And there's a board that meets once a month in the evenings, so you'll get to meet all those folks when you come to those. But for now, we're a small group." She smiled at me.

"So, it's pretty much just you and me?"

"We're a nonprofit organization, and at this point we don't have the funds to pay for any other staff. But maybe that's a project you'd like to take on while you're here. Fund-raising. Fund-raising and getting the word out about our organization." *Organization* was a generous term for this one-woman operation, but Naomi had to think positively, I supposed.

We finished up with Naomi leaving me a big, fat folder detailing the history of the organization and the procedure for handling hotline calls. She said I could tackle the material when I returned on Monday. I didn't see why I couldn't take this bad boy home with me and read it in front of *Days of Our Lives* next week, but I just nodded and smiled and otherwise did my best to look breathless with expectation about my

110

new line of work. How I was going to survive the year cooped up in this little room with Naomi was beyond me. "See you Monday," I called with false cheer as I swiftly made my exit.

I'm free! I'm free! On to my weekend! Oh, damn. I had Eric's funeral tomorrow. What was happening to my life?

I found my car in the lot and felt grateful that I'd had the foresight to park in a garage. Even though Friday afternoon traffic in Boston was going to be rough and I probably could have made it home faster on the T, this way I could be alone in the car rather than pushed up against some smelly frat boy starting his night early. I pulled up to the parking booth and handed over my ticket. "Fourteen dollars," the burly woman in the booth called out.

"That can't be right. I was only here for, like, an hour?"

"Fourteen dollars," she repeated sternly.

I sighed and reached inside my purse for my wallet, where I found nine dollars. It'd been a while since I'd parked downtown, but it didn't seem possible that it could cost this much. I leaned out the window. "Um, I only have nine dollars in cash. Can I use a credit card?"

"Cash only." She laughed and shook her head at my naïveté about the big city.

"Okay, well, let me just pull back into one of those spaces, and I'll go to an ATM." What a nuisance.

"Sorry. Those spaces are reserved. And this ramp is

a one-way, anyhow." She was having more fun by the minute.

"I can't just pull into one of those spots for five minutes while I get some money?"

She shook her head firmly. I looked at her in disbelief. What was she going to do? Keep me hostage here in the garage until money magically appeared in my purse?

"Should I just leave my car *here* then?"

"If you'd like me to have you towed, sure, go ahead."

I should've strangled her, but I'd seen enough murder for one week. Dammit. I started rummaging around my car looking for change. I finally pulled together another two dollars and forty cents and offered up my findings in the hope of release.

"Honey, you're still short over two bucks. Can't let you go."

I snarled at her and continued ripping apart my car for money. I even climbed into the backseat, pulled up the floor mats, and dug in between the seats, where, to my delight, I uncovered some additional change, including a couple of quarters covered with a revolting semisoft crud. Still, money was money, and I'd found enough to get me out of there. Smiling smugly, I handed my encrusted findings to the beast in the booth.

She peered at the coins and looked up at me with satisfaction. "I can't take two of these quarters. They're Canadian."

For a few seconds, I hated Canada. Then I revved my engine and shot the woman a menacing glare that apparently persuaded her to end the battle. She let me go.

I wormed my way out into the downtown traffic and poked through it feeling sorry for myself. On the radio, horrible Mariah Carey shrilled the message that love takes time, and I felt myself drift back into that teenage stage of dreaming about young love and first kisses, and dancing in the school gym to Jamie Walters, Color Me Badd, and other musical mistakes of the early nineties. Had the dreams been mistakes, too? If not, when was I going to meet my true love? Where was my sweaty hunk? When was I going to make out to "Stairway to Heaven"? It was probably going to be a high school dance song until the next millennium, so even now, long after high school, there was still time, wasn't there? Okay, I did dance to that song once in tenth grade with Billy Lajewski, but that damn Billy warned me at the beginning of the song that because it was *really long,* he wouldn't be able to dance with me through its entirety. And even with only half a song, he'd had plenty of time to kiss me, which he hadn't, so "Stairway to Heaven" didn't count at all. I'd been so hopeful back then that I'd find a perfect love or that I'd at least tumble so quickly from one passionate relationship to another that I'd barely have time to catch my breath. So far, I was not living up to my high-school expectations. And that just about defines failure, doesn't it?

EIGHT

Saturday morning marked the one-week anniversary of Noah's philandering and my Internet dating error. The one-week anniversary of my enrollment in nightmarish social work school was approaching. Yay. And I had Eric's funeral today. Yay, again.

I called up Adrianna to find out what to wear. "If I were you, I'd wear something loud and obnoxious, gobs of makeup, and big hair. Don't play into their impression of you as the grieving girlfriend."

Ade could've pulled it off, but I went ahead and scrounged up something that my mother would have deemed appropriate: black pants, sleeveless black top, and black blazer, all in different shades of black, since God forbid that I ever get it together to take things to the dry cleaner's and prevent all my clothes from fading. The day was gorgeous and sunny, and I'd have to spend most of it dealing with the Raffertys while sweating in black. But between rescuing Oops paint and consoling the Raffertys, I felt as though social workers far and wide would be proud of me.

I found the funeral home in Cambridge with no problem. Reluctant to commit even my car to the Raffertys, I avoided the funeral home's lot, parked on the street, and fed the meter. After last night's fiasco with the parking booth bitch, I had actually remembered to bring quarters. So here was my plan: I'd sit through the funeral service, make proper remarks to fellow mourners, briefly stop by the Raffertys' after the service, and run home to change my phone number so they couldn't find me ever again.

I entered the funeral home through big wooden doors. A man in a suit asked for my name and then quickly escorted me down the aisle. The room was about half full, mostly with middle-aged people. My usher took me through the main room to the first row and presented me to a scrawny, pale woman in an expensive-looking black dress. "Ma'am? Ms. Carter has arrived."

"Darling, I'm Mrs. Rafferty. I cannot *believe* we're meeting under these circumstances." Eric's mother leaned into me and wrapped me tightly in her bony arms. She eventually pulled back, but kept her grip on my upper arms and stared at me. "Oh, you must just be sick about all this." Sheryl Rafferty had carefully styled gray-blonde hair. She'd managed to pull herself out of her grief long enough to accessorize with elegant jewelry and to put on makeup, but her perfectly applied blush didn't hide her fatigue and obvious sorrow. She turned to the man next to her. "Dear, this is Eric's fiancée." Either Eric had been a pathological liar, or Sheryl Rafferty had gone psychotic following her son's death. "Chloe, this is Phil, Eric's father."

Phil Rafferty was quite a handsome man, probably in his early sixties, with a full head of jet black hair, a color that wasn't, I guessed, natural. The problem with men like this is that they don't have the sense to just go ahead and dye their eyebrows to match their dyed hair. I mean, really, who has black hair and gray eyebrows? Mr. Rafferty looked as haggard as his wife but hadn't gotten it together enough to look as collected as she. His tie was askew, his shirt rumpled, and his fake-black hair uncombed.

"I'm so sorry for your loss," I offered meekly.

Mr. Rafferty practically fell onto me as he threw his arms around my neck and pulled me toward him. Ah, whiskey breath. That could explain his disheveled appearance. The poor man started sobbing as he hugged me tightly. At a loss about what to do, I lightly patted his back.

"I can't believe he's dead. I can't," he cried. This hardly seemed the same loud-spoken man I'd talked to on the phone yesterday. But grief hits people in different ways and at different times, and I was sure that the morning whiskey hadn't improved this man's ability to cope with pain. "Thank God that damn Veronica hasn't shown up. I was afraid she'd try to make this day worse than it already is and come in here screaming and crying and making a big scene and saying how much she and Eric loved each other. I would've had to have her thrown out. I'm so glad you don't have to see that stupid bitch and listen to her lies." Actually, Veronica was beginning to sound pretty entertaining. And she could've taken the focus off me.

Sheryl tugged me away from Phil's grip. "You'll sit with the family, of course, Chloe." Of course I would: no hiding in the back pew by myself. Sheryl introduced me to some aunts, uncles, and cousins sitting nearby. "Now, we've had Eric cremated." Sheryl paused as if uncertain about how to continue. "You can see the urn right up there among the daylilies. After the service, we'll take him home where he belongs. Oh, here comes the minister. Should be a lovely service. Just what Eric would have wanted." She patted my knee as I sat down between her and her husband.

The minister began speaking about Eric. I thought I might learn a little something about who this dead man was, but the minister's eulogy consisted mainly of general remarks about death and loss, many of which were drowned out by Phil's choked crying. I found myself checking my watch. I did perk up, though, when the minister began to speak about Eric's love of food. The minister evidently knew Eric quite well. He discussed Eric's interest in investing in Essence ("sure to be a huge success") and then read an alphabetical list of Eric's favorite foods. By the time he hit wasabi, I was losing interest again. Finally, he introduced Madeline Rock, owner of the famous Magellan restaurant.

I brightened up and looked to my left as an attractive woman rose from her seat and took center stage. She was wearing what Adrianna had told *me* to wear. This restaurant diva strutted confidently up to the podium in a blue wraparound dress, high heels, and a silver necklace. Madeline had long brown hair that she had pulled back in an elegant knot tied at the base of her neck—hard to pull off unless you had the stunning face and body she did: beautiful ivory skin, shapely legs, and perfect breasts. I wasn't sure whether I was going to admire or detest her. She arranged herself in front of the audience and somehow managed to look sensational without appearing disrespectful.

"As we all know, Eric loved the restaurant world. He was a big fan of my restaurant, Magellan, and was a frequent diner at my establishment. When Tim and I owned Magellan together, we used to joke that Eric was like an unpaid member of the staff. He adored the smells and sounds and sights of a bustling restaurant on a Saturday night. He loved the chaos and the excitement and the energy that came from a successful restaurant. Our staff knew his favorite dishes and could always count on him to order that evening's special. I remember the night we ran the duck marinated in Calvados with Bhutanese red rice, pearl onions, and apple-pear chutney. He was so thrilled with the dish he thumped the table with his hand and yelled, 'That's how you do it!'"

I heard some laughs and murmurs of understanding among the mourners. *Way to kick this funeral into high gear, Madeline.*

She continued, "And that's the Eric we'll all miss. His enthusiasm and support were unmatched. I don't think Tim and I would have survived the ups and downs of the past few years without Eric's positive energy. When Timothy looked into opening his new restaurant, Essence, I know how much Eric wanted to be part of that opening and that partnership. And now that Eric is gone, we must continue to support Essence as Tim and his crew work to make it a restaurant Eric would have been proud of."

Now that was pretty generous of her. From what I knew, restaurants opened and closed faster than you could say, "Check, please," so encouraging diners to go to the competition was admirable. But Eric had said that Tim and Madeline had had an amicable divorce. It seemed to be true. Madeline smiled affectionately at Timothy, who was seated beside her empty seat. "Now I know this a difficult day for us all, but I think the best way to remember Eric is to enjoy what Eric enjoyed—food. So the chefs at Magellan have prepared some of Eric's favorite dishes, and the Raffertys have kindly invited us back to their house, where I hope we can all benefit from the healing power of gourmet food and share memories of Eric together. Thank you." Madeline finished her speech and returned to her seat right next to Tim. They looked so perfect together that I couldn't imagine what had broken them up.

Sheryl and Phil each held one of my hands as the minister continued the service. After thirty more minutes and four more speakers who waxed poetic on Eric's seemingly endless appetite for cuisine, I was starving. When things finally wrapped up, I asked Sheryl for directions to their house. "Oh, just leave your car here. You can ride back with Phil and me, and someone will drive you back here when the party's over."

Party? Interesting choice of word, but the idea was, after all, to celebrate Eric's life. Odd, though. There was no way I was going to be stuck in a car with these loons and then get trapped at their house—that would totally ruin my getaway plan.

"Oh, it's okay. I can drive myself. Just give me directions," I said hopefully.

"Nonsense. You're too upset to drive," she insisted.

I dutifully stayed with my dead date's parents as they hugged and exchanged proper words with the funeral attendees. Mrs. Rafferty left briefly to retrieve the cobalt blue glass urn that now held her son's ashes, and then we made our way out to their car.

"Chloe, dear, would you please hold Eric for me. I'm so upset I'm afraid I may drop him."

Her fear was, I thought, justified not only because she was shaky but because the urn was fragile. About twelve inches high and six inches wide, it looked like a flower vase inexplicably topped with a lid. Fortunately, its blue glass was opaque. Still, gross, gross, gross! I should have been grateful that there was no revolting graveside service or, God forbid, an open casket, but holding human remains was still pretty vile.

"Sure," I relented. I tentatively took the urn from her and felt my stomach roll over. I was not going to make it all the way to the Raffertys' house holding this thing. What if the top came off and I got sprinkled with Eric's ashes? What if we had an accident and the vase shattered? As we turned the corner at the end of the street, I placed Eric, so to speak, next to me in the rear driver's side seat and buckled him in with the seat belt. There. Safe and secure. Sheryl Rafferty turned her head around and stared at me in horror and disappointment, clearly hoping I'd have held her beloved in my arms.

The Raffertys and I, with Eric in his urn, made a silent fifteen-minute drive to an upscale section of Cambridge and parked in their driveway off Brattle Street. Their house was phenomenal. Really phenomenal, like old-money phenomenal. A massive old gray Victorian, the house was surrounded by a fence with an electronic gate that let us in to park. The yard was beautifully landscaped with late-blooming flowers. A bright yellow Nissan Xterra was parked next to us. I hopped out of the car quickly before anyone made me carry what was left of Eric and waited while Phil Rafferty reached in the backseat to unbuckle his son.

I followed the Raffertys inside the house, which had crown molding, hardwood floors, and high ceilings. Mrs. Rafferty excused herself to go to the kitchen to check on the food preparations. Mr. Rafferty led me to the living room to await the arrival of the other guests. He placed Eric's ashes on the mantlepiece, presumably to give everyone a view of the guest of honor. We sat uncomfortably together on an antique couch while I tried to think of something to say.

"It was a lovely service. I'm sure it was just what Eric would have wanted," I managed. A fresh crying fit overcame Phil, and I looked around the room, hopelessly wishing someone would come and rescue me.

Someone did. Madeline swooped in through the front door. "Oh, Phil. I am so sorry for your loss," she said as she crossed the room and seated herself in an armchair near us. "This is a terrible day for you. Why don't you go freshen up and splash some water on your face. I'll make sure there's hot coffee waiting for you when you get back." Phil nodded, rose numbly from the couch, and plodded across the room to the staircase. Madeline turned to me. "Hi, I'm Madeline Rock." She stretched her hand out to mine. "Call me Maddie."

"I'm Chloe Carter. Nice to meet you. Eric spoke very highly of you."

"So you and Eric were . . . ?" she started.

"Honestly, no. But I can't seem to get anyone to understand that. I was on a blind date with him the night he died, but somehow everyone seems to think we were much more. His parents seemed so excited about the idea, I just haven't had the heart to try to clear things up."

Madeline actually laughed. "Oh God, what a mess! And now you've been dragged to the funeral and all this? How ridiculous! I heard you were the one who found Eric. Not much of a first date, huh?"

"I've had better. Today I thought I'd just stick it out and break it to Eric's parents later if I have to," I explained. "You own Magellan, right? Eric had been telling me about it and how he got hooked up with Tim."

"Right. But between you and me, Eric made such a pest of himself at Magellan, the only good thing about getting divorced from Tim was that he got Eric. Eric used to hang around all the time, bothering the chefs and giving unsolicited input. I know I shouldn't speak ill of the dead, but he was irritating. Not mean or anything, just annoying. But I couldn't exactly say that during the funeral service, could I?" Finally, someone who understood!

"Yeah, I kind of got the same impression during our date. But he certainly seemed to be a fan of yours and Tim's."

"Oh, he definitely was. Totally enthusiastic and genuinely thought he was helpful. But he annoyed the crap out of me. Tim didn't mind him so much and was actually excited that Eric wanted to invest in Essence. I don't know what's going to happen to Essence now, though." Madeline pushed up the sleeves of her dress, thereby jangling a set of bangle bracelets. "This is bad news for a young restaurant. I'm not sure Tim can pull it off. I really thought he was going to make it, too. Good chef, good staff, everything was in place. I love Tim to pieces, and even though we just couldn't make our marriage work out, he's a damn good restaurant owner, and he deserves to have Essence survive this. But who wants to go eat at a place where someone was killed? I mean, would you?"

I shook my head. "Truthfully, if I heard this story on the news, I don't think I'd be running out to eat there. So what's going to happen to Essence now?"

Madeline crossed her perfect legs and leaned forward. "If Tim wants to pull through, he's going to have to work hard. I told him I'll do whatever I can to help him. And the police had better solve this murder quick. The faster they can reassure the public that they've caught the killer, the faster customers'll be put at ease. But still, something as awful as this is hard to overcome." She sighed and stood up. "Listen, I've got to run into the kitchen and help get the food out. It was nice talking to you. I'm sorry you got dragged into all this, but hang in there. At least the food today will be good, right?" She winked at me and headed off to supervise. I liked her already.

The doorbell rang, and Sheryl emerged from the kitchen to answer it. Looking more pulled together than he had, Phil came down the stairs and joined his wife in the foyer. I watched as the two now-childless parents greeted their guests. It seemed miraculous that they were getting through this day without collapsing. A bar had been set up at the far end of the living room, so I headed over and asked the bartender for a gin and tonic. I was not going to make it through this day without a little liquor.

"Is there any food out yet?" I asked the server. I'd watched how much gin he'd poured into my glass. Drinking on an empty stomach could lead to an inappropriate display of my dancing skills atop the Raffertys' antique coffee table.

"There are appetizers on the table in the dining room." He gestured behind him. I nodded thanks and went to investigate. The dining room was huge and set up more for a wedding reception than a funeral service, with lighted candles and fresh flowers. Wonderful smells floated my way. The walls were painted a deep periwinkle blue, a perfect color probably not found in the Oops section at Home Depot. Three long tables lined the walls, each covered with china, silver flatware, embroidered napkins, and platters of luscious-looking food. Most people avoid being the first to dip into a buffet, but I was hardly going to hold out. As far as I was concerned, the food was here to be eaten, and from the little I knew about Eric, I was sure he'd have approved of my sampling the goods. Each dish had a printed card beside it with its name. A small side table was set up to promote Magellan. A pile of menus was neatly stacked, and copies of newspaper and magazine reviews had been pasted to a large poster board. Madeline's business savvy was evidently such that she never missed a PR opportunity.

I grabbed a plate and perused the cards that gave the names of the dishes. Lime and Coriander Marinated Smoked Bluefish on Wonton Chips with Wasabi Vinaigrette; Raspberry and Goat Cheese Stuffed Endive; Steak-au-Poivre Crostini with Fresh Horseradish and Fried Sage; Cold Seafood Salad of Shrimp, Lobster, and Calamari Tossed with Lemon, Thai Basil, and Brunoise Vegetables. No deli platters, no boring cheese trays! And this was only the first table! I refrained from doing a little dance of excitement as I set my drink down and served myself a bit of everything.

Other guests entered the room, and I was hoping to be left in peace to savor my meal. I sat down in a window seat and gazed out at the garden in an effort to look as unapproachable as possible. This endive thing was amazing . . . and the seafood salad better than any I'd had before. Divine. Love at first bite! All the other guests now seemed as engrossed in their food as I was and were too busy discussing the delicacies to bother me. Feeling pleased that my crummy week had suddenly and dramatically improved, I was startled out of my bliss by the most amazing man.

Gorgeous, sweaty, white chef's coat open at the top. Dirty blond hair—and not mousy like poor Eric's, either. Striking blue eyes and smooth, arched eyebrows. Slim build, average height. Super attractive, and I mean super. He seemed to strut into the room in cinematic slow motion. I nearly dropped my plate when he walked toward me, but I managed to save my bluefish from toppling to the floor. As it turned out, he wasn't so much walking toward *me* as he was walking to the food to see what needed to be refilled, but I could still hear my heart pounding.

The gorgeous one glanced at me and smiled as he grabbed an empty tray and headed back into the kitchen. *Argh, don't go!* I silently pleaded. And like magic he was back! Heading into the living room. What was I supposed to do? Follow him like some sort of groupie? And here I was at Eric's parents' house, supposedly mourning my dead boyfriend, while actually having the hots for another man. Too bad. My new boyfriend reentered the dining room holding a beer and stood at the back of the room, surveying the food situation. I stared at him until he finally looked my way. I raised my plate and nodded my enthusiastic approval at the food. I practically leaped out of my seat when he grinned and walked my way.

"Hi, I'm Josh Driscoll. I'm the chef from Magellan. Enjoying the food, I see?" he said as he looked down at my nearly empty plate. My stomach got all jumpy. I took a big swig of my gin and tonic.

"Unbelievable. I mean, really. Everything is out of this world," I gushed. "I'm Chloe. It's so nice to meet you. I've heard so much about Magellan, but I've never eaten there. I've read every amazing review, though. Is this all food from the restaurant's menu? I mean, do you normally do catering and this is from a different menu, or . . . it's all really good, I was just wondering . . ." *Oh, I'm talking like an idiot. Somebody shut me up before I scare him off.*

"No, we don't usually do catering, but Madeline, the owner, wanted to do this for Eric's parents since he loved Magellan so much. How did you know Eric?"

Oh God, don't let him think I'm unavailable. I explained the confusion regarding my relationship with the deceased.

"You found the body? Oh, my God! Well, between you and me, his parents seem a little screwed up to me. I don't blame you for playing along." There is a "you and me" already? Oh, I'm in love.

"Yeah, well, at least the detective I talked to that night believed me, so he didn't make me hang around too long answering all sorts of personal questions. He seemed to be the only one who believed that I'd known Eric for all of two hours. I was so freaked out that night I just wanted to get home." I took another gulp of my drink. "Did you know Eric well?"

"Nah. I mean, he hung out at the restaurant a lot and was always putting his two cents in about everything, but I wouldn't say I knew him well."

One of Josh's assistants stuck his head into the room, looked around until he saw Josh, and called over to him. "Josh, we need you in here."

Josh turned to me. "Sorry, I gotta run. Maybe I'll find you later, though?" Another handsome smile, and he was gone.

I reloaded my plate and made my way back into the living room, where Madeline cornered me. "I see you met Josh. Cute, huh?" I blushed furiously and nodded. "He's single, you know." She gave me an exaggerated wink and nudge.

I laughed and quickly silenced myself when I caught Sheryl staring at me. When I'd put on my serious face, I said casually, "He seems very nice. The food is outstanding. I see why Magellan gets such glowing reviews. And please don't make me laugh, or Eric's parents will wonder what's wrong with me."

"Oh, forget about them. I love matchmaking, and you two could be a great match. If you ask me, Josh had a little skip in his step on the way back to the kitchen. How old are you?" I told her twenty-five, and she practically jumped for joy. "Good! Josh is twenty-eight, so that's perfect. Well, we'll have to get you in one night for dinner. Come on, let's get another drink." Beautiful Madeline was looking more beautiful by the minute. She led me to the bar, where we ran right into Timothy. I hoped this wasn't going to be awkward.

"Hi, there," Madeline chirped to Tim. "You've met Chloe, right?" Tim and I nodded and smiled at each other. "Oh God, right. The night of the murder. What was I thinking? Sorry. Listen, I was talking to Chloe earlier about Essence. You need to come up with a game plan to keep everything running. This is a pivotal time, what with this awful incident, but I think you can get through it. Let me know what I can do."

"I know. You're right." Timothy nodded emphatically. "I've been giving the story to the newspapers in the best light possible. You know, playing up the fact that nobody in the restaurant was involved, et cetera. Just explaining that it was in no way connected with Essence. I don't know what else to do. But the police have been all over everyone at the restaurant trying to find out if the murderer worked there . . ."

"Well, first of all, the police have been all over Magellan, too, trying to make it out like someone on our staff was out to get you and your new restaurant. Which is bull, since everyone there knows you from before and loves you. And obviously Eric's parents aren't worried, or they wouldn't have had us all here.

So the police investigation will run its course and be over soon. And if you ask me, Eric's murder isn't restaurant related. I think it's personal. We all know that Eric was an annoying little snot who happened to have a lot of money. Someone in his life probably got fed up with his bullshit and got rid of him."

Tim started to protest, but Maddie stopped him. "Don't say it. Realistically, people get murdered for money all the time. More importantly, Tim, you should have pushed the Raffertys to let you do the food here. I mean, I was happy to do it, but you have to use every opportunity possible to promote yourself. It may seem callous, but you know as well as I do how this business is. You have to fight tooth and nail for every customer. Don't let this murder send you into a downward spiral. You'll be okay." Madeline leaned over and gave her ex-husband an enormous hug. "Essence can make it. It can."

"Thanks, Maddie. You're right, you're right. I'm going to do some serious work on promotion," Tim agreed.

"Good. Call me this week. Maybe we can get together and pound out some ideas?"

"Definitely. Oh, there's Phil and Sheryl. I'm going to go talk to them. I'll see you two ladies later?"

Two drinks, one mini fruit tart with gooseberries and citrus cream, and one mini fried-banana cheesecake later—and no further Josh sightings—and I was ready to call it quits. After a few more uncomfortable encounters with Eric's parents, I'd run out of patience with the bereaved-girlfriend act. Madeline rescued me.

"Sheryl. Phil. I think it's time for Chloe to go home. She must be as tired as you both are, and she needs to get some rest. I'll make sure she gets home safely." With an Oscar-caliber look of sincerity, she whisked me toward the kitchen so swiftly that I barely had time to say good-bye. Bless her.

"Josh?" She called out into the kitchen.

Although thrilled that Josh was walking over to us, I did stop to take notice of the immense kitchen, which was equipped with stainless-steel Viking appliances, granite counters, and ceramic floors. There were five or six people working there, most of them beginning the monumental task of cleaning up. I wondered who was left at the restaurant.

Madeline the matchmaker spoke to my new favorite chef. "Josh, can you please take this poor girl out of here? One more minute with Eric's parents, and I think she's going to slit her throat. Sorry, bad choice of words. But it looks like you're in good shape here, and the rest of the crew can finish up."

Embarrassed to be foisted off on Josh, I said, "It's okay. I can call a cab. Don't worry about it—you don't have to drive me." *Please want to drive me, please want to drive me!* Josh looked so adorable, all sweaty from the kitchen, hair tousled, jacket spatted with grease and covered in food stains . . .

Josh spoke up eagerly, "You're not taking a cab. I'll drive you home." He put a hand on my shoulder, and

I almost fainted. "Maddie, everything should be under control here. And Duff and Brian are chefing tonight for you. I talked to Brian earlier, and he's all good, so no worries there. These guys'll be done soon and back at the restaurant in time for dinner. We prepped everything last night, so they're in good shape." He looked back at me, "I just have to grab my toolbox, and we'll go. And, Maddie, I'll see you Monday." I didn't know chefs had toolboxes, but I would've waited all night for a ride home from him.

I said good-bye to Madeline and in an undertone thanked her for heroically saving me from the Raffertys' clutches. In an overly dramatic voice she called after us, "Have fun, kids! Don't be out too late! Drive safe! Fasten your seat belts!" She giggled and whirled back around.

I followed Josh out through the kitchen door to his car, the Xterra I'd seen in the driveway. Following Maddie's instructions, I buckled my seat belt and gave Josh directions to my condo. I felt way too giddy for someone leaving a memorial service, but I was riding in a cool car with a cool boy. Yay me!

"I didn't know chefs carried toolboxes. What do you keep in it?" I asked.

"Oh, I use it to carry around my knives and other kitchen tools. And top secret recipes," he teased.

Josh and I talked during the short ride home. He was just as captivating as I'd hoped. I said nothing about leaving my car near the funeral home. If he dropped me there, how could I invite him in? And from what

I'd gathered, he was off work for the rest of the day. I had him pull into my parking spot at home.

"Thank you for the ride. I hope it wasn't too much out of your way?"

"No, not at all. My pleasure."

"Where do you live?" I asked.

"Over in Jamaica Plain." This was *totally* out of his way!

Time to be brave. "Listen, do you want to come up for a while?" I asked.

"Yeah, sure. Um, but listen." Josh shifted in his seat, and I braced myself for the inevitable: He has a girlfriend. He thinks I'm a dork. "I feel uncomfortable saying this, but I should probably tell you that the police have been questioning me about Eric's murder. And, well . . . at the moment, I'm their prime suspect."

Oh, crap.

NINE

"Detective Hurley thinks *you* killed Eric?" I was in disbelief. I finally find a seemingly normal, attractive man who *cooks,* and he's a murder suspect? This would not do at all.

"He's not ready to haul me off to jail just yet, but he questioned me for a long time about where I was on Sunday night, which I had off. He seems to think that I could've been trying to sabotage Essence by killing off one of their investors. I'm as competitive as the next guy but not *that* competitive." Josh looked simultaneously depressed and annoyed at the thought of being a suspect. "Um, and, well, the knife used to kill Eric was mine. But anybody could have gotten hold of it. It was in my toolbox that I keep all my knives and stuff in, and I just leave it open in the office at Magellan."

Although Josh's owning a knife used as a murder weapon wasn't necessarily a good sign, I decided that my newly acquired social work credentials provided me with excellent insight into the human personality and that I was amply qualified to determine that Josh was indubitably innocent. In other words, Josh was way too cute to be a killer.

"Okay," I said, "but if the detective thinks there's competition between Magellan and Essence, why isn't he questioning Madeline? I mean, she *owns* Magellan, so I'd think she has more to lose if Essence does better than Magellan." I liked Madeline and all, but she wasn't the one making me all sweaty with lust.

"The detective has talked to her, but it's pretty obvious to everybody how well she and Tim get along and how much help she's given him starting up his new place. There's no evidence to show she'd want anything bad to happen to Tim. Plus, she was at Magellan that night with plenty of witnesses. And it's true that they get along. I know both of them, and I know Maddie would never hurt Tim. Much less murder anybody, that's for sure."

I tried to smile reassuringly at Josh. "Well, I'm not worried you're going to hack me to death if you come inside. Why don't you come up and tell me the rest."

Josh returned my smile and took the keys out of the ignition. I led him up the side of the house, deliberately stomping past Noah's door and up the fire escape to my condo. Josh sat down on the couch while I went to the kitchen to get something to drink.

"Hey, this is a great place," Josh said, looking around. "I love the colors in here."

"Thanks, I just repainted. I have a bit of a painting disorder, actually. I keep repainting everything and then a few months later change my mind and redo it. It's a decorating illness, and I expect you to refrain from making fun of me." I heard Josh laugh in the other room while I rummaged in the fridge for something to drink. "Josh, I have water or milk. I'm sorry, I don't seem to have anything else."

"Any chance you have any coffee? I'm sort of beat from today."

"Um, possibly. I'll give it a try," I muttered. I set the coffeemaker up and went back to sit next to Josh. I was all tingly again, seated in my place beside this chef. His chef's coat was full of cooking smells, and although most people would have said that he stank to high heaven, I thought he smelled delicious.

Josh must have caught me sniffing. Suddenly, he looked embarrassed. "Sorry, I'm sure I reek from being in the kitchen all day. I'm going to go grab a change of clothes from the car and just freshen up."

"No, no! I'm sorry. You do smell. I mean, not in a bad way. I like it, really." Wonderful, now I've told him he smells.

"You're funny and very nice, but I'm still going to change."

Josh left to get a change of clothes, returned, and disappeared into the bathroom. As I was pouring us some coffee, I heard Josh talking. "Hello, how are you?" he said. "You're cute. You and I are going to be friends."

He thinks I'm cute? And we're going to be friends? Hmm . . .

"Are you talking to me?" I called out.

"No, I'm talking to this cat sleeping in your sink."

"Oh, that's Gato," I said, relieved that Josh wasn't defining our relationship as destined to be purely platonic. "He sleeps in the sink all the time. Just push him out of the way."

I heard a meow, a long apology from Josh, and then the water running.

Josh talked from behind the closed bathroom door. "So you and Eric ate at Essence when you went out, huh? What did you think? Aside from the murder, obviously. But what did you think of the food?" He emerged, hair and face slightly wet, wearing worn jeans and a red T-shirt, and looking more scrumptious by the minute.

"Well," I said as I walked back to the couch with two mugs, "the menu looked phenomenal, but some of the food wasn't all that great. I feel bad saying that because Timothy seems like such a nice person, but a couple of the dishes we had were pretty awful."

"Really?" he said. "What did you guys order?"

"Some stuff off the menu, but also food Garrett did as specials for us. So we had some soggy oysters, mealy foie gras ravioli, and a terrible tuna with mustard greens. But the lobster and venison we had were wonderful."

"Yeah. Garrett is an all right chef. Great sous chef material, but probably not cut out for an executive chef job yet. Or maybe ever, if you ask me. My own sous chef, Brian, he's eventually going to be a great executive chef. Right now he isn't near being ready to handle his own place. I mean, he's only twenty-one. But he's hardworking and definitely ambitious. He just needs more experience." Josh settled himself on the couch and turned his body to face mine.

"Do you know Garrett well?" I asked.

"Yeah, actually Garrett and I went to culinary school together, and I wouldn't exactly say we're the best of friends. I don't mind him, but he doesn't like me much. Not to sound cocky, but we're both pretty competitive, and I was always a better chef than he was. He's good, don't get me wrong, but he pretty much hated me because he knew I could outcook him anytime. There are plenty of other chefs just as good as Garrett, and he knew it. But he knew I was in a different league, and he resented it. And still does."

"He did look pretty harried the night I was at Essence, and the food was certainly not spectacular."

"He was a strong sous chef, but I don't think he's good enough to make Essence anything special. See, my guy, Brian, is different. He can *cook*. And I show

137

him exactly how to make all the dishes, which is helping him a lot. But he's still trying to learn all the other parts of being a chef and managing a kitchen. Brian fell to pieces when I was off last Sunday, but I can still tell that he learned from what went wrong and that eventually he'll be ready. He tends to be sort of accident prone, and when he gets nervous, like when I'm not there, it gets worse. He dropped a vat of veal stock all over the floor and made a mess."

Josh stretched his arms above his head. "But it's a drag, because now whenever I'm off, I'm worried about what's going on in the kitchen at Magellan and whether or not Brian's managing things okay. Most nights he does fine, but like, tonight, since I'm off, I'll probably call there a few times to check in and see if he's got questions for me. I'm not usually *ever* off on a Saturday night, but Maddie wanted me to have a break after working all day for the funeral."

"I don't know why Tim had all that much confidence in Garrett as a chef," I said. "I mean, enough confidence in him to give him the job. First Tim hired Garrett, then, from what I heard, Tim had you help Garrett with the menu." I paused. "Oh God! I'm sorry. I just said the food at Essence was terrible! And you helped Garrett—" Now he was going to run away for sure.

"No, that wasn't me cooking, so don't feel bad," Josh assured me. "But, yeah, I did sit down with him and write up the menu."

"Why would Tim hire him if he can't even write his own menu?"

"Well, Tim doesn't have to pay him that much because Garrett doesn't have much experience. Tim works him seventy hours a week and probably doesn't even give him health insurance or any other benefits. You get what you pay for sometimes. Garrett's not a bad guy, though, he's just a little bitter about the fact that we went to school at the same time and that I'm in the position I'm in, and he's struggling where he is."

"So you helped out Essence? That was generous of you."

"Maybe . . . see, I like Tim, but I was a little irritated about it, because for one thing, I have enough to do at Magellan, but mostly because chefs don't like sharing their recipes. The detective was right when he asked me about the competition between Magellan and Essence. On the one hand, I like Tim and want him to do well, but on the other hand, I don't want him to do *that* well. The truth is that there's only so much room for top restaurants in one city, and I'm only so interested in helping out the competition."

"But the menu at Essence looked so great, so you must have helped Garrett out quite a bit?" I didn't understand how the chef who created today's food could have been responsible for some of the disasters I'd eaten at Essence.

"Sort of. He had some okay ideas, but his dishes were very simple. Not the kind of high-end food Tim wanted to serve. I helped him come up with the concept for the dishes, but I let him figure out how to make everything. I'm betting that's where the problem is—he's been trying to cook *my* dishes, and he's screwing them up because he's frankly just not *that* talented."

He sighed and continued, "So, like I said, I basically screwed him over." Josh looked down. "Like, he wanted to do my fennel and orange side, so I basically just gave him the general idea of how to make it. But I didn't tell him all the ingredients, and I definitely didn't give him step-by-step instructions. I know for a fact that instead of using fresh orange slices and fresh juice, he uses canned Mandarin oranges, which totally changes the quality of the dish. And I shave my fennel, and Garrett just chops it—which means the fennel doesn't absorb the flavor in the same way. So," Josh admitted, "I screwed him over."

"It's like if you told me all the ingredients in a beef stew, but didn't tell me exactly how to make it? Instead of roughly chopping the vegetables into big chunks, I might finely mince up the carrots and pota-toes, which would make for a sort of disgusting stew, right?"

"Exactly. Tim probably would've done better to let Garrett do his own simple food rather than try to cook something beyond him."

I was starting to see the detective's point. "So you intentionally set him up to fail? And is that what Detective Hurley thinks?"

"I probably did without realizing it. I went in there with good intentions, but Garrett copped such an attitude with me the day I showed up to help him that I guess I wrote up items I knew were mine, items I was the only one who could do just right. He was being such a dirtbag. It was just like we were in school all over again. He kept acting like he didn't need my help and kept walking away in the middle of talking to me. I know this doesn't make me sound like the greatest guy in the world, but he pissed me off, and that's what happened." He paused. "But if Madeline brought in another chef to help me do my dishes, I'd probably be an asshole, too. Garrett was probably embarrassed and just took it out on me. But it sounds like he pulled off a couple of the dishes, which is better than I thought he could do." Josh smiled sheepishly.

He leaned back on the couch and ran his hands through his hair. I noticed his hands were covered with burns and blisters and calluses, signs of battle from the kitchen. Although his beat-up hands might have put off some women, I thought he looked manly and, for some reason, heroic. But I did start to worry about the impression Josh's self-assurance might have created on the police. To me, Josh seemed justifiably confident about his ability as a chef; he'd probably paid his dues and deserved to gloat a little bit. To me, his attitude wasn't arrogance; it was pride. But maybe the police had seen him otherwise; maybe his self-confidence had made him a likely suspect.

"Look," I started, "I don't think it was the nicest thing to do, but I can understand where you were coming from. If you two were old rivals, it doesn't seem to make sense to put you together to work on a menu. And Garrett should've known that he was reaching with those dishes and figured out something else."

"I do feel bad about it, because I probably could've helped him plan dishes he could've done well. But I didn't. And I think that's made Detective Hurley suspicious."

"So you were off last Sunday, the night Eric was murdered, right?" I asked.

Josh nodded. "Yup, and that detective is still trying to 'verify my alibi,' as they say on TV. I'm not that worried. It'll be fine. I was home alone, though, so he's having trouble confirming that. My roommate, Stein, was working late that night and didn't get home until after midnight. And there's the problem with the knife being mine. But the detective actually seems like a nice guy, and he has to do his job. And it's not like I've been arrested or anything."

"Josh, what kind of knife *was* that? I saw it, unfortunately, when I found Eric in the men's room. I've never seen a knife like that before. Kind of curved."

"It's just a specialty knife called a cimiter." The word sounded like *scimitar: a saber.* For someone talking about an object remarkably like a sword, Josh sounded casual when he went on to say, "It's used for cutting down meat." He paused and looked right at me. "So, are you ready to kick me out yet?"

Maybe it was the gin-and-tonic-induced love goggles, but all I could see was a sincere, talented, driven guy, a guy I wasn't about to kick out of my condo. I shook my head, "Of course not."

"Look, for the most part, the culinary and restaurant world is not nice. Everyone's overworked, usually underpaid, and totally chaotic. We don't get weekends off, we work nights, it's tough on families, it's tough on relationships. And everyone in this business is sort of whacked in one way or another. We're all kind of manic, which I guess we need to be to keep up with the pace. But I don't want you to get the impression that I don't like other chefs and that I think I'm the greatest chef. I have plenty of friends that are chefs, and there are lots of chefs out there that I totally respect. But it's still, well, pardon the expression, cut-throat."

"It's okay. I don't think you killed Eric. I'm starting to understand how tough your chef world is, but that doesn't make you a killer. Now we just have to convince Detective Hurley of that."

Josh looked up at me. "We?" he asked.

"Yes," I said firmly. "I just met you, and I want to get to know you better, so I'm not about to let you rot in jail."

Sometimes it happens: an instant connection. Even my recent disasters with Noah and Eric couldn't prevent me from putting myself out there. Heather was always warning me that I fall too hard and too fast for men. I didn't care. I hated playing games, feigning indifference, taking things slow. When I liked someone, I just went for it, and I wasn't about to start holding back now. If Josh decided he wasn't interested in me, then I'd survive. Maybe I'd get burned. Maybe I'd find love. In fact, maybe I'd found it.

"You know what?" I said to Josh. "Let's not talk about the murder anymore, okay? It's all going to work out."

"I'm sorry. I've been talking your ear off about this and the restaurant and Garrett. You must be bored stiff. I guess I just needed to get some of this off my chest. Thank you for listening." One week of social work school, and I was already a highly skilled therapist.

"No, don't apologize. I love hearing about restaurants. I'm completely obsessed with food, which is probably why I thought Eric would be a good date for me. He *was* interested in restaurants. But we know how that turned out." I rolled my eyes.

"So, I guess this means you're single, then?" Josh asked adorably.

"Very single. Yes." I got that nervous feeling that happens right before you get kissed for the first time . . . was he going to kiss me?

Yes.

Josh leaned forward and gently placed one hand on the back of my head as he moved in for the sweetest kiss ever. What a relief that he kissed as well as he cooked. It was always such a disappointment when a first kiss was seriously flawed: a monstrous tongue darting in and out, saliva everywhere. Nauseating. Unfortunately, common. I'd dumped people after the first bad kiss. If the kissing is bad, you're pretty much guaranteed that any other physical pursuits will be a letdown.

Josh eventually pulled back and whispered in my ear. "You know what, Chloe?"

"What?" I asked, a little too breathlessly.

"I'm starving." Josh said. "I'm sorry, it's just I haven't eaten much today."

"Oh, I'm sorry. I should have offered you something. I'm a rotten host," I apologized.

"You," he said as he kissed me again, "are a wonderful host. It's just that I don't usually get to eat when I'm working."

"I'm not sure what I have. Probably leftovers and scraps. If I'd known I was having a chef over, I'd have stocked up," I teased him. We went into my tiny kitchen and peered into the fridge. I was dismayed to find nothing I'd consider offering to a man of such gourmet taste. "I don't have much." I pushed a wilted head of lettuce out of the way to reveal a one-inch cube of cheddar.

"Here, I'll find something for us to snack on." Josh placed his hands on my waist and moved me gently aside. "Can you grab a plate for us?" he asked as he busied himself pulling jars and Saran-wrapped items from the depths of the refrigerator. Within minutes he had created an antipasto-like appetizer of three cheeses, pickled vegetables, stuffed peperoncini, sliced apples, crackers, a few raspberries, and some stray deli slices. Now, if I'd arranged exactly the same ingredients on the platter, it would've been nothing more than a group of mangled food bits; Josh, however, performed magic.

"Here we go, my lovely one," Josh said, placing the platter on the kitchen table.

"I don't know how you put this together. I didn't know I had half this stuff left in the fridge." We sat down together and talked while we ate.

"So, Ms. Chloe Carter, tell me about yourself," Josh said with a look of sincere interest.

And I did. We talked for over two hours. After debating whether or not to portray myself as a pulled-together social work student with a clear plan for my future, I decided to put the truth out there and see where it led. I confessed that I was a bit muddled. Josh was slightly amused but supportive; he didn't show the slightest hint of disapproval.

Of course, we talked food. I would've assumed that Josh had grown up eating like royalty or at least like ordinary French people, same difference, but he'd existed on frozen dinners and canned vegetables until he'd left home to go to culinary school on a scholarship. He'd lived in a pretty rough section of South Boston with his parents and a sister, Angela, who was eight years older than he was. Josh used to bake with his grandfather quite a bit, but making pies and cakes was the extent of his cooking experience until he announced his intention to become a chef. "I'm not even sure how I decided that's what I wanted to do. I just knew it. No one in my family got it . . . well, except my grandfather, who said, 'You're gonna cook your ass off, kid.'" After graduation, he worked his way up at a number of Boston restaurants until he eventually got the job at Magellan.

"All of your girlfriends must've loved the fact that you're a chef?" I had to broach the subject of women. How many ghosts or exes were still hanging around?

"Actually, no. Most girls don't want to put up with a chef's hours. I work holidays, weekends, and I'm not usually done until anywhere between ten at night and one in the morning. I've had a couple of people break up with me because they resented how much I work." Josh shrugged. "But what are you gonna do? I just love being a chef."

"Well, I think that's horrible. If you want to be with somebody, then you work it out, bad schedule or not." I'd wait up until three in the morning every night just to catch a glimpse of Josh. "Well, they must have loved your cooking, though. Didn't that make the hours worth it?"

"I dated one girl for two years, and her favorite food was a well-done turkey burger on a roll." Josh rolled his eyes. "So I can't say she was a big fan of my cooking. God, I never want to see another turkey burger as long as I live. And she couldn't deal with my hours, so she dumped me."

"Turkey burgers? With everything you make, *that's* what she wanted? You've got to be kidding me."

"Yeah, obviously that relationship was doomed. And she was pissed that I didn't make more money. Believe me, most people who cook aren't in it for the money. A handful of top chefs have great salaries, but people like me and like Brian? We don't make a lot. In fact, sometimes sous chefs and line cooks work second jobs to pay the bills. If they have the time to, that is."

I can't say that I was too upset that someone else had cast off this great guy. But what woman in her right mind would break up with someone this wonderful? Murder suspect or not.

As tempted as I was to jump out of my chair and into Josh's lap for a more in-depth interview, I figured we'd better wrap up our first date, which wasn't exactly a date but was better than most actual dates and consequently counted as one. Josh must have had the same feeling I did. He stood up and started loading the dishes in my minidishwasher. "Listen, I was wondering if maybe you'd like to come into the restaurant for dinner this week. You could bring a couple of friends if you want."

I refrained from fainting with delight and collected myself enough to agree to come in at seven on Friday night. I said I'd bring Adrianna and her boyfriend, Owen. No sense in flaunting Adrianna without Owen on her arm.

"Excellent. I'll seat you guys up by the kitchen so I can talk to you while I work," he promised. "I can't wait to see you again," he murmured as he leaned over and kissed my forehead.

"I can't wait to eat again," I joked, pulling him back in for another full-on kiss.

TEN

As much as I didn't want to see Josh go, I was exhausted from the funeral as well as from my day of food and new love. I puttered around the house for a while and thought about Josh and how cute and sexy and gastronomically gifted he was. I couldn't believe I'd be at his restaurant on Friday. I left Adrianna a voice message demanding that she and Owen come to dinner with me to check out my new love interest, rate his food, and keep me collected during my first real date with Josh. Even though he'd be working, as far as I was concerned it would still qualify as a date. And a date at Magellan! Probably with dishes even better than his catered funeral food.

I hated going on dates where the guy took you to some boring restaurant with mediocre food and didn't notice that anything was wrong. In fact, I can remember what I've had to eat on most of the dates I've had, and for me, the sharing of food can make or break a relationship. The first date I ever had was in the spring of my sophomore year in high school. It was with George Rosenthal, a junior who worked part-time at a fishmonger (good sign). He took me to the Ground Round (bad sign), where in quintessential teen fashion, I made like I never ate anything and lived exclusively on Diet Coke. George scarfed down two plates of fries and a huge burger and, clearly not impressed with my soda dinner, took me to see *Die*

Hard: With a Vengeance and then promptly drove me home. That was the last time I starved myself on a date. If a guy is put off by the fact that I like to eat, too bad for him.

The quality of the food on a date doesn't necessarily have to be great, but we do have to agree about whether a meal is sensational, forgettable, or just plain offensive. The first time my ex-boyfriend Sean made dinner for me at his cramped studio apartment, he somehow managed to burn the spaghetti while it was boiling (something I hadn't known was possible) and to oversalt the red sauce so horrendously that we both kept puckering our mouths as we tried to eat. Sean got high marks for effort and agreement: he couldn't cook, but we agreed that the burned and oversalted dinner was awful. We dated for two years.

After Sean and I broke up, I briefly dated Zach, who was definitely not my type, but I was lonely and taken in by his muscular build, strong jaw, and fully loaded black Jeep Cherokee. I predicted his good looks and cool car would eventually enable me to overlook his deficiencies, among them, that he was not very bright and not particularly interesting. He lived two hours away in Connecticut, and after the novelty of his body had worn off, the distance had meant tiresome drives followed by insufferably long weekends during which I made ineffectual attempts to find something intellectually redeeming about him. When that strategy failed, I decided that if cognitive capabilities weren't his strength, I'd address the food angle. So far, his dinners had consisted of baked beans and franks, but maybe he just needed some culinary education. After all, it wasn't his fault if he didn't know any better; it was up to me to teach him about meals that didn't come out of plastic wrappers and tin cans.

One cold Saturday morning in February, I drove to Zach's place with my car full of fresh produce and two beautiful cod fillets. I slaved in the kitchen finely slicing red peppers, onions, zucchini, tomatoes, garlic, and cilantro. I laid the fillets in foil packets, slathered them with the veggies, and doused the fish in white wine and butter pats. Zach looked on in bewilderment, having probably never even seen a piece of fresh fish before. When his virgin kitchen was filled with the heavenly aroma of the bubbling cod purses and audible sizzling was erupting from the oven, Zach curiously went over to the radiator to see if the pipes were hissing again. I explained that the unusual noises were the result of *actual food* cooking. As proof, I had to crack the oven to show him. I served the fish packets with plain couscous and French bread. Zach diligently tasted his fish and, surprised, pronounced it "not bad." He then devoured the whole dish in seconds, leaned back in his chair, and reached for the remote to check in on Sports Center, which he'd grudgingly turned off when dinner was ready.

I was about to give up on Zach but went to see him the following weekend after he'd called me to say that he wanted to make me dinner since I'd done so for him. I made the tiresome trek to his place that Friday night with the hope that some sort of miraculous transformation had occurred following his first fish dinner. Much to my dismay, Zach had gone to the local grocery store and bought some frozen haddock fillets that he bravely slapped onto a dry skillet while I sat frightened in the living room. I mustered all the graciousness I could and bit into the miserable fish, which was accompanied by a side of canned green beans. Zach, who didn't seem to notice much difference between his fish and mine, once again pronounced the meal "not bad." The declaration marked the demise of our relationship. I fled after dinner, pausing outside his building to vomit in the privet hedge before speeding back to Brighton.

Josh was clearly on a whole new culinary level. I went to bed that Saturday night feeling like Christmas was coming.

On Sunday morning I decided I'd better go retrieve my car from the funeral home in Cambridge, where I'd probably amassed nine hundred dollars in parking tickets. I called Heather, hoping she'd take pity on me and drive me to collect my Saturn.

"Well, where have you been, my long lost sister? Huh?" Heather said as she picked up the phone.

"Come get me, and I'll tell you. You won't even believe the week I've had. Drive me to my car in Cambridge, and you'll hear all about it," I said, knowing Heather would do anything for a good story.

"Fine. I'm heading over to Mom and Dad's with Walker and Lucy. Let me just get them ready, and I'll come over. Meet me outside your house."

Twenty-five minutes later I was comfortably seated in Heather's Mazda minivan tickling my adorable niece and nephew. "All right," Heather demanded, "spill it. What the hell is your car doing in Cambridge?"

"Hell! Hell!" Walker chirped from the backseat.

"Dammit, I have to stop swearing in front of the kids. Walker, don't say that word, please. Mommy shouldn't have said that. And, Jesus, don't say it in front of your grandparents."

"Jesus! Jesus!" Walker echoed.

"I'll just have to tell Mom and Dad he's an extremely religious child," Heather sighed. "Okay, Chloe. Go."

I caught my cursing sister up on Eric and Josh and the whole murder investigation. With the kids in the car, however, I had to spell out a lot of the story to avoid having Walker scream "dead body" or "sexy kisser" in front of my parents.

When we reached my car, I'd finished feeding Heather most of the story. With an exasperated look, she warned, "We're not done talking about this. I don't like the idea of you hanging out with this Josh character." Heather's bad attitude and the two orange parking tickets on my car couldn't kill my giddy mood. I started the engine and followed Heather to Newton.

Heather and I had grown up in a white Spanish-style house on Farlow Road. Both of my parents, Bethany and Jack Carter, were professional landscapers and had created an incredible outdoor utopia with raised garden beds, cobbled pathways, and stucco walls. Vegetables, flowers, shrubs, and berry bushes and vines left little room for a lawn, and each year the few patches of grass that remained became smaller and smaller, overtaken by new plantings. My parents had published a successful series of books for the home gardener and spent much of their time testing out new ideas in their own yard.

Heather pulled out her key and let us all in the front door. Heather and I had been out of the house for so many years that our bedrooms had been taken over and turned into greenhouses. The outside of my parents' house was a shrine to taste and style, but the inside was a ghastly display of my mother's obsession with hideous craft projects.

"Lord, what has she done now?" Heather wondered aloud as we entered the living room. "Well, Chloe, at least we know where you got your warped decorating sense."

A series of wreaths made of yarn and silk flowers adorned the main wall. I stared at a particularly garish wreath constructed entirely of fake sunflowers. "Why couldn't Mom have discovered a less obtrusive hobby, like jewelry making or scrapbooking? *Why* has she become obsessed with objects that have to be displayed?"

"Just be happy she hadn't discovered wreaths when we lived here. Could you imagine bringing your friends over to see this garbage?"

"There are my babies!" Mom shrieked as she ran into the room, followed by our father, who was busy rolling his eyes and pointing to the new wall hangings. "I've missed my girls so much!" Tanned and fresh looking from their vacation in Acadia National Park, my parents showered us with hugs and kisses and immediately whipped out presents for the two kids.

In typical sister-ratting-out-sister style, Heather proceeded to announce, "Guess what Chloe's done? She's going out with the man suspected of murdering the blind date she had last week!"

"Jesus!" Walker said.

"Thank you, Heather," I said. "*And* Walker."

"What in the world are you talking about?" Mom said.

How many times am I going to have to retell this? Can't we all just focus on the news that I may have just met my future husband?

"Heather left out a few details. Josh, the guy I'm going out with, is a very unlikely suspect," I said.

After I had yet again given the short version of the date-and-murder debacle, my father asked, "So the food stinks? Bethany, cancel the reservations we made at Essence for next week with the Morrisons."

"Definitely," my mother agreed. "But you're going to Magellan on Friday?"

"I know! Can you believe it?" I squealed.

"Have you all lost it?" Heather said. "This Josh person shouldn't be at the top of Chloe's dating list

155

right now. He shouldn't be on it at all. He could be a murderer!"

"Oh, please, Heather. You're so paranoid. Chloe wouldn't go out with a murderer—she has excellent judgment. Besides, chefs hack up food, not people," Mom said. "And you're the one who sent her on this Back Bay Dates date with this poor Eric. You're the one who started the ball rolling."

Heather defended herself. "Are we all supposed to *ignore* the fact that Chloe has been through a traumatic event? She saw a dead body, for Pete's sake. All bloody. And now she's behaving irrationally, eating food cooked by a murder suspect!"

"She looks fine to me. In fact," Mom continued, smiling at me, "I think she looks happy and excited about this boy. And he sounds better than that Daniel. I didn't like the sound of him when I thought he was a platonic friend of yours, Chloe, and then Heather called him your 'fun buddy.' Do I have that right? What a horrible expression."

Even though Daniel had refused to come to my aid by fooling around with me in front of my building during the Noah crisis, I felt some loyalty to him. Mostly, though, I was furious at Heather for passing on private information about me to our parents.

I hoped to God that my mother was right about Josh and that Heather was wrong. "Finding Eric was upsetting," I admitted. "So was his murder. It was awful, but I'm dealing with it. I don't want to speak ill of the dead, but I'd just met Eric, so there's a limit to how devastated I'm going to be, okay? But fortunately for me, Josh is alive and well, and I want to go out with him."

"Not alone, I hope," Heather said. "I don't think it's one bit safe for you to be alone with him."

I sighed. "Adrianna and Owen are coming with me." They hadn't yet accepted the invitation I'd left on Adrianna's voice mail, but I didn't say so.

"Why don't we all go?" Dad piped in. "I'd love to eat at Magellan."

"Oh, wonderful!" Mom said, delighted. "The whole family will go!"

"No!" I said incredulously. "The whole family will *not* go. I'm not into sicko family group dates. I will be fine with Ade and Owen."

Looking hurt, Dad said, "If that's what you want. But we expect a full report on your meal. Okay, now come help us taste-test the tomatoes."

It was that time of year again. When all my father's tomato plants had produced their bounty, he whipped up a chart, and as a family, we meticulously rated each variety according to overall appearance, skin thickness, flavor, texture, color—a tomato beauty pageant, if you will, only without the obligatory swimsuit competition.

Baby Lucy had the good sense to sleep through most of the tomato tasting, which lasted an hour. At the end, Dad's chart was filled in, with a yellow pear variety deemed this year's winner. Walker's face and hands were stained with tomato juice, and Heather sent him off to play in the sprinkler while I told my parents about the exciting world of social work and workplace harassment.

"Sounds boring," Dad declared. "On a happier note, I'd like to announce the official end of this season's Soft Shell Crabfest." Each year my father set himself the goal of eating one hundred soft shell crabs during crab season, and Fresh Pond Seafood was so thrilled with his attempts that they created a chart for him, hung it on the store's wall, and x-ed off one box for each of his purchases. They also gave him the last three crabs for free. Yesterday, when he'd bought his hundredth crab of the year, the shop's owners had framed his crabfest chart and presented it to him.

Dad proudly raised the trophy above his head, declaring, "I am the crab king!"

"The fact that you've eaten a hundred crabs over the past few months is revolting. You should be embarrassed," Heather scolded.

"Heather, leave him alone," I said. "I think it's admirable. I love soft shell crabs, but I can only eat a few a season. But Dad has really proven himself."

"Yeah, proven himself to have a few loose screws," Heather said, but went over and hugged Dad.

"Okay, family," I said. "I'm goin' home. I've got about a zillion pages of reading for school."

"Lock your doors when you get home," instructed Heather.

I nodded in mock seriousness, kissed her kids, and headed home—with every intention of locking my doors.

ELEVEN

I spent Monday and Tuesday incarcerated in the horrible Boston Organization Against Sexual and Other Harassment in the Workplace. Naomi had left me a note to remind me that she was attending a two-day rally for some worthy cause outside the State House and that I should familiarize myself with the monstrous folder she'd left out for me. I was welcome to come find her later that afternoon.

If she thought I was going to sit in this room reading from nine to five, she was nuts. After two hours of trying to digest harassment facts, I decided to start on a social work school assignment I'd been putting off. Our General Practice professor had assigned us the task of detailing our field placement experiences in a journal in which we were free to write about whatever we wanted.

"Day 1," I wrote. "Am forced to read lurid stories of workplace harassment while confined to poorly decorated minioffice. Management has opted not to include windows in decor so as to keep staff (me and Naomi) diligently focused on work at hand. Have avoided answering calls all morning since cannot recall exact name of organization. Every time the phone rings I must pretend to be so engrossed in literature that have not even heard incessant ringing. Naomi has encouraged me to take on projects on my own and am considering painting office and creating new filing and storage space. (May not be traditional social work per se, but would contribute to staff morale and psychological well-being.) Will order tons of stuff from Hold Everything catalogue and write off for tax deduction. Will discuss with Naomi next week. Am pleased that am not forced to work in community mental health center or hospital psych ward, like some peers, and do not have to deal with those with schizophrenia or other pathological disorders. Although, may go cuckoo in this office come May. Naomi seems to be a hands-off supervisor since is not here today or tomorrow—very nice. Looking forward to stimulating field placement this year."

I left at two on Monday. On Tuesday I left at one, having written Naomi a note to say that on the previous day, I'd looked everywhere for her in front of the State House and that although I hadn't found her, I'd still stood with other women chanting and holding a sign that read No More! I had, in fact, only passed through the crowd on my way to the T and, unable to determine exactly what the group was protesting, had chosen to participate in a protest of my own by objecting to being stuck in a dimly lit office on a sunny September day.

That afternoon I finally reached Adrianna on the phone. "You found a date at Eric's funeral!" she screamed with delight. "That's the Chloe I know and love!" After a short rendition of "Back in the Saddle," she wanted every detail about Josh. "He sounds amazing. And a chef! Oh my God! I can't believe we're going to Magellan. This is going to be unbelievable!"

Now that's a best friend. No irritating questions about guilt or innocence—she knew that the only concern here was what the hell I was going to wear.

"So," I begged, "will you come over on Friday and help me get ready? And can I borrow something to wear? The nicest thing I have is the blue dress you made me, but it seems sort of disrespectful to wear it again since that's what I had on when I, uh, went out with Eric."

"I'll be there at four, okay? Um, make it three o'clock. Miraculously, I'm off for the weekend after eleven, so I'll come over early. Will you be done with classes by then?" she asked.

I said I would, and she promised to bring over an assortment of outfits for me to choose from. Owen would pick us up and drive us to Magellan so we could both drink. At the very least, I'd need some wine to calm my jitters.

Josh had left me a message on Monday to make sure we were still coming. So far, I'd replayed it about forty times, just loving the sound of his voice. When I told Adrianna about the message, she squealed, "Oh, I want to hear it!" I gave her my voice mail password and hung up. A minute later she called back. "He sounds totally dreamy. I can't wait for Friday."

"Tell me about it," I agreed. We said good-bye, and I went back to reading the Social Work Code of Ethics for class on Wednesday. I had Group Therapy first and

General Practice after that.

Group Therapy met at eight in the morning, which I thought totally went *against* the social work code of respecting all individuals (and allowing them to sleep late). But on Wednesday, I managed to show up on time and found an empty seat between two women, one about my age and one who was probably in her forties. I'd noticed that approximately half my classmates were middle-aged, and last week when we were all forced to introduce ourselves in each class, learned that a lot of people were making drastic midlife career changes by coming to social work school. The woman next to me was in another of my classes, and I remembered her telling my Research Methods class last week that she had left her job as a CPA and had a field placement at a homeless shelter.

Professor Buckley entered the room and instructed the class to move their chairs into a large circle, a ploy I hated, a transparent technique meant to encourage participation. So now I couldn't hide in the back and watch the minutes tick by. Professor Buckley pulled his own chair into the circle and sat back. We all waited for him to start lecturing or leading or doing something. Anything. But he just sat there, expressionless, looking around at his students. We all looked around at each other, wondering if perhaps our professor was having some sort of amnesic episode. Uncle Alan was paying for *this?*

After another few minutes, the change-of-career student next to me spoke up. "Should we be doing something?" she asked expectantly.

"This is it," our professor said. "We are doing it."

Students looked at one another in confusion. Oh, shit. I wasn't confused. On the contrary, I knew what was going on here. This was supposed to be some sort of self-analytic group where we all "processed" what was happening in the "here and now." I'd read about this crap in college psych. We were in for a long two hours.

Students began trying to get the professor to elaborate, but his only responses were things like "This *is* the group," and "There *is* no agenda," statements that did little to appease his annoyed class. I decided that I could sit there and listen to the squabbling or I could do something to make time fly by faster.

"Okay, I know what this is," I announced with unusual boldness. The class stopped talking and looked at me. "This is some sort of Gestalt therapy thing where we discuss what's happening right now, the dynamics of the present, and lots of other abstract stuff. How we're relating to each other, blah, blah, blah." I was barraged with questions and could only reply that since this was a course on group therapy, we were apparently expected to partake in our own group therapy process right here. Groans and whispers followed. The professor smirked and nodded his head slightly.

"So what are we supposed to talk about?" demanded a man from the other side of the room.

I said, "Anything we want. I think that we determine

how to use our two hours."

We all sat there quietly, waiting for someone to come up with a topic.

"All right," I started. "How about this," and I launched into the story of Eric's murder. I omitted the details of my kissing bonanza with Josh, and in accordance with the Code of Ethics of the National Association of Social Workers, I changed everyone's name to protect privacy, even though in reporting the murder, the media had used real names. In a flash of genius, I dubbed Eric "Mr. Dough." Faced with this audience of students, all glued to my every word, I realized that I did need impartial advice. Maybe this group could help absolve Josh of any wrongdoing in Eric's murder. After I finished, I sat back and waited.

"I heard about this on the news," someone said. "And they still don't know who did it, right?"

I nodded.

A tall brown-haired woman spoke next. "I'm Gretchen, and I'm a first-year student here." Continuing slowly and emphatically, she said, "As a *social worker,* my first concern would be to address *your* feelings of loss and find out whether you're having any symptoms of post-traumatic stress." Although she seemed like a caricature of the touchy-feely social worker, her sincerity was apparent. She continued. "Death is hard on all of us."

The rest of the class nodded in sanctimonious agreement, thus tempting me to rebel by arguing the opposite, namely, that death was easy on all of us if we were survivors who hadn't known or cared about the deceased. Or had outright hated the deceased. Exactly how hard was death on the murderers who caused it? What if they weren't remorseful at all, but were thrilled with the consequences of their deeds?

Gretchen went on. "And I think that one of the ways we cope is through denial. Denying the grief that we're experiencing deep down. I wonder if maybe you've been so caught up in pleasing Mr. Dough's parents and everyone else that you've failed to take the time to process how this experience has affected you?"

Oops. While I'd been summoning examples to counter the death-is-hard platitude, I'd become the group's client. Abandoning my silent rebellion, determined not to flunk out of social work school, I fought platitudes with platitudes. "Actually," I said, "I feel as though I have done a lot of introspective thinking about the impact that finding the body may have had on me. I've talked at length with family and friends, who've all been terrific. And I feel that I have tapped into the painful reality of man's inhumanity to man."

"Person's inhumanity to person," someone piped from across the room.

"Person's inhumanity to person," I corrected myself. "I have borne witness to one of the world's atrocities, murder, and have come out stronger and more driven to understand human nature. And whoever committed this murder may not have had access to proper mental health counseling. There may have been some familial dysfunction that caused an intrapsychic break that led this person to kill another."

Thankful that I'd done my psychopathology reading last weekend, I paused dramatically. "But you're right. Discovering a murder victim was devastating. So I'm glad I have this forum in which to process my feelings." I covered my mouth and faked a coughing fit. "And I think that part of my recovery process might be to figure out who the murderer is."

Gretchen nodded. "It's important that you have a support system in place to get you through this. So, have you had disturbed sleep, a change of appetite, any generalized anxiety?"

I shook my head. Gretchen looked disappointed at my failure to display symptoms of stress or depression.

"I think we should discuss Mr. Dough's family," came a voice from the circle. I looked to my right and was happy to see Doug, my bookstore savior. "Hello, everyone. I'm Doug. I'm a doctoral student, and I'm your TA for the class." Rather sneaky of him to covertly embed himself in the group as though he were a first-year student. I liked him.

A girl named Julie joined in the discussion. She was a petite twenty-something dressed in all black with tiny black eyeglasses that kept sliding down her nose. "I think it's clear that Chloe is in good shape emotionally and that her real concern here is who the murderer is. She seems to have the sense that this chef that we're calling Chef Tell"—she rolled her eyes—"isn't a likely suspect. She's highly motivated to clear him of any suspicion since he appears to be a possible romantic interest?" She looked at me.

I nodded slightly.

She pushed her glasses back in place. "So, Chloe, what about Mr. Dough's parents?"

"You think his parents killed him?" I asked.

"It's worth exploring. I gather Mr. Dough was well off financially. Maybe they were hoping to get hold of his money." Julie cocked her head to the side. "If you ask me, I think their behavior following their son's death was erratic and odd."

"They certainly were weird," I admitted.

"And I think we should question their inability to grasp the true nature of your relationship with their son. Why were they so eager to believe that you and Dough were engaged? Why, on the day of the funeral, did they latch on to you so intently? I'm sure they must've had close family members who would've been more appropriate supports to them."

"I don't know why they wanted to believe Mr. Dough and I were a couple. But I didn't feel like I could tell them the truth. And I don't think they would've believed me even if I tried. They were both so upset that I just went along with it. I mean, what's the harm?"

"I'm not sure," said Julie. "Maybe none. If they thought you were engaged to their son, then maybe they needed to be close to the person they thought was closest to their murdered child. If one or both of them is guilty, though, maybe they clung to you to demonstrate their *supposed* grief. They couldn't exactly show up at their son's funeral jumping for joy."

I saw Julie's point. And liked it. Better Eric's parents than my Josh. "So you think they were in his will?" I asked. "And they knew that and they killed him? But they seemed to have plenty of money of their own, so why would they need more?"

Julie had an answer. "It might not be about *needing* more money but about *wanting* more. For some people, there's never enough money. And who knows what their relationship with their son was really like. It doesn't sound like this set of parents was connected in any meaningful way to their only son. To them, his money may have represented a symbolic way to tie themselves to an emotionally unavailable and distant son. If they couldn't have him in any appreciable sense, they may have taken what they could from him. His money."

By now, the group members were on the edges of their seats. "Hm . . . that's possible, I suppose," I said. "And by grabbing onto me, they could at least pretend that they'd had enough of a relationship with their son that they could grieve with his fiancée? In other words, me. One united and loving family mourning a common loss. So they could be completely nuts, huh? Delusional enough to think that murdering him would bring them closer to him?" Scary thought. "Or they're just peculiar people, of which there are many in this world, and they were overwhelmed by a real loss."

Doug stepped in again. "And what about the owner? Mr. T?" (That's what I'd called Timothy.) "Was his divorce friendly? It sounds like it, in fact, was. But what else?"

"What about this?" began a student who introduced herself as Barbara. "I used to work in marketing, and we all know the saying that bad press is better than no press. Mr. T could have murdered Mr. Dough to publicize his restaurant. Although it might seem like having a murder at your restaurant would be bad for business, the opposite may very well be true. Think about how much press coverage you get. The restaurant's name is all over the news and the papers. And we all know what advertisers do. They bombard you with a product's name until it's so ingrained in your head that when you go shopping you're more likely to buy their product. Same thing here. The more the public hears about the restaurant and the owner, the more likely people are to check it out. Out of curiosity if nothing else."

People looked to me for a response, but I kept quiet.

Giving up on me, Barbara elaborated on what she'd been saying. "And it depends on what happens now. If Mr. T seems appropriately upset but continues to do interviews and press about this story and acts like he was the victim here, too, it might work for him. Now everyone knows about his restaurant, and if he's smart, he can turn the focus onto promoting the food, the staff, the location, et cetera."

"That's not a bad theory," I said excitedly. Tim had

been all over the news last week, tearfully talking about how wonderful Eric had been. Tim had lied: anyone who'd ever met Eric had known he was obnoxious and arrogant. "Except for the fact that Mr. T honestly just seems like a guy devoted to his restaurant and his food and his customers. He doesn't seem like a murderer."

"Of course he doesn't," Barbara said. "He has to come off like that. Murderers don't usually walk around flailing guns and knives about. But your chef, he admitted to not being perfect. He acknowledged that he tried to hinder the competition by giving its chef partial recipes and leaving out ingredients. He was honest. He admitted that he'd done something unfriendly, let's say, or competitive, but not murderous. Same thing with Mr. T's ex-wife, Mrs. M. She sounds tough, but she's so *outwardly* tough and true to herself that she has nothing to hide. She's got control of her life, while Mr. T is having to start fresh after the divorce and is probably more desperate for success. He left a great situation business-wise and has everything riding on this new place. Considering the circumstances, I think Mr. T is acting a little too perfect."

"I hadn't thought of that," I said slowly. "I hadn't thought of that at all. Mr. T did rush in and come off like a hero when he tried to 'save' Mr. Dough. And he got his fingerprints all over everything."

Professor Buckley finally spoke up. "I'd like to hear how the class feels about the fact that Chloe has dominated this conversation today. What does that say about her and the kind of participant she is in a group setting? Are we, as a whole, resentful?" We all ignored him and continued with our theorizing.

I turned back to Barbara. "But why kill off a potential investor? If he's so driven to make his restaurant succeed, why get rid of a source of income?" I asked. "Is that less important than publicity?"

"Good question. But you don't know everything about their relationship. It does sound like Mr. Dough was becoming more of an annoyance than a great investor. He latched onto this group of restaurant owners and their world, and he was intrusive and bossy and generally made a pest of himself. And how do you know that Mr. Dough was really going to invest, anyway? Maybe he was so desperate to work himself into this crowd of people he obviously admired so much that he only pretended he was going to get involved. He certainly doesn't sound like the most personable person. Maybe he was desperate for friends."

I nodded enthusiastically. "Now that I think about it, it does seem like, uh, my date had been toying a bit with Mr. T, you know, getting as many free meals as he could, acting like he ran the place, ordering the staff around. And at the same time that he was yabbering about all the money he had to invest . . . I don't know, but he also seemed like a pretty serious cheapskate. Maybe he wouldn't have wanted to part with his precious money if he wasn't going to be guaranteed a return."

171

"Again," began our exasperated professor, "let's shift the focus to the current dynamics in this room. To what's going on right now. What processes are present here?" He looked around hopelessly. "All right, let's take a break. Everyone back here in ten minutes."

Doug caught up with me in the hall. "I knew you were going to be trouble when I found you in the bookstore. Good group work today, Chloe."

I smiled. I was beginning to enjoy Group Therapy. So far we'd cast suspicion off Josh and onto other possible suspects. Unfortunately, when the class resumed, Professor Buckley slipped out of his nondirective role by insisting that we quit talking about the murder, and then a lot of students got annoyed with him, so the remainder of the class was somewhat satisfying in terms of group process but disappointing with regard to exonerating Josh.

Still, the class had been productive. As soon as it ended, I went home to call Detective Hurley and let him know what my social work cohorts and I had come up with.

Detective Hurley miraculously picked up after the first ring. "Aren't you supposed to be out catching criminals?" I asked him.

"Yeah, theoretically. Only this case isn't moving as quickly as I'd hoped. Did you remember something that could help?" he asked.

"Well, I've been talking to Josh, and I have the impression that he's your main suspect right now. But I definitely don't think he did it."

Hurley groaned. "Let me guess. You and Josh are . . ." He didn't bother to finish the sentence.

"Well, yeah. No, not exactly. But listen," and I ran through my social work class's alternative theories. "I suggest you look at Tim and at Eric's parents. I didn't see Tim during the *exact* moment Eric was murdered. And his parents are whacked, if you want my opinion. Where were *they* that night?" I also stressed that Josh had been up-front about sabotaging Garrett's food, and I dished out some of my classmates' theories about restaurant promotion, parental pathology in relation to an emotionally distant son, and so forth.

"Chloe, I can't tell you who to spend your time with, but I'd advise you to stay away from all suspicious parties. You don't have any connection to these people. Leave it that way."

But Detective Hurley was wrong. I *was* connected to Josh.

TWELVE

I called Josh late Thursday morning after class. I wasn't trying to follow any rules about calling or not calling within a certain number of days since I thought that was all a bunch of BS.

"Hey, cutie! How are you?" he said cheerily.

"I'm good. I just got home from class, and I thought I'd check in with you about Friday night. Is it still okay if we come in for dinner?"

"Of course. You're going to bring your friends Adrianna and Owen, right?"

"If that's okay with you. I'm sure the restaurant will be swamped on a Friday night. I don't want us to be in the way."

"Not at all. I told Maddie you were coming in, and she's going to have places set up for you at the kitchen. We've got an open kitchen like Essence does, but I hope you'll have a better time at Magellan than you did there. So, what've you been up to the past few days?"

I told him about visiting with my parents and sister, and my idiotic field placement. I left out the discussion I'd had in group therapy. Why ruin the conversation by mentioning that he was murder suspect?

Josh thought my father's crabfest story was hysterical. "You want me to make you soft shell crabs? This is your last chance before the season's over."

"That would be wonderful. Ade and I love soft shell crabs. But Owen has some sort of seafood phobia that dates to a bad shrimp he ate ten years ago. He hasn't eaten anything that's lived in the ocean since," I said apologetically.

"No problem. I'll make him something else, and you girls can have soft shells, okay?"

According to BCGSSW's policy on avoiding non-sexist language, *girl* was an unacceptable term for someone over the age of eighteen. Suggested non-sexist terms included *female adolescent* and *woman*. Obviously, *You adolescent females can have soft shells* wouldn't do at all. *You women can have soft*

174

shells? Possibly. But for really good soft shells, I'd have been willing to tolerate even egregiously sexist language, particularly because Josh, however manly, struck me as more boyish than as adolescently male, and his use of "girls" was clearly intended to convey affection.

"I don't want to be a bother . . . ." I started.

"Stop. I want you to have anything you want on Friday." Hm. Double meaning there? I hoped so.

We hung up and, even though I had a full day ahead of reading about the atrocities of the health-care crisis in this country, I did a happy dance around the kitchen.

On Friday, Adrianna showed up precisely at three. For a minute I thought she might be going out of town: she had a three-piece luggage set with her. I looked at her questioningly.

"Supplies." She smiled. She lugged the suitcases into my room and started unzipping them. "Now, I wasn't sure what you'd be in the mood for, so I brought a little of everything."

I sat down on the rug as Ade began showing me various outfit options for the night. Even though she was skinnier and leggier than I was, she wore her clothing even tighter and shorter than I did, so her things usually fit me well enough. "Okay," she said. "Strapless black knee-length dress?"

I shook my head violently. "Not unless I want to be flashing my boobs at Josh while he cooks."

"So, we'll save that for your next date?"

"Ha-ha. Keep going. And nothing white. You know I'll spill food on myself."

We ran through a few more outfits before we settled on a stretchy, short-sleeved pale green top and a matching short skirt with tiny flowers.

"Now we're highlighting your hair," she announced. "Your roots are disgusting."

I could always count on her for honesty, if not for tact.

Adrianna spent the next hour weaving chunks of my hair into completely unflattering foil sheets. "If my hair turns green, I'm going to kill you," I threatened.

"Shut up. I've done this a million times. Besides, would I ever make you look like a freak? It would reflect badly on me." She giggled and continued to torture me.

When she'd finished glopping on the vile-smelling chemicals, I stood up and looked in the mirror. Aluminum foil stuck out all over my head. "This was not at all what I was going for," I moaned pitifully. With my luck, Noah would show up at the door any moment and I'd have to answer it like this.

"Then don't look in the mirror until I'm done."

Within an hour, the foil and glop were gone. So were the dark roots. As if by magic, I had snazzy highlights in my red hair. After I'd showered and dried off, Ade blew my hair out. Twenty-five minutes of yanking, I was done. As she rubbed a defrizzing serum through my smooth style, she said, "It's a tiny bit humid out tonight, and I do *not* want you frizzing up. Now," she ordered, "start your makeup while I get dressed."

I turned on the oldies station while we finished beautifying ourselves. I listened to Adrianna sing along to "Don't Pull Your Love (Out)" and was satisfied to realize that she was completely tone deaf. Ha! One thing she wasn't good at!

When she'd finished getting dressed, I said, "You don't look like yourself." She had on the kind of boring, conservative outfit she never wore—gray dress pants and a long-sleeved, button-down white shirt—and her newly brown hair was pulled back in a low ponytail. I should have felt insulted. "I know what you're doing," I said, "and you don't need to. I'm not worried about Josh trying to pounce on you. I want you to look like *you* again. Wild and hot. Okay?"

"This is your night, and I didn't want you to think I was trying to . . . can I go back to blonde tomorrow?"

I nodded and hugged her. "You'd better. Now, put on something low-cut, skimpy, and sexy, okay?"

"Yay! Chloe's back! This Josh Driscoll must be something special if you're so relaxed and happy," she teased. "And I'm ready for a margarita."

I blended up our drinks while she changed into a fuchsia tank dress, shook her hair out, and applied more makeup. "We've got half an hour before Owen gets here," she said, "so I say we drink up and discuss your love life a little more." She leaned in to me and whispered, "Did you shave your legs?"

Two strong drinks later, Owen picked us up in his beat-up Blazer, which was possibly the ugliest car I'd ever seen, dark brown with yellow stripes on the sides. "Ugly and reliable, just like me!" Owen always said. Please. He was gorgeous. Very Irish looking, Owen had fair skin, dark hair, and bright blue eyes. He and Adrianna actually made a strange-looking couple, since she was always glamorous and style conscious, and he bought most of what he wore at a vintage clothing store in Harvard Square. We jumped into the Blazer, and Owen hit the gas.

"Owen! What in God's name are you wearing?" Adrianna yelled.

"What? You don't love it?" He grinned devilishly. He'd gone all out for our big night by dressing in a deep orange polyester suit and brown cowboy boots.

"Apologize to Chloe for this ghastly ensemble. I told you to wear something *normal*. And preferably something made in this decade."

It could have been the margaritas talking, but I had to laugh. As foolish as the outfit was, Owen managed to pull it off. Besides, as atypical as the suit was of Magellan's clientele, everyone always liked Owen. He was charming and funny and loyal—and could put up with Adrianna's headstrong, not to say occasion- ally obnoxious, personality.

"Owen, I think you look dashing," I insisted. "And I won't lose either of you tonight in your bright colors."

Adrianna shrieked, "Oh, Jesus. I'm not sitting next to you, Owen. We'll totally clash!"

"So, Chloe," Owen said, cutting off another car, "are you nervous?"

"Actually, no. I don't know why," I answered. Butterflies on amphetamines were flying around in my stomach, but mostly I felt happy at the prospect of seeing Josh again.

We reached the South End in record time, thanks to Owen's terrifying driving skills, and parked with the valet outside Magellan. "And I don't want to see any marks on this baby when I get back." Owen winked at the attendant. Ade rolled her eyes, glancing at the wreck Owen called a car.

Suddenly nervous, I said, "Ade, you go in first."

"Don't be a loser."

"What if he's wearing one of those silly tall white hats? I'll be so embarrassed for him," I said, panicking.

"Only dorks wear those, and Josh doesn't sound like a dork." She pushed me through the door.

The restaurant was so full that we had to squeeze through a crowd to get to the hostess, who was apologetically explaining to a couple that there would be an hour-and-a-half wait for a table.

"Hi," I said to the hostess. "I'm Chloe, and I think Josh made a reservation for the three of us?"

"Oh, sure. He said you'd be coming in tonight. Nice to meet you all. I'm Margaret. Just follow me back here. Josh has set you up by the kitchen."

Déjà vu: I again followed a hostess through a restaurant for a date.

Magellan was so high toned that I tried not to giggle as Ade in her hot pink dress and Owen in his orange suit followed behind me. We walked past a square bar area and past tables of customers in the center of the room to get to the open kitchen. There was another dining area ahead of us, but the kitchen was clearly the heart of this restaurant. Although Essence had been attractive, with its own open kitchen, I now saw that Magellan was the original and Essence a copy.

"Oh, look at that rack of lamb," I heard Owen say. For once, my own eyes weren't on all the food around me but were scanning the kitchen for my chef.

Once again, I had an eerie reminder of my visit to Essence: we were seated at a counter that ran the length of the kitchen. But this was a spacious counter covered with rustic-looking stone. As we took our seats in plush bar-height chairs, I felt sure that other customers of Magellan and Essence had noticed the similarities between the restaurants. Who could have missed them?

"Wait, Chloe, you have to sit in the middle. Owen and I cannot be next to each other in these outfits," Adrianna insisted.

"You two are weird," I said but agreed that it would be best for other diners if they didn't have to witness the pairing of my fashion-extremist friends. Maybe my green outfit would tone them down?

Once settled, I looked up to see Josh off to my left furiously chopping onions. How cute was he? He looked so serious and focused and lovable. He suddenly whipped around to the grill behind him and flipped a piece of meat. I could tell, even from a distance, that it was perfectly seared.

"That's Josh, I bet, right?" Ade asked.

I nodded.

"How did he know that was done? He wasn't even looking."

Owen, Ade, and I continued staring at Josh while he worked. We watched in awe as he sharpened a chef's knife on a steel with a bright blue plastic handle. The sharpening steel reminded me of something a fencer would use, probably because of the swift, smooth way Josh dragged the knife blade across the top and then under the bottom of the metal rod. I was able to watch in comfort only because he held the knife with the blade facing away from him. When satisfied with his knife, Josh reached under the counter and pulled up a bunch of leeks that he speedily sliced and tossed with the onions into the hot skillet behind him. The sweet aroma brought a smile to my face.

Ade nudged me. "If slicing onions makes you smile like that, who knows what could happen later."

I rolled my eyes. "But seriously, isn't he cute?" I couldn't stop staring at Josh, who was a Josh I hadn't seen before, Josh at work.

"He's adorable," she agreed.

After shaking the pan of onions and leeks, Josh finally looked over and caught my eye. "Hi, beautiful!" He leaned across the chef's counter to give me a little kiss. "I've been waiting all week to do that."

He called me beautiful! And kissed me!

I introduced Adrianna and Owen and was happy to

see that Josh appeared not to notice Ade's supermodel looks.

A dark-haired young man appeared by Josh's side. "You want me to pull out the sea bass?" he asked.

"Hey, Brian. Yeah," Josh said. "Brian, this is Chloe, Adrianna, and Owen. Here for dinner tonight as my guests, so we have to impress them. My future happiness depends on what we cook for them tonight," he said with mock seriousness.

"Oh, so this is Chloe?" Brian poked Josh's side with his fingers. "Let me tell you something. I've never seen Josh burn anything until this week. But so far, he's burned a salmon and two steaks, and I'm betting you're the reason."

I was pleased to note that Josh blushed as he playfully shoved Brian away. "That's enough of that. Just go get the sea bass. We've got a three top that's all ordered the special."

At a guess, a "three top" meant a table of three people. Before I could ask my chef what tops had to do with anything—top hats? tops of people's heads?—he turned back to us and said, "Okay, kids, you ready to eat? I thought I'd start you off with my spring rolls. And then I've got soft shell crabs for the ladies and a duck for you, Owen. Sound good?"

Owen clapped his hands together eagerly. "Bring it on, baby! We're ready!"

Josh looked at me and smiled, holding my gaze for a moment.

"Josh! The leeks!" Brian yelled.

182

Josh spun around, saw the burning mess in the pan, and threw his hands up. Brian laughed, "One cute girl and look what happens."

Josh started chopping fresh leeks just as Madeline approached our group. "Hello, again, Chloe," she said. "I'm so glad to see you. You made quite an impression on Josh." She smiled conspiratorially. "I guess the ride home worked out well, huh?"

"It did, it did," I agreed, unable to stop grinning. I introduced Ade and Owen. "And this is Madeline Rock. She owns Magellan."

We all chatted for a few moments before Madeline offered us drinks from the bar. Adrianna asked for wine, and Madeline said she knew exactly the right bottle for us, on the house, no less.

"Excuse me, folks." A young waitress dressed in all black spoke from behind us. "The chef asked me to bring these out to you."

She placed the plates of spring rolls in front of us. These spring rolls bore so little resemblance to any I'd ever seen before that they seemed to demand a different and far more grand name. The rolls were about five inches across and had been sliced in half at an angle and placed artistically on the brilliantly white plate. Brightly colored shredded vegetables were wrapped tightly in the golden brown wrapper, and two sauces had been poured on either side of the roll.

"Whoa, these look awesome," Owen said.

We started eating, and I started smiling again. Truly, they were fabulous. The vegetables were crisp and flavorful. And the sauces?

"Oh my God," Adrianna murmured with her mouth full. "Unbelievable."

Josh shouted over to us from the grill. "Happy?"

We all nodded enthusiastically. "Dude," Owen started, chewing a huge bite, "*what* is in these?"

"I'm glad you like it. Um, let's see . . . onions, zucchini, squash, cabbage, peppers, carrots, roasted garlic, cumin, and coriander. And the sauces are a sesame-mango sauce and a port wine syrup," he said proudly.

Josh looked to me, and I could tell he wanted to know what I thought. But I didn't need to say anything: he saw my happy expression and nodded. "All right, all right," he said softly.

We polished off every bit of our spring rolls and ordered another bottle of wine while we quietly discussed what a catch Josh was. The meal only continued to get better when our waitress brought our entrées. Josh had done a lavender-glazed duck for Owen with, our waitress told us, a sweet soy sauce and aromatic spices, jasmine rice, and Chinese long beans. Adrianna and I were presented with soft shell crabs fried in cornmeal on a vegetable "hash" made with finely diced onions, red peppers, carrots, potatoes, and fresh thyme, all served in an orange-scented fish fumé with truffled pea tendrils.

"Man, if you don't marry him, I might," Owen said as he admired his duck.

I smiled. "Hey, back off. Besides, I think you're taken already."

"He certainly is," Adrianna said. "But I wouldn't mind if you could cook like this, Owen." Owen was famous for his ability to make noodles and sauce à la Lipton and not much else. He and Ade ate out all the time. They knew good food but couldn't cook it.

The three of us worked our way through the delicious plates Josh had prepared for us, and Owen even asked for a bite of the crab dish. "I never thought I'd see the day when you ate seafood," Adrianna said in disbelief as Owen plunged a fork into a juicy bite.

"Me neither," Owen agreed. "But I can't help myself, that looks so good." He practically moaned as he bit into the crab.

"Guess I know how to get you in the mood now," Adrianna teased her boyfriend. "We're coming here every night, I think."

The restaurant was still full when we'd finished our meals, and Josh had been busy cooking and plating food. Besides Josh and Brian, two other people were in the kitchen helping prep ingredients and dunking more spring rolls into a deep fryer. Things had just started to calm down by the time our plates were cleared when suddenly we heard a loud bang from the back of the kitchen.

"I dropped the tray of guinea fowl!" Brian growled. "What's wrong with me!"

"Brian, take it easy," Josh called back. He headed toward the scene of the mess.

He returned a moment later, looked at me, and shrugged. "I love Brian, but he's so clumsy," he said

185

with real affection. "Let's hope no one orders the guinea fowl tonight."

"Could he get fired for that?" I asked Josh, knowing what high hopes he had for his protégé.

"He could probably set the whole kitchen on fire and Maddie wouldn't let him go. She knows a few lost birds here and there aren't worth getting rid of him. Oh, hey, Maddie," Josh called as the owner crossed into the kitchen. "Our boy just dumped the guinea fowl on the floor. You'd better go check on him. He feels pretty bad about it."

"Oh, that Brian," she shook her head. "I'm going to sign him up for ballet lessons and try to teach him some grace."

While Josh chatted with Ade and Owen, I watched Madeline head to the back of the kitchen. I saw her bend down and talk to Brian, and had the impression that she was trying to calm down the upset sous chef. She tousled his hair before standing up and calling another worker for a mop.

I elbowed Adrianna, and she looked up in time to see Brian looking desperately after Madeline. Poor Brian. I knew how much Josh wanted him to do well and wondered whether the clumsy sous chef understood that Josh was eager to have him succeed.

"Ready for dessert?" Josh asked us.

"Always," Adrianna said.

"Let me go grab Perry. He's our pastry chef. He's been downstairs tonight working on some cakes for a party here tomorrow. He's a little crazy, but he makes the best desserts."

"What do you mean by 'crazy'?" I asked Josh.

"You'll see."

Josh returned a moment later with a paper-thin guy of about thirty who rushed over to greet us. "Hey, I'm Perry!" he yelled manically. "So desserts, huh? Two ladies and a gent. Let me see what I can come up with!" He dashed off to work on the finale to our meal.

"See what I mean?" Josh said. "He's a little wired and off the wall. I try to keep him hidden in the basement when I can."

We had cappuccinos and waited for our mysterious desserts to arrive. Fifteen minutes later, Perry returned with three plates. "For lady number one," he said to Adrianna, "we have the Chocolate Goddess." Owen frowned as he looked at a giant chocolate tube that ascended from his girlfriend's plate. "This," said Perry, "is filled with lemon sponge cake, chocolate ganache, white chocolate mousse, and fresh raspberries."

Perry set a plate down in front of me. "And for lady number two, Kahlua crepes with banana pastry cream and Valrhona chocolate." Two long rolls lay across my plate. Like the Chocolate Goddess, this dessert was distinctly phallic. I couldn't imagine what Owen was going to have.

"And finally, for the gent, we have a succulent passion fruit and guava tart with fresh whipped cream. Enjoy!" Perry took off faster than I could say "erotic desserts."

Owen scowled at Ade. "I mean, come on! Look at that! It's a giant chocolate penis shooting up at you. I'm sitting right here next to you. Didn't he notice *me? With* you?"

Adrianna and I got the giggles. The gazillion glasses of wine I'd had did nothing to squelch my laughter. "What do you think it means that I have *two smaller* ones?" I pointed at my plate.

"I have no idea." Ade said. "And how about Owen's succulent fruit tart? A *succulent tart?*"

Josh passed by with an armful of foccacia. I love that stuff: flattish Italian bread saturated with olive oil and seasoned with wonderful herbs. Ordinarily, I'd have been wondering how to manage a taste of it. Tonight, the only armful I had eyes for was Josh. "So," he asked, glancing at our plates, "what did Perry do for you? Wow, Adrianna. Perry must really like you!"

My crepes were actually delicious. In some sort of metaphorically group-sex manner, the three of us traded bites. "I don't know what it means," Ade said, licking her spoon, "but I love that tart. Call me open-minded."

As I emptied my wineglass, Josh appeared behind me and put his arms around me cozily. "Listen, I'm going to be out of here in a little while. Do you want to meet up somewhere?"

I looked at my friends, who nodded yes. "Definitely," I told Josh. "Where do you guys want to go?"

Adrianna mentioned a bar across town, a suggestion

that Owen rejected quickly. "No way. If I have to listen to one more idiot play Van Morrison or John Mayer covers again, I'll puke up this delectable dinner. Either we're going to be cool and go to a jazz or blues club, or we're going all out cheesy and heading over to Boylston Street. I've got the good suit on, folks, so let's not waste my look." He moved his eyebrows up and down dramatically.

Adrianna and I voted for cheesy bars. Josh said he'd be at our chosen bar in about an hour. "I'll get everything settled here. The good thing about being the chef is that I don't have to clean up, so once all the food is out, I'm outta here." He leaned over and kissed me slowly on the mouth. "I'll see you soon," he whispered to me.

"Thank you so much for dinner, Josh," I said. "This was by far the best meal I've ever had."

Owen and Adrianna jumped in with praise and thanks for the night. I asked if Madeline was around so I could say good-bye. "She's talking to Brian right now. Probably trying to make him feel better. He tries so hard to impress everybody that whenever he screws something up, he feels awful about it." Josh shrugged. "I'm not worried about him. He just needs to toughen up a little. He's too sensitive."

"Well, please thank her and Brian for us. And, uh, Perry. And I'm sure we'll be back," I said, kissing Josh again. "So we'll see you in a hour or so?"

We left enough money to give our waitress a generous tip and went outside to get Owen's car from the valet. Adrianna and I had been responsible for most of the wine consumption and tipsily made our way into the car. After we'd tipped the valet, Owen headed toward Boylston Street while Adrianna and I gushed over Josh and his cooking.

Uninterested in girl talk, Owen decided he was going to play his favorite car game, "Taking My Driving Test." He'd invented this asinine game a few years ago and periodically subjected us to it. The so-called game consisted of driving as though you were in the midst of your driving test, in other words, driving very slowly and law abidingly, thus pissing off every driver around you as you came to full stops at stop signs and drove below the speed limit.

"Owen, cut it out!" shrieked Adrianna as a black car almost rear-ended us at a major intersection. "We don't have time to waste filling out accident reports!"

"Okay, okay," agreed Owen, chuckling as he resumed normal Boston driving. "I just like to prove the point that this city is full of driving-impaired citizens. I'm trying to be a role model."

We continued raving about the food until Owen reminded us of Eric's murder investigation. Owen and Adrianna agreed that they didn't see anything at all sinister about Josh, and both felt confident that even though he lacked an alibi for the time of Eric's murder, he couldn't be the killer. It occurred to me that I should somehow lure Detective Hurley and his associates to Magellan for dinner. Once they'd tasted Josh's food, he'd be off the hook.

THIRTEEN

I woke up the next morning and snuggled up to Josh, who was spooning me tightly. My head was throbbing from one too many beers the night before, and it took me a few groggy minutes to recall that I hadn't committed any cardinal sins. Except attempted sexual assault? The happy thought crossed my mind that if I confessed to Naomi, I might get fired from the Boston Organization Against Sexual and Other Harassment in the Workplace. My bed wasn't exactly a workplace, of course. Even so.

To the best of my recollection, Adrianna and I had knocked back quite a bit at the bar as our dates had been nursing a few pints of Guinness. After last call, Ade and I had decided that a slumber party was in order and had yanked the boys back to my place to crash. I'm pretty sure I attacked Josh on my bed but was too inebriated to do much more than drunkenly kiss and grope him for a few minutes before falling asleep. At some point I'd apparently put on striped pajama bottoms and an extremely seductive Sponge Bob T-shirt.

I peeked back under the covers to find that Josh was shirtless but still had on jeans. I guess I still hadn't scared him off.

"What in God's name is wrong with this coffeemaker?" Owen demanded from the kitchen. I smelled the familiar reek of burning and heard the ghastly burping noise that the stupid machine made when attempting to brew a pot.

I sat up in bed, rubbed my eyes, and hollered, "Just back away and let it finish. Whatever you do, don't touch it!"

Josh suddenly grabbed me and pulled me back down onto the bed. "Don't touch it?" he asked, rolling on top of me and kissing my neck. "I hope you're not talking to me," he said coyly.

"No, Owen's trying to make coffee." I paused while Josh continued kissing my neck and shoulders and . . . why had I brought Adrianna and Owen over here? I could have been alone with Josh right now.

"Owen, go out and get us some real coffee, okay?" Adrianna moaned from the living room. She sounded as hungover as I was. She and Owen had slept on my pull-out sofa, which had a mattress primarily composed of lumps and springs. Even if she'd gone to bed sober she'd have felt a violent need for caffeine.

"Hey," Josh called out, "you guys want to go get breakfast? My roommate Stein works at Eagles' Deli down in Cleveland Circle."

"Bless that man!" Owen shouted. "I'm starving! Everybody up!"

"I love Eagles'," I told Josh as I rummaged around my room for clothes. "I didn't know you had a connection there. I wonder if we've ever run into each other before."

"Oh, I would've remembered you, baby," he teased. He looked around my room in the light of day, and I cringed. My unfinished paint job was now tragically highlighted by the sun glaring through the windows. "What's going on with that stripe there?" Josh asked innocently.

"I'll tell you later," I muttered with embarrassment.

Ade and I met up in the bathroom and gossiped for about thirty seconds while we threw on clothes. I barely got to whisper to her about mauling Josh before Owen thumped the door with his hand.

"Move it! We're not going to Spago."

We hurried up, and I didn't notice until later that I hadn't even bothered to put on makeup or worry about my hair. Josh, my self-image therapist. I could practically hear the outraged reaction of my feminist classmates at social work school to that idea. *Dependent on a man for—* Still, I wasn't worried about my appearance, and that had to count for something, didn't it?

When we emerged, Josh and Owen were talking.

"So, Stein's your roommate?" Owen asked. "Was he around the night this Eric dude got killed?"

"No, he was working the night Eric was murdered. He can't give me an alibi. But"—he smiled at us—"he makes a mean omelette."

"Don't worry, man." Owen patted Josh's back. "I have a feeling Chloe's not going to let you go off and rot in jail."

"Good. A conjugal visit isn't exactly what I had in mind." He winked at me. "The good news is that I haven't heard from the detective in a few days. I'm not sure how strongly he suspects me. I mean, he's actually been pretty nice to me this past week. You know, polite and formal, but I get the feeling he's just trying to do his job. I don't think he's out to get me just to pin the murder on someone. I'm the easiest suspect right now. All right, that's enough. No more murder talk today."

"Yes, sir." Adrianna saluted Josh. "We're ready to go!"

As we were heading out the back door, the phone rang. "Let me just grab that before we go, okay?" I rushed back inside and picked up the phone. "Hello?"

"Chloe? It's Sheryl Rafferty, dear." Dammit. I hadn't heard from her since the funeral and thought I was free.

"Oh, um, hi. How are you?"

"As well as can be expected, I guess," Sheryl's shrill voice ripped through my hangover headache. "Phil and I would like to have you over for dinner tonight. We'd like to talk to you about some things. Can you come? Around six?"

Now, the last thing I wanted to do was have dinner with the Raffertys. The only reason I even thought about accepting the invitation was the possibility of learning something about Eric that would point to a suspect other than Josh. I agreed to dinner, but said I wouldn't be able to stay long. School work and all that, I lied.

"Who was that?" Adrianna asked.

"Actually," I hesitated, not wanting to freak out Josh, "it was Eric's mother, Sheryl. She and Phil want me to come over for dinner to discuss something. I said I'd go."

"Are you nuts?" Ade yelled. "I thought you'd gotten rid of them."

"I haven't gotten around to it. Yet. I haven't even talked to them since the funeral. I'll tell them tonight that I wasn't Eric's fiancée. But I was thinking that if I talk to them and find out more about Eric, maybe I can find a good suspect to pass on to Detective Hurley. With luck, maybe the real murderer."

Josh looked at me. "Chloe, you don't have to do that. Please. I'll be fine. Call her back and tell her no. Just explain everything over the phone. You don't have to suffer through dinner with them for my sake."

"I want to. We all know you're not the murderer, but *somebody* is. Maybe the Raffertys are. Both of them. Or one of them. And maybe I can get some useful information. Besides, they're still mourning their son's death. At least I guess they are," I said, thinking about my Group Therapy class's hypotheses. "All right, we said no more murder talk. So let's get out of here."

We walked down the back stairs and ran smack into Noah.

With the trashy blonde.

I hadn't noticed her car outside, but I'd been too focused on half-naked Josh to see much of anything else.

"Noah," I said cooly, grabbing Josh's hand.

"Veronica?" Josh said. Owen, Ade, and I whipped around to stare at Josh.

Noah spoke first. "You two know each other?" he asked the skank.

195

"Yeah," she bubbled. "I do the books for Magellan, right, Josh?"

What the hell is going on? Eric's ex-girlfriend is dating my ex? Is everyone part of a conspiracy, some freakish plot centered on Eric's murder? Is every guy I get involved with connected to this idiot Veronica? And most of all, God, I hope Josh hasn't slept with her, too.

"Yes, you do a lot of things at the restaurant," Josh responded. The condescension in his voice told me that he hadn't been with her. Huge relief.

"Oh my God! Did you hear about Eric Rafferty? I couldn't believe it."

We ignored her.

"Let's go." I started down the stairs again.

"Hi, I'm Noah." The jerk extended his hand to Josh while ignoring Owen. I stopped and eyed Adrianna, silently begging her to help move us along. But she looked pretty interested in checking out the male dynamics going on here. Consequently, I was stuck standing there waiting to see which guy would be the next one to try symbolically marking me as his turf.

Josh shook Noah's hand but looked far from pleased about it. "So, how do you two know each other?" he gestured to Veronica.

"Oh, she's Tyler's bookkeeper," Noah answered. "He's a chiropractor who lives downstairs," he explained to Josh. "I met her when she came by to drop some papers off for him."

"Brilliant," I said. "Now we all know each other. Let's get going."

We started the five-minute walk to Cleveland Circle. "That was weird," mumbled Josh. "Veronica sure gets around. She and Eric had something going . . . and now this kid? And before that she and—"

I cut him off. "Wait! Josh, hold on."

Veronica was a link between Eric and Noah. According to Adrianna, Noah had a violent attitude. So . . . Veronica could have wanted Eric dead for some ex-girlfriend reason, and she could have convinced Noah to murder him. Maybe. But what would have been in it for Noah? Veronica's undying love and devotion? I highly doubted that. The promise of unconditional sex with no desire whatsoever for a relationship? Still not likely. But Noah was a sneaky, untrustworthy person. A person with the makings of a murderer?

Or Veronica did it herself. When Noah had asked how she and Josh knew each other, she'd mentioned Magellan and hadn't said a word about working at Essence, too. Of course, Magellan was the place she and Josh had in common. Even so.

My question was how to run the possibility of Veronica's guilt by Josh while conveying a minimum of uncomfortable details about my past with Noah. So far, I'd managed to omit any information about my ex downstairs. I gave a quick summary and actually ended up enjoying the spark of jealousy in Josh's eyes. When I'd finished, Josh quickly grabbed my hand, thus claiming his position as my new (and improved) man.

"I didn't like that kid." Josh shook his head. "I don't

know what it was, but I just didn't like him."

"Turns out I didn't like him much either," I agreed.

"Yeah. He's an asshole," Ade said. "But . . . so what do you think he was doing with Veronica?" She paused for a second. "Okay, I know *what* he was doing with her. But Chloe's right. It's a creepy connection. With this whole Eric-getting-chopped-up situation."

"Could you not say 'chopped up'?" I pleaded.

"I don't know," Josh said. "I'll have to think about that. Small world? It might just be a coincidence." He pulled me in close to him as we walked, his arm securely over my shoulders. "Let's just forget about it for now." Josh kissed the top of my head as we strolled toward the Circle.

"You two are ridiculous. Aren't they, Owen?" Adrianna said. "Any more ogling each other, and I'm going to puke."

"Ew! Kissing? Girls?" screeched Owen. "Yick!" He gave Adrianna an impressive, slobbery kiss.

"Owen, stop! I'm hungover and all smelly!" Adrianna protested, laughing.

Josh and I walked ahead while my two friends acted like fifth-graders in the playground, chasing each other and squealing.

When we got to Eagles' Deli, there was a long line just to get to the front entrance. Ade and Owen caught up with us, still giggling.

"Oh God. Look at that line," Ade moaned. "It's going to take forever to get in today."

"Ah, don't worry about it. Come on," Josh said, leading the way past the college students lined up along Beacon Street and into the deli. "Hey, Fatty, what's up?"

I looked behind the long deli counter to see a six-foot guy assembling an English muffin sandwich. "There you are. I was wonderin' what happened to you." He smiled at Josh.

"Chloe, this is Stein. Stein, Chloe." I gave him a little wave. "And Adrianna and Owen."

"What do you guys want to eat?" Stein asked us. I looked up at the menu posted above Stein and asked for pancakes, fried eggs, and a side of sausage. When everyone had ordered, we wove around the deli and grabbed a table together.

"I've definitely seen Stein before. In fact, I think he's been working every time I've been in here," I said to Josh. Stein was built like a linebacker. I silently wondered how he managed to maneuver around in the skinny area between the counter and the grills.

"Yeah, he's hard to forget. And he works all the time."

"God, I'm starving." Owen rubbed his stomach. "I don't know how I can be after last night, but I am. And I have to eat a big meal now because I won't be able to eat again until I get home from work."

"Where do you work?" asked Josh.

Owen beamed. He loved telling people. "I work on a blimp. We do all the football games and stuff like that around Massachusetts. I'm actually going out later today to fly over a parade in western Massachusetts."

"No way!" Josh gave the typical reaction to hearing Owen's unusual line of work. In other words, he barraged Owen with blimp questions.

Owen looked over our heads at the wall behind us. "What are all these Polaroid pictures for?"

The walls at the Eagle were plastered in Polaroids with personalized phrases written underneath.

Josh laughed. "Oh, those are people who've eaten one of the big burgers here. You don't know about the Riley Burger?" he asked Owen.

Owen shook his head. Anyone with Owen's appetite should practically have been born knowing this famous Cleveland Circle eatery.

While we waited for our food, Josh gave us some deli history. "See, the owner, Robert Chiller? A while back, he came up with the idea for the Godzilla Burger, which is a one-pound burger with a pound of fries. Anyone who finished it got their picture on the wall. There's no time limit, and that started to seem too easy, because too many people were doing it. So then came the Megaburger, a one-and-a-half-pound burger with fries. Then the Cowabunga Burger, two pounds of meat with two pounds of fries. Next, the ATB Burger."

"Let me guess," Owen said. "Two and a half pounds of meat?"

Josh nodded.

"What's ATB stand for?"

"The Almost There Burger," Josh answered.

"Now, wait," Adrianna said. "This isn't one big, disgusting burger?"

"No, no," Josh explained. "It's eight-ounce patties stacked on top of each other on one bun. But then there came the Riley Burger. This kid named Shawn Riley came in one day and said he could eat a three-pound burger with three pounds of fries. So Robert said that if Riley could do it, he'd name a burger after him. And the kid did it. So he was the burger champion for a while. Until the Collette Burger, which is three and a half pounds."

Even though the images of gluttony were making me queasy, it was still satisfying to listen to Josh recount the legends. Revolting though they were, they weren't about anything he'd done, and his enthusiasm proved that although his own cuisine was just that, he was no food snob.

He went on. "And the deli was on the Travel Channel, where this Collette kid ate his way through the burger. He did throw up, though. On the show, Robert said that anyone who could eat the biggest burger would have it named after them." Josh paused. "Which led to the Paul Jones Burger. Four pounds. But Robert started getting too many people who could eat these huge burgers, so he created the Chillarama Burger, which is five pounds of meat, twenty slices of cheese, twenty slices of bacon, and five pounds of fries. No one's eaten that yet."

I shook my head in disbelief. "No one has any business eating that much food. And, Owen, don't even think about it." I could see that Owen, deep in thought, was pondering the challenge.

Josh got up to get us some coffee and check on our food. When he returned with Stein, both of them were carrying trays of food. Big Stein set pancakes down in front of Ade and me. "I made you the Mickey pancakes, even though you just ordered regular," he said shyly. I looked down to see two pancakes shaped like Mickey Mouse.

"Oh, he likes you two." Josh winked at us. "Not everyone gets the Mickey pancakes, you know."

"Hey, I'm cute. Where are my special pancakes?" demanded Owen.

"Aw, I'll share mine with you," promised Adrianna while pouring syrup all over her plate. "Thank you, Stein." She beamed at him.

Last night, the desserts. Now, the pancakes. I'd never noticed the phenomenon before. How general was it? And were plain-looking people doomed to spend their lives being served food that was unfairly unspecial?

"So Stein, what are the Godzilla Babies?" I asked. "I've seen them on the menu and always wondered. Are they just little burgers?"

"Yeah. They're three-ounce burgers, but they never really caught on. We don't even have them anymore, but we used to have special little buns for them and everything." He shrugged. "I thought they were kinda cute."

Stein went back to deal with the unruly and very hungry college crowd while we worked our way through our heaping plates.

"So, Josh," I wondered aloud, "is Stein's name really Stein?"

"No," he laughed. "It's Mark."

"Mark Stein?"

"No, Mark Seland. Stein's a nickname. Just look at his belly." Josh grinned. "I come in here all the time to make fun of him." His comment didn't come across as mean. On the contrary, it sounded like the kind of ritual insult that little boys exchange only with good friends.

When I'd been to Eagles' before, it had always been for takeout, and, of course, the deli hadn't yet enjoyed the romantic association it now had, so I'd never really looked at the place. There was a jukebox in the front corner, flowering plants filled the window, and memorabilia covered the walls. I asked Josh about all the pictures.

"Oh, those," he said. "Well, a lot of times girls from Boston College will send in pictures of themselves from formals and stuff and ask if they can be on the wall. All the girls around here have crushes on Stein, so they're always sending in pictures of themselves all dressed up and stuff. And then there's one over there of Steven Tyler. He came in one day by himself and let them take his picture. And I guess Joey McIntyre showed up at a party around here, so the girls sent in that picture of them all huddled up with him."

203

"Watch out." I warned Josh. "Adrianna might try to take that home."

"I would not!" she insisted angrily. "It was a fleeting crush I had years ago, and I'm properly mortified about it, okay?" Poor Ade had fallen prey to a New Kids on the Block infatuation, an embarrassing addiction that was replaced only by the wretched release of the Spice Girls CD.

"Ade used to have a severe dependence on boy bands. And everything else irritating from the nineties." I giggled. "Her mom wouldn't let her watch *Party of Five*, so she used to come over to my house and pretend we were studying."

"Shut up! That was a good show!" she practically hollered at me.

"And then," I continued, "the famous night of Bailey's intervention, she showed up at my door with a backpack full of Corona she'd stolen from her parents. We hid in my room and drank beer while Claudia whined that she'd always loved Bailey best out of all her siblings and that he'd better get help for his alcoholism or she'd disown him as a brother." I made a connection. "Hey! And now you're going out with someone named Owen! Just like the little brother on the show!"

In an attempt to defend her honor, Adrianna tried to maintain a serious face. "I don't know how we all started making fun of me, but Chloe was just as bad. Yeah, she thought she was so cool pretending to listen to No Doubt and Alannis. But I know about that Jon

204

Secada CD hidden in your bedroom, so don't act all high and mighty like you weren't listening to crap music and watching crap TV, too. And my dating someone named Owen is just a coincidence." She frowned. "I think."

"All right," I surrendered, finally composing myself. "We were both products of popular culture, so we shouldn't blame ourselves for bad taste. Not that we're much better now."

Ade and I eventually quit teasing each other and called a truce by vowing never to mention shows like *Melrose Place* or songs like "Tubthumping" again. Owen, who wasn't part of the peace accord, kept humming "Rhythm Is a Dancer" under his breath so persistently that Ade and I found it nearly impossible to finish eating.

Josh, still smiling, looked over at the crowd still waiting to place orders or even to get in the door; the sidewalk was jammed. "Listen, I'm just gonna hop on the line for a minute and help Stein out before you all discover something about my past. I don't know who else is supposed to be working today, but he looks swamped. I'll be right back." He hurried behind the counter and started cracking eggs onto the large griddle.

As Ade and Owen cleaned their plates, I sat back in my chair, sipped my coffee, and, in between catching glimpses of Josh at work behind the counter, wondered about dinner tonight with the Raffertys. I'd have to keep the evening short and to the point without letting on that I wanted to pin the murder on my host and hostess to exonerate my new man. For the twenty minutes Josh was gone, I was uncharacteristically quiet.

When he returned, he apologized and said, "The new kid they hired never turned up, so Stein is alone. But Robert just showed up, and he's going to help out until someone else gets here." Stein was now accompanied by a man in his mid-fifties whose head was mostly bald, with gray and brown fringe on the sides. A long, bushy mustache hung down around his mouth and curled slightly at the ends. "Listen," Josh said, "I didn't realize how late it is. I have to get home and get ready for work. I'm supposed to be there at two to prep for tonight. And I have to do a bunch of ordering."

"I forgot you have to work tonight." I made a mock-pouty face at him. "So when do you get off?"

"You tell me." He smiled devilishly.

"Ha-ha. *What time* are you done working?"

"Oh. Probably not till late tonight. I've got a late party coming up that I have to take care of. Sorry." He'd warned me about chefs' hours. "I've got a long day again tomorrow, but how about I come over on Monday and make you dinner? You're home at like, what? Five?"

I nodded. I'd leave my field placement early by pleading emotional turmoil resulting from the intensity of the job. I didn't want Josh to leave, but I knew I could endure two days if the delay meant another amazing meal. And possibly more.

We all headed for the door, waved good-byes and thanks to Stein, and walked outside.

"I parked my car down here last night, remember?" Josh pointed up Beacon Street.

"Um, vaguely." I searched my drunken memory.

"There are a couple of meter-free spots down here, so hopefully I won't have a ticket." Josh gave me a hug. "Listen, Chloe. Be careful tonight, okay? I appreciate that you want to help me, but if you think the Raffertys are dangerous . . . well, just watch out. I don't want anything to happen to you."

"I don't want anything to happen to me either, but I have to get clear with them. I'll leave you a message on your cell when I get home to let you know I'm alive and well, okay?"

"Fine. But I won't relax until I hear from you."

"Good. I like to keep my men on edge," I said, kissing him good-bye.

FOURTEEN

After Ade and Owen left, Ade to go back to blonde and Owen to fly around in the blimp, I decided to let Heather know that not only had I had survived my dinner at Magellan but that Josh hadn't even *tried* to murder me.

"Aaaah! Help!" I screamed into the phone when she picked up. "I'm being mauled by a murderous chef! Heather! I love you, big sis. Always remember that!"

"You're hilarious," Heather said with exasperation. "I gather you are, in fact, alive?"

"Yes, and I got Adrianna and Owen's approval. They think Josh is a doll."

"Yes, I'm sure Owen called this guy a doll. But whatever. I'm glad you're safe. I worry about you sometimes."

"Yes, Mommy, I'm fine. And now that I've reported in to you, I'm going to take a nap."

"What did you do last night that you need to take a nap?" my sister demanded.

"Unfortunately, nothing. But I'm still tired."

"Tired? You don't have a clue about tired until you have a baby and only sleep in two-hour increments all night. Lucy was up nursing the whole night. I'm more tired than you, and I don't get to take a nap because I have to take Walker to his Gymnastics for Tots class. So don't tell me about tired!"

Heather's excellent, if unintended, argument for birth control reminded me that I needed to get to a drugstore.

"All right," I said. "You're more tired than anybody else in the entire world, but I'm still going to enjoy my nap. Good-bye." I hung up.

I took a blissful two-hour nap and watched *E!* for a few hours to catch up on the celebrity gossip before getting ready to go to the Raffertys. When I left my building, I had the misfortune to run smack into Harmony, who was again grilling outdoors in her negligee dress. "Hi, there! I told you there's otha fish in the sea,

208

didn't I?" Just what I needed—having Harmony keep tabs on my love life. There was, however, one minor point about Harmony and the fish: she'd been absolutely right.

When I arrived at the Raffertys', I had to park on the street because their driveway was filled with luxury cars. I rang the bell and was greeted by the wiry Sheryl, who ushered me through the foyer and into the living room. "Come in, dear, and meet everyone."

Until I'd seen the cars, I hadn't realized there'd be other guests, but I was quickly introduced to Sheryl's two brothers, John and Brent, their wives, and Phil's sister, Emma. I knew I'd never be able to confess the truth about my nonengagement in front of the entire family. Phil came over and hugged me. Even though his eyebrows still needed a trim, he looked better than he had the day of the funeral.

I sat down in the formal living room and immediately noticed some cardboard boxes that had been pushed to one side of the room. I accepted a glass of wine from Phil and tried to peer inconspicuously into a study off to my right. More boxes.

"Are you moving?" I asked Phil.

"Yes," Sheryl jumped in. "Well, we're going to keep this house, of course. But we're going to be spending part of the year in a new house in Huntington Beach, California. We've had enough of New England weather, so we'll likely stay in our new place most of the year."

Phil shuffled across the room to a bar set up on a

coffee table. "With Eric gone, it seems like this is the time to do it. We've always wanted another place. I just retired from the bank, so there's no reason we have to stay."

Murderers on the verge of escape! Fleeing the scene! But I just nodded silently.

Sheryl passed around a tray of flavorless cheese on flavorless crackers while the group conversed quietly.

Phil took a seat next to me.

"When are you moving?" I asked.

"Oh, in about six weeks. Sheryl and I are flying out for a quick trip to check out the house again and make some arrangements for everything to be settled when we get there. Sheryl is busy trying to figure out what to take and what to leave here. If you ask me, I think we'll just end up buying new furniture when we get out there. We're still going to use this house, so we should just leave it as it is."

"I didn't realize you were moving. Did you just decide?"

"No, it's been in the works for a while. We had some technicalities to work out before we finalized our plans."

Technicalities that had to do with inheriting Eric's money? If, of course, Eric's parents were his beneficiaries. If so, his money wouldn't yet be theirs; inheritance didn't happen immediately after a death. But what kinds of monsters would kill their son for a beach house? And if the Raffertys wanted another house, they probably had enough money of their own to buy one. Still, my classmates had raised the idea that for some people, there is no such thing as enough money. Also, according to the members of the group, I was supposed to be on the lookout for signs of pathology within the family system or for anything else I could report to Detective Hurley to divert his attention from Josh.

Unfortunately, the most pathological thing I discovered during dinner was that the entire Rafferty clan was exceedingly boring. Conversation centered around the Raffertys' move to California and the upscale gated community in which they would play golf and tennis. Worse, the food was terrible. Eric's good culinary taste was apparently not genetic: dinner consisted of iceberg salad and bland roast pork with overcooked broccoli. If the Raffertys actually enjoyed this horrible food, they must have hated the divine concoctions Josh had prepared for the gathering after the funeral. Fools.

"So," I said, trying to steer the conversation toward the murder investigation, "have you heard anything from the police? Any leads on Eric's killer?"

Looks of horror appeared on the faces of Phil, Sheryl, the aunts, and the uncles.

"No, Chloe, we haven't," answered Sheryl, her face as pinched as ever. "I didn't want to speak about this over dinner, but I suppose we can't just ignore the pink elephant in the middle of table now, can we? The detective has been by several times. In fact, he was here yesterday. We gave him what information we could, but he doesn't have enough evidence to arrest anyone. Yet. He was asking us whether we'd done any painting around the house. And, good Lord, he specifically wanted to know whether we'd painted anything *orange!* Can you imagine?" Sheryl Rafferty was someone who'd choose tasteful shades of Ralph Lauren and hire a professional to do the painting. The image of her teetering on a ladder with a roller of orange paint in her hand was ludicrous.

"And," she continued, "he wanted to know about that Veronica, that, uh, girl Eric was seeing before he met you. I told him the truth, which is that Veronica was a gold-digging tramp and that she probably murdered our son once she . . . well, once he broke things off with her."

"When exactly was that?"

"Oh, don't worry, dear. He wasn't seeing her when you two started dating. I suppose it was about six weeks or so before he died. I know you two hadn't known each other long, but when it's right, it's right. We didn't even know he'd been seeing someone else after her—you, of course, as we know now. But Eric was probably afraid to introduce us to you after the Veronica fiasco. We all despised her. In fact, we had just found out about you the day he died. I'd spoken to him on the phone earlier in the day, and he told me that he was taking a young woman named Chloe to dinner. He said you'd been out together a bunch of times and that he was absolutely *smitten*." Mrs. Rafferty's eyes twinkled at the memory of that last phone call. "I just

212

know you two would have been together forever."

"That's enough, Sheryl." Phil, who struck me as the more grief-stricken of the parents, looked miserable. "I don't want to talk about this anymore. Can we just get through dinner, please?"

I excused myself to use the bathroom but just needed a breather. Eric, it seemed, had invented a relationship with me and had lied to his parents, probably because he'd wanted to convince them that he was hooked up with someone other than the despised Veronica. Sheryl had not only believed him but had gone on to fantasize about our supposed romance and to cultivate the image of her son heading down the road toward blissful matrimony.

Only when I'd walked out of the dining room did I realize that I had no idea where the bathroom was. I wandered through the living room and once again glanced into the study, where a computer screen illuminated the stacks of boxes. If I was going to play the amateur crime-solver, I was obliged to take a quick peek in there, wasn't I?

I stuck my head in the study and looked around. Only a few yards from where I stood was a rolltop desk on which rested a computer and a phone. The monitor told me that someone, Phil or Sheryl, was in the middle of losing a game of hearts and favored a tropical fish desktop theme. Most of the desk's surface was thick with piles of bills and torn-open business envelopes. Immediately recognizable were envelopes from the same bank I used and bills from the same cable and electricity companies that sometimes dunned me for overdue payments. My own desk was often cluttered with unpaid bills, but even at my most impoverished or lazy, I'd never begun to create anything remotely like this picture of financial disaster. How could the wealthy Raffertys have fallen so behind in paying their bills?

I tiptoed to the desk and took a peek at a bank statement that was lying open across one of the stacks.

It was Eric's bank statement. Maybe I could find out how rich he'd really been.

I held the green paper close to the light from the monitor and scanned it as quickly as I could. The late-August date showed that it was the most recent statement.

And Eric had been nearly broke. His final balance barely broke seven hundred dollars. I looked around quickly and grabbed an envelope from a credit card company. The account was also Eric's. He'd owed a whopping amount of money for just that one card, an amount that did not, of course, include all the bills for utilities, other credit cards, and who knew what else. Oh, and his car was about to be repossessed.

I left the study and headed back to the dining room. Although I hadn't had time to think through the meaning of Eric's debt, my new knowledge was giving me the creeps. The last thing I wanted to do was hang around here with the Raffertys for the rest of the evening.

I stood in the dining room doorway and stared at the

Rafferty family. "I'm so sorry," I announced. "I'm not feeling well. I think I have to leave. Thank you for dinner." Pivoting smoothly, I made for the front door.

Having caught up with me, Sheryl had to rush to keep up. "Chloe? Are you all right?"

"I'm just feeling sick. Probably all the stress. I need to go home and lie down. Thank you again for dinner." I barreled out and practically ran to my car.

I turned the key in the ignition, locked the doors, and sped down Brattle Street. Eric was broke. More than broke. In *serious* debt. Probably on the verge of bankruptcy. *And* he was planning to invest in Essence? I'd been convinced that he'd had money to invest. Had he successfully deceived his parents as well? When had Phil and Sheryl Rafferty discovered the truth about the dismal state of Eric's finances? Had they known all along? Or found out only after his death?

I fumbled in my purse for my cell phone and called Josh, who picked up almost immediately. I could hear the noise from Magellan's kitchen in the background.

"Chloe?" Josh asked.

"Yeah, I just left dinner."

"So you're okay? I was worried about you. But since you're all right, did you find out anything useful?" Josh asked over the banging of pots and the sound of running water.

"Well, they didn't exactly throw down their forks and confess to killing Eric, but I did find out something interesting. It looks like Eric was broke."

"That's impossible. Eric ate out all the time, he

215

drove a nice car, and he was going to put all that money into Essence. Besides, he bragged about his financial-planning business all the time. He said he could hardly keep up with all his clients."

"He may have spent money like he was loaded, but I saw his bank statement at the Raffertys. His account is nearly empty. He could've had other bank accounts, but I don't think so, Josh. There were piles of unpaid bills in his name. His car was going to be repossessed. And he had the biggest credit card bill I've ever seen."

"His parents told you all this?" To someone in the kitchen, he shouted, "I haven't boned it yet."

"Um, no," I admitted. "They didn't tell me. I kind of snooped in their study. Very briefly, though. I didn't see everything that was there. When I excused myself from the table, I said I had to go to the bathroom, so I didn't want to stay away too long."

"Chloe! What if they'd seen you?"

"Too late now. I ran out right after that. I said I wasn't feeling well. Anyway, Eric was broke!"

"Chloe," Josh said in disbelief, "do you realize what this means? Eric conned Tim. He never could've invested in Essence. Do you think Tim found out?"

"I have no idea. I haven't had time to put any of the pieces together. But, hey, don't say anything to anybody about this yet, okay?"

"Yeah, sure. Of course not," Josh agreed. "I'm coming!" Josh hollered away from the mouthpiece. "It's in the walk-in." To me, he said, "Listen, I have to go. The kitchen is out of control tonight. I have to work tomorrow, too, actually, because we've got another party coming in, but I'm still cooking dinner for you on Monday, right?"

"Definitely," I said. "I can't wait."

I sighed and continued my drive home. Cursing chefs' hours, I went to bed early and slept late. Alone, of course. I spent Sunday working my way through the long list of required readings for school and writing a short paper for my General Practice class. In the paper, I was supposed to address how my newly defined sense of self as a social worker had shifted my thinking, heightened my awareness, and impacted daily interactions with those around me. Impacted daily interactions! That's a direct quote. Ugh. I turned out four pages of bull in an hour. But I have to admit that as I did the required readings and wrote the paper, it occurred to me that if I'd been taking my classes seriously, I could've improved the interviewing and information-gathering techniques I'd been using with my . . . clients. Well, not clients, exactly. In fact, not clients at all. The Raffertys. Anyway, if I'd followed the standard intake format we were being taught in class, I'd have learned about their physical health, socioeconomic status, and family trees. I might even have been able to entice Eric's parents into revealing the details of their history with Eric, their parenting experiences, and their mental complexities. My thought processes momentarily halted. Did a couple so exceedingly boring actually *have* mental complexities? I nonetheless resolved to take my educational endeavors more seriously than I'd been doing.

With that resolution in mind, I headed off the next morning to face Naomi, the minioffice, and harassment of employers about sexual harassment. On the T ride downtown, I even tried to convince myself that I enjoyed being packed like a smiling sardine among cranky commuters.

Naomi was barely visible behind her desk, the top of which held about six thousand manila folders. "Is that you, Chloe? How are you?" Braided as ever, she emerged, walked toward me with open arms, and embraced me. Energized as I was about learning what social work school had to teach—and not knowing what else to do—I hugged her back.

"I'm fine. How are you?"

"Wonderful. I think we should start each day with a hug and a short staff meeting about our inner goals for the day. This is a stressful line of work, and we need to begin with all our emotional ducks in a row, don't you think?"

I suppressed the impulse to quack.

Naomi smiled broadly and pulled two chairs together so that they faced each other with little space in between. "Okay, now grab a seat, and we'll get started."

Braids, I thought, must have taken too many antidepressants. Empathic social worker that I was becoming, I played along. We took our seats, our knees practically pressing together.

"Now," Braids began, "I myself am not a terribly

religious person." She brought her hand to her chest. "But I still take the time every morning to thank a higher power for giving me the strength to rise to the challenges I face every day here at this organization." She took my hands in hers and closed her eyes. "I'm so grateful for the opportunity to work with Chloe. I welcome her today, and every day, as we share in our determination to protect the women of Boston from hostile work environments. I will work hard to be the best possible supervisor I can be, and I will put aside my own troubles while I help women whose needs are greater than mine."

She opened her eyes and pursed her lips as if to contain overwhelming emotion. Were those tears in her eyes? She squeezed my hands and let out an enormous breath. "Okay. Now, your turn. If you're religious, you're free to say a prayer if you'd like."

"Oh, no thanks. Um," I stammered. There were probably thousands of traditional thank-you prayers and asking-for-strength prayers out there, not one of which I knew. I closed my eyes and did my best. "I, as well, am grateful for the opportunity to work with you. And I, as well, want to have my emotional ducks nicely aligned so that I may perform to my full capacity as a social worker." I opened one eye to see Naomi swell with pride at my willingness to expose my inner self.

"Wonderful!" she leaned over and gave me another hug. "Now, on with our day!"

I spent a good part of the morning pretending to

organize the filing cabinets and reviewing procedures for answering the hotline calls I had so far avoided.

Naomi was on the phone when the dreaded hotline phone rang. I glanced over at my supervisor, who was in the middle of informing a caller that the practice of referring to female employees as "babes" was outrageous and unacceptable, and needed to be stopped immediately. It belatedly occurred to me that when I'd been invited to pray, I should've asked God to divert Naomi's attention from comparatively minor deviations from feminist ideals and toward the existence of genital mutilation and other truly horrifying crimes against women. She looked up at me and signaled me to pick up the call.

I lifted the receiver from the ancient-looking phone. "Hello? Boston Organization Against Sexual Harassment and Other . . . Things." What the hell were we called?

"Hi, this is Ellen," a young-sounding voice told me. "I spoke with Naomi a few weeks ago about my problems at work, but I wanted to see if I could talk to her again."

"Oh, I'm sorry," I said with relief. "She's busy right now. Can I take a message?"

"No, Chloe," Naomi called from her desk. "You take it. You can do it! You're ready!" Then she returned to her own call.

"Naomi is on another line," I told Ellen. "But she asked me to try to help you." Feeling a little panicky, I scrambled to find my oversized binder with its hot-

220

line-call instructions. "Um, can you tell me what's wrong at your workplace?"

Ellen proceeded to tell me about her job as an office assistant for a small private law firm in Needham. There were three male lawyers, and Ellen was the assistant to one of them. Although she loved her work, got along well with the two other lawyers and their female assistants, and wanted to keep her job, her boss was a dirtbag. He made passes at her, told offensive jokes, and showed her his favorite pictures from the latest *Penthouse*.

"I did everything Naomi told me to do. I documented every incident on my computer and then printed it out and mailed a copy to myself. I told him clearly that his actions made me uncomfortable and that he needed to stop. But then he tried to make me sit on his lap while he dictated a letter, and that was the last straw. The firm is so tiny that we don't have a human resources department I can turn to for help. And the other girls don't want to help because they like their jobs and their bosses. I don't know what to do. I don't want to go to the police, because I don't have any real proof. Besides, he says he's just joking around and doesn't mean any harm."

Oh God, how could I help this poor woman? I flipped to the appropriate section of instructions in my binder and desperately tried to imagine what Braids would say. "Well, okay. Ellen, my name is Chloe, and I work with Naomi," I said as I scanned the page for advice. "Have you thought about trying to get together with the other women from the firm outside of the office?" Ellen used the word *girls,* but I wanted to spare Naomi a fit of feminist apoplexy. "Maybe you could meet in a neutral setting so you could explain how truly upsetting your boss's actions are to you. See if you can elicit some help from your coworkers. Maybe they could talk to the other lawyers in the practice?"

"I can try, but to be honest, I just don't think that's going to help," Ellen said sadly.

Naomi walked by me, gave me the thumbs-up sign, and headed out the door.

"All right, look," I said to the harassed Ellen, "Naomi would kill me if she heard me, but I don't think that's going to work either. So, as I see it, you have two choices. The first is to tell this idiot off, quit, and get the hell out of there. There's no reason you should have to put up with him."

"Yeah, except the pay is good, and I don't have that much work experience, so I don't think I could get another job like this."

"Got it. Well, then, if I were you, the next time he makes a pass at you or whatever, you accidentally-on-purpose kick him solidly in the crotch, apologize profusely, and go about your business. If he says anything, you insist that you didn't mean any harm. Do that two or three times, and I'll bet he backs off. It's simple behavioral conditioning. Punish bad behavior!"

"You think that will work?" Ellen asked.

"Good chance it will. Call me back and let me know how it goes."

"I definitely will! Thank you so much for all your help and for listening to me. It feels good just being able to talk about it with someone who understands."

As I hung up, I felt more than pleased with myself. Finally, this poor woman had been given some sensible advice!

Naomi returned a few minutes later. "Chloe, I am so proud of you. You handled that call like a real professional," she gushed. "Doesn't it feel wonderful to help someone?"

"Yes. I really think I did help," I agreed.

I worked on my field placement journal by faking some new entries. "Am in charge of all harassment hotline calls now and am struggling to maintain professional distance while providing empathic ear to distressed callers. Am following guidelines well and developing more confidence in own abilities to handle calls independently. Also working on defining own personal counseling style as advised in General Practice class. Building strong relationship with wonderful supervisor."

While Naomi was on a bathroom break, I also put in a call to Detective Hurley. I got his voice mail and left a message to inform him that Eric Rafferty had been horribly in debt and would not have been in a position to invest in a hot dog stand much less in a fancy restaurant. I felt sure that the detective would later thank me for my brilliant discovery.

After telling Naomi that I wanted to do research on the Internet about my field placement, I ducked out of the office early. The real story was, I wanted to make a trip to CVS to buy condoms for my date with Josh.

I hit the local CVS in Cleveland Circle and, as discreetly as possible, dropped a big package of Trojans in my basket. Better to stock up now than to have to repeat the mortification of sliding birth control across the counter to some smirking teenage cashier. I browsed the aisles in search of anything to cover up the lifetime supply of condoms. The razor blades I added to the basket were too small to hide anything. But look at that! A wonderful new alternative to shaving! The product, a Smoothie Pad, was a small exfoliating cloth that promised to rub the hair off with no messy shaving cream, no nicks, and no painful wax. Yes! I could hardly wait to get home to Smoothie Pad away all unwanted body hair and be all silky for Josh tonight.

When I walked past Eagles', Stein was by the window. So happily preoccupied was I that I raised the CVS bag up as I waved to Josh's roommate. He waved back and then smiled broadly. No wonder. The damn see-through bag had prominently revealed enough condoms to halve the birthrate throughout Greater Boston for the next ten years. Blood rushed to my face. Stein must've assumed that I'd been flaunting the contents of the bag. Oh God. Any explanation I could offer would make matters worse. What's more, if I went inside the deli, I'd either have to carry the bag with me, its contents plainly visible, or park it outside and then retrieve it when I left as if I were a madwoman who'd mistaken a wholesale purchase of Trojans for her bicycle.

Wishing that I, in fact, had a bicycle and could make a quick getaway, I rushed home. When I got there, I read the Smoothie Pad directions as I ran a hot shower. All I had to do was rub the cloth over my legs and bikini line while showering. Easy enough. The pad turned out to feel just like a loofah, so I was delighted to realize that I was ridding myself not only of hair but of all dead skin cells. Visions of passionate, wild love-making raced through my head as I sloughed away stubble. Only an hour and a half until Josh arrived!

FIFTEEN

Josh showed up at my back door with oversized stainless-steel containers piled high in his arms and two bags that hung from his forearms.

"Hello, beautiful." He headed right to the kitchen.

"How many people are you cooking for tonight?" I asked. Following him, I stared in disbelief at the dozens of containers he was distributing across the kitchen table.

"Just us. I prepped almost everything at the restaurant today. Maddie said she didn't mind. Anything for love and all that."

"I can't believe you went in to work on your day off just for me."

"It was easier than trying to do everything from home. Madeline let me use whatever vegetables and seasonings and everything I wanted from Magellan. And"—he spun around while holding up a covered container—"gorgeous fresh tuna steaks on the house."

"Oh, I love tuna. This is so amazing." I peered into bowls and peeked in bags.

Josh pulled a bag out of my hand, but he was grinning. "Hey, no snooping! Wait here for a second. I still have to get a few things out of my car." My handsome chef raced to his car and returned with two bottles of wine and an enormous, stunning bouquet of flowers.

"Oh, Josh! These are just beautiful." I leaned in to smell the oversized lilies and pink roses. I couldn't remember the last time anyone had given me flowers—unless you counted the time Noah had yanked a flower off a neighbor's fence and jokingly recited, "He loves me, he loves me not." He hadn't loved me, of course. But then, I hadn't loved him, either. Thank God.

After Josh and I had made out in the kitchen for a good five minutes, he peeled himself off me and started our dinner.

"Can I do anything to help?" I asked.

"Just open one of the bottles of wine and sit back and relax," he instructed. I could get used to this.

He made himself at home in my tiny kitchen and worked on plating two salads for us. "Bibb and radicchio with chèvre and a three-tomato vinaigrette," he said, whisking the dressing. "I'm going to let the cheese come up to room temp, so we'll just wait a few minutes."

I helped Josh locate a small pot and a skillet, and pulled out a cutting board for him. Mortified, I noticed that my wooden cutting board had warped so radically that it formed an arc when placed on the counter. "I'm sorry. My kitchen tools aren't what you're used to," I apologized.

"Not to worry. I can chop and slice on anything. And your cutting board has real architectural interest." His eyes smiled.

I poured two glasses of white and sat down to drool. Over Josh *and* the food.

Josh had mercifully brought his own knives, so I didn't have to embarrass myself by showing him my pitiful collection of Kmart cutlery. I watched as he held a sharpening steel out in front of him and worked on placing razor edges on what looked disconcertingly like murder weapons. The steel was the same one I'd seen him use at Magellan, a foot-long rod with a blue plastic handle. The sight of the knives bothered me. I wasn't sure I could ever look at a knife again without having visions of the curved knife that had killed Eric. A cimiter, Josh had called it. Josh's knife, I thought as I watched him hone a blade. Then, as if I were awakening from a light trance, I saw the absurdity of my attack of suspicion. A chef sharpening a knife? Nothing was more ordinary. What was Josh supposed to do? Cook with dull knives?

Josh took the tuna out and began rubbing it with a

mysterious and aromatic mixture. "Okay, let's let the tuna marinate in that for a few minutes while we start the salads."

The Bibb lettuce and radicchio salads were dressed with tomato vinaigrette. Josh spent a few moments rearranging the green Bibb lettuce leaves and the red radicchio leaves before wiping the edges of the plates clean and setting our dishes on the table.

"Okay," Josh started. "So, tell me about dinner at the Raffertys'. I still can't believe Eric was broke."

"Yeah, I know. But what we don't know is who knew that. And when." I cut a piece of lettuce with my fork. "What if Tim found out that Eric was never planning on investing in Essence? And in a rage, he killed Eric? Tim probably could've gotten hold of your knife. No one would've thought it was strange to see someone from Essence over at Magellan. Especially Tim, since he used to be one of the owners."

"And he would've been pissed off that Eric had been milking him for free food and bugging him with all his suggestions for the restaurant." Josh laughed. "Except Tim just doesn't strike me as a killer. And from what you've said, Tim was out to impress Eric the night Eric was killed. So unless Tim found out during your dinner at Essence that Eric was scamming him, that theory doesn't work too well."

"Well, Tim might've found out *before* we went in for dinner and just acted like he still needed to impress him. He lured Eric in for a free dinner so he could kill him!" I beamed. Chloe Carter, the next Sherlock Holmes!

Josh raised his eyebrows at me.

I continued. "And Garrett! He had a motive, too. I'm sure he wanted Essence to do well. He's the executive chef. He has to want Essence to be a big success. And with Eric's money, Garrett would've had access to better ingredients, better equipment, and all that. He'd have been furious that Eric was a big fraud, too. Or what about Eric's parents? Maybe they *thought* Eric was loaded and that they'd inherit his money. Imagine their surprise when they discovered they'd killed their son and he was in major debt!"

"The odds that his parents were in some sort of sick conspiracy to murder their son is pretty unlikely. Possibly *one* of them might've done it, but not both of them."

"And, did I tell you they're moving? Well, buying a second house. Out in California. Phil said they'd had plans to do it for a while but that there were some things to work out first. Like maybe getting more money to close their new real estate deal," I said excitedly.

Josh looked at me skeptically. "But I don't see how they could've needed Eric's money so badly. They certainly seemed to have enough. I was in their house, and I saw their cars. That doesn't make any sense. And Garrett and Tim aren't good suspects either," he said. "Garrett had no reason to want bad press around Essence."

"And I don't see how he would've had time. I didn't have my eye on him every minute, but just before I fainted, I was pretty sure I saw him cutting a piece of meat. He would've had to hop out of the kitchen, kill Eric, and jump back into cooking. The restaurant was swamped by then, and I'm sure someone would have missed him."

"Any others on your list?" teased Josh, evidently enjoying my desperate attempts to pin this murder on someone else.

"What about Veronica? I wonder if she thought she'd inherit his money. She probably knew Eric and his parents weren't particularly close and that he was pretty serious about her. She might have wormed her way into his will. Maybe they broke up and she killed him before he could change his will."

"I know you want to help me, but I still think you're reaching here." Josh polished off his salad and took the plates to the sink. I couldn't believe he actually rinsed them off and put them in the dishwasher.

"Have you talked to Detective Hurley again?" I asked.

"Yeah. I went down to the police station this morning to talk to him. He is not pleased that my knife was the one used in the murder. Obviously my finger-prints are all over it. And I don't know how to convince him I was home. It's a boring alibi, but I can't help it. I was tired and stayed home and watched television. I even told him about every show I watched. It was shark week on the Discovery Channel, so I gave him a lot of facts about sharks and shark attacks," he explained. "But that doesn't help much since anyone can look at a TV schedule or the Internet and get plenty of information about what was on. But I'm still not in jail. And I explained to him that he couldn't arrest me since I had a very important dinner to cook tonight." Josh winked at me, turned the front burner up to high, and placed a skillet there to preheat. He then filled a small pot with a precooked rice mixture. "Do you have a lid for this, by any chance?"

I shook my head. "Sorry, no. Um, I might have a bigger lid you could use. Would that work?" I resolved that Uncle Alan would buy me a nice set of cookware, which I'd somehow justify as a necessary student expenditure. Oh, and a cutting board and some knives.

"That's okay. I can just use plastic wrap." Josh sealed a sheet across the top of the pot and turned the heat up. I didn't think you could put Saran Wrap on top of the stove, but soon enough the plastic began to puff up like Jiffy Pop. Josh, I reminded myself, had gone to culinary school and worked as a chef, whereas I was a social work student who did unpaid work for the Boston Organization Against Sexual Things I Couldn't Remember. In other words, if I tried covering a pot of steaming rice with plastic wrap instead of a lid, there'd be an explosion that would leave me with rice all over the kitchen and burns all over my face.

"The rice smells delicious. What's in that?" I asked curiously.

"Cardamom. Goes perfectly with the tuna."

Josh threw the fish steaks onto the hot pan and seared each side briefly. I could smell garlic but couldn't figure out what the rest of the aromas were. Josh must've caught me sniffing inquisitively because he said there was a mix of spices that made up the beautifully seared crust. He pulled the tuna off the burner and began slicing half-inch-thick strips to reveal the rare middle. When he put our plates together, the tuna slices fanned out on top of the cardamom rice. He garnished the dish with baby bok choy slaw he produced from one of the plastic containers.

The artistry of the food and the delicious aromas made me wish for a dining room with a small, intimate table set with linen, china, crystal, and silver. Once I tasted the meal, however, I realized that Josh's culinary skills had triumphed over the humble setting of my kitchen. I gushed to Josh and savored every bite.

"Oh, I was going to ask you," I began, swallowing a crunchy piece of bok choy, "what's up with Madeline and Brian?"

"What do you mean?"

"Well, Ade and I noticed her sort of playing with his hair and being kind of touchy with him."

"Yeah, they kind of have a flirty thing going on. I don't think anything has happened, though. Brian looks up to her—you know, attractive older woman, successful in business, who encourages him and supports him. Even when he screws up, she's really patient. And Maddie likes the attention she gets from a younger man. I try to keep out of it, though. As long as they don't get in my way, I don't care what they're doing."

"But do you think Brian expects Madeline to make him the executive chef? Is he going to try to charm her into giving him your job?" I said with some alarm.

"Not a chance. Brian isn't experienced enough, and Madeline knows it." Josh refilled our wineglasses. "There are nights he does great, and then there are times that he just totally makes bad decisions. Like if we run out of an ingredient, he'll run over to Essence to borrow it. Which is fine, but he should do that before service and not leave me alone in the middle of mayhem. It throws everything off balance, and food goes out late, and then Madeline has to deal with unhappy customers. He's just too eager to please sometimes, so he doesn't stop to think that we'd better just substitute something else for whatever we're missing. He gets completely thrown off if anything unexpected comes up. Which it does all the time in this business, and you'd better know how to roll with it, or you'll lose it."

Although I was paying attention to Josh, I was practically licking my plate as well. "God, this is delicious," I raved. "Well, Madeline seems to have a good head on her shoulders. She seems like the kind of person that can stay calm when things get busy at the restaurant."

"Yeah, not much rattles her anymore. She's been doing this long enough that she's seen it all. Most

233

people in this business are pretty nuts, just because everything is always so stressful, so I'm lucky to work for someone who's as normal as she is. Don't get me wrong, she can get mad, and I've heard her yell at Brian before, but it's usually justified. Perry—you remember him? the pastry chef?—he told me that the night of the murder, Maddie ripped into Brian for botching a bunch of orders, and the two of them, Maddie and Brian, had to step into the office downstairs to work things out. I felt bad for Brian when I heard it, but it's actually nice to know she keeps everyone in line. And I don't want to be the bad guy all the time, so it's good he hears things directly from her, too."

"Tim doesn't seem like the type to take charge and be tough when it's necessary, though. I wonder how he's going to do without Madeline," I said.

Josh got up from his chair and turned the oven on. "Dessert." He winked at me before sitting back down. "You're right. Tim is much too nice sometimes, and I'm afraid someone's going to take advantage and just walk all over him. He'll learn to toughen up, though. At least Maddie is all over him about Essence. I think she's a little worried, too. She's always checking up on him, finding out how many people have been in for dinner, what Garrett's food costs are, et cetera. She calls him all the time to make sure he's doing okay. I heard she even talked to him a bunch of times the night Eric was killed. She wanted to know how the meal was going, what Eric was saying about the food, and if he'd made a decision yet, so I guess she kept calling over there all night."

"If they care about each other so much, why did they get divorced?" I wondered aloud.

"Well, Tim was the one who wanted the divorce, but apparently Maddie doesn't hold it against him. I think they were just better business partners than they were husband and wife. Madeline could probably care less. She's all about her restaurant and making money. Obviously Tim is driven, too, but I don't think Maddie was putting as much into their marriage as Tim wanted." Josh reached over to take my hand in his. "And I bet being married to Maddie was hard. She's so stressed out all the time. Not bad for a non-social-work student, huh?"

I laughed. "Yes," I said with mock formality, "I'm impressed with your insightful remarks regarding their relationship. But why is Madeline so stressed? Magellan is thriving, she's got a great chef," I said, blowing Josh a kiss across the table, "and a pretty good sous chef who still needs some work but is coming along nicely, thanks to you. So mostly, she's got a great life, right?"

"True. But there's a lot of pressure to keep up. Restaurants go out of business left and right, and just because Magellan is doing well now, it doesn't mean that it couldn't fold anytime. One bad move, one bad decision, one lousy review, and it could be over. That's reality. Boston has a lot of great restaurants, each of them just waiting for another one to fail so they can take their place."

"Yeah," I said, "that's pretty much what Madeline was saying to Tim and me at the Raffertys' house. And she was really pushing Tim to play up Essence with the press."

"Did you see her on TV the other night? She was on the news plugging Magellan *and* Essence."

I nodded. I'd seen part of her interview on a local news magazine show. Not only was Madeline totally beautiful in person, but the camera loved her. She'd given the reporter a quick tour of Magellan, showed some of Josh's dishes, and then described Essence as a worthy competitor. She'd brushed off any concerns about the murder at Essence. According to Madeline, it had been an unfortunate event that happened to occur at the restaurant. She'd assured viewers they were safe to test out both restaurants and judge for themselves. "Friendly competition is what drives us to keep getting better," she'd said, smiling.

"Yeah, why weren't you interviewed?" I asked. "They showed all your food." To my mind, Josh should've been the star.

"Maddie thought it would be better if I stayed low until the investigation is finished. I mean, she knows it's silly, but she figured it would be better to play it safe. At least my name hasn't been in the news."

I more or less understood: *And here's our wonderful chef! He's currently under investigation as a murder suspect, but never mind that because he makes a bang-up bouillabaisse!*

Josh got up from his chair and took out two small tin

molds from one of the bags. "I'm going to put the cakes in for us, okay?"

I nodded and practically started drooling as he poured chocolate batter into the little molds, placed them on a cookie sheet, and slid it in the oven.

"I'll be right back." Josh walked toward the bathroom.

Oh, no. A few years earlier, I'd been casually dating a seemingly normal guy named Tom and had had him over at my place to watch a Patriots game. At the start of halftime, he'd nonchalantly stood up from the couch, grabbed a section of the Sunday newspaper, and disappeared into the bathroom. *For twenty-five minutes.* He'd returned as though the duration of his absence were totally fine. Tom was not invited back for any more football games. Mercifully, Josh reappeared in about thirty seconds.

We cleared the plates and tidied up while the gorgeous aroma of chocolate took over the room. I was beginning to suspect that I'd exfoliated too much with my new beauty secret, since I had to keep adjusting my jeans as I loaded the dishwasher. Feeling a little itchy in certain areas, I decided that another glass of wine would remedy the discomfort. I refilled both our glasses while Josh removed the cakes. "They're done already?" I asked.

"Yup. Warm chocolate cake with a molten chocolate center. You just half-bake it so it's all gooey and runny inside," he explained. He flipped the molds upside down onto a large plate, added toasted marshmallow ice cream from Christina's in Cambridge, and carefully placed fresh strawberries and raspberries around the edges. He carried the dish to the table and pulled his chair close to mine.

The next ten minutes proved to be the most romantic of my life. Josh fed me bites of the warm cake and, in between spoonfuls of chocolate, kissed me and whispered how beautiful he thought I was, how much he wanted me, and . . . not needing any more persuading, I went to the bathroom to get a good scratch in—by then, I was itching like anything—and dig into the CVS bag.

I slipped into the bathroom and lowered my pants. In possibly the most horrifying moment of my life, I discovered something worse than razor burn: I had a viciously contagious-looking rash all over my legs, with the worst of it right on my bikini line. "God dammit!" I screamed. Well, that explained the itching and the growing burning sensation I'd been feeling. I cursed myself for buying that stupid Smoothie Pad. Smoothie? Ha! I might as well have taken sandpaper and rubbed it all over my body. I gently eased my pants up over the skin I had left.

"Are you okay?" Josh called with concern in his voice.

"Um, well, no," I said pitifully. I was all prepared to have passionate sex with this wonderful guy, and now there was no way. If his beautiful body rubbed against mine, I'd break out in screams of agony. "I sort of have a problem."

"Oh, is it . . . that time of the month? You know, that's okay."

238

"I wish. No. I've done something so stupid. I'm too embarrassed to tell you." *I'll just stay in this bathroom forever,* I decided. *This is totally humiliating, and he's going to bolt out of here thinking I have some crazy STD.*

"Chloe, what is it? Are you going to come out of there?" I heard Josh just outside the door.

I was just going to have to tell him the truth. How else could I explain why one minute I'd been ready to leap into bed and the next I was wailing in the bathroom? To get the ordeal over, I spoke as fast as I could. "This is awful, Josh, but I wanted to be all cute and sexy tonight, and I thought something might happen, see, so I got this thing that was supposed to rub off all the hair on my legs better than a razor, and now I have something that looks like some freaky jungle rash. I think I took off half of my skin!"

To his credit, Josh started laughing. "Are you okay? It sounds like it probably hurts."

"No, I'm not okay." I moaned from behind the closed door. "You better go. I'm way too dorky to ever come out of here. I'm going to spend the rest of my life locked in this bathroom."

"Let me see," he insisted. "It can't be that bad."

"Yes it can! In fact, it already is."

"Chloe, please open the door."

"Fine. But promise you won't laugh anymore. It is not in the least bit funny." I cracked the door. "All right, come in."

"Okay, pull your pants down," Josh said.

"That's romantic," I said sadly. "This isn't at all how I pictured it."

"I'm serious. I want to help you," he said. "I'm not coming on to you. Well, not right this minute. Just let me see."

I sighed and, thanks to all the wine I'd consumed, lowered my pants.

"Man, that must sting." Josh grimaced. "But I think I have an idea."

He led me to the bedroom. "Okay, take your pants off," he instructed.

"More romance," I sighed.

"I'm going to get the cold packs I used to bring the food over, and we'll put those on the worst spots. That should make you feel a little better."

I lay down on the bed and covered my eyes with my hands. "I can't even look at myself!" I screamed. "This is awful!"

My beloved returned with ice packs wrapped in paper towels and placed them on my bikini line. "There, now keep those on for a while. I'm going to pour us more wine, and we'll watch some TV together, okay?"

"Can you turn off the light?" I begged. "Neither of us should have to look at me."

"I think you look gorgeous, rashy legs and all, but I'll turn it off if you want." Josh kissed me deeply before getting our drinks and hitting the lights.

Josh and I spent the rest of the evening with me sitting in front of him, leaning back on his chest and exposing my poor legs to the air. I thanked him a hundred times for the amazing dinner and apologized even more times for not being able to ravish him the way I was dying to. He ran his hands through my hair, kissed the top of my head and my cheeks, and promised there was no rush. We channel surfed and talked and cuddled until midnight, when we both fell asleep. I woke up for a few minutes around three and got up to turn off the television. I crawled back into bed next to Josh and drifted right back to sleep. I'd found a cure for my insomnia, yes. But how permanent a cure?

SIXTEEN

Brimming with frustration, I dragged myself into my field placement the next morning. In between yawning from a late night, scratching my itching, burning rash, and muddling my way through hotline calls, I called my parents.

"How's the chef?" my mother asked eagerly.

"Amazing. Dinner at Magellan was fantastic. And then he came over last night and cooked for me, too." In all seriousness, I announced, "I may have to marry him."

"Well, that's wonderful, dear," she said distractedly. "I have to go now and check on Mrs. Ainsley's yard. She seems to think her water fountain is bubbling too loudly. Love you!" I'd just have to confide all the details to Ade.

I called Detective Hurley again and left him another

message telling him that Eric was not the wealthy bachelor he'd made himself out to be and that I'd be happy to discuss the implications of this matter at his earliest convenience.

Josh called to say he was off on Wednesday night and wanted to take me to Essence, in part to check out his old rival's food and in part to support Tim's restaurant. Of course, I agreed. Maybe my legs would've healed by then. If I hadn't sanded off half my skin last night, I could've been basking in a sexual afterglow. As it was, I was still itchy. In more ways than one.

When Wednesday finally arrived, my Group Therapy class proved to be more irritating than it had been the previous week. This time, instead of continuing to learn about group process by discussing Eric's murder, each of us was forced to pair up with a partner and play the roles of client and therapist as a way to improve our counseling skills and encourage the expression and verbalization of emotion. We didn't even get to pretend to be a single parent fighting poverty or a person with bipolar illness struggling with medication; instead, we were stuck being ourselves. Worse, each team had to sit in front of the class and demonstrate its techniques.

The only positive note was that Gay Doug grabbed me and rescued me from having to partner with someone to whom verbalizing emotion was a new and foreign experience.

Doug and I sat together in a corner of the room and practiced.

"I don't want to do this," I informed him.

"Yes, I can tell. Can you expand on that feeling?"

"Yes. If I wanted to be in therapy, I'd do it on my own. Why am I paying eighteen thousand dollars a year for this?"

"So you're frustrated?" *Ah, reframing and reflecting back.*

I sneered at Doug.

"Chloe, look, part of being a good therapist is learning to understand yourself, so just behave."

When it came time for us to present our skills in front of the class, I noticed an unusual amount of interest from my fellow students. Before Doug had a chance to try to engage me in a scintillating interview, Gretchen cut in.

"Chloe, we were just talking about you." She gestured to a few women near her. "And this seems like a good opportunity to catch up on where you're at emotionally with the murder. Are you maintaining your support structures? Have you disentangled yourself from the victim's parents?"

With eager social work faces on me, I looked to Doug to bail me out. Instead, he said, "Yes, Chloe. Can you express to us how this experience is affecting you?"

Thanks, Doug. I gave a summary of my dinner with the Raffertys and noticed eyes widening when I mentioned Eric's financial woes and his parents' imminent move.

"And how does it make you feel to be caught in this

lie with his parents?" Gretchen wasn't going to let up until I'd had a meltdown, preferably one complete with hurling objects and bawling.

I sighed. "I *feel*," I emphasized, "cranky that I'm stuck in the lie, and I blame my downstairs neighbor for being such a dork and making me so desperate to find a boyfriend that I went on the Internet for a blind date and now have to deal with this stupidness. And I just want to have my chef without all this other nonsense."

Determined to be the responsive social worker, Gretchen said, "But you need to own your part in this. Your neighbor didn't *make* you do anything. You have to accept responsibility for your choices. And perhaps you're more angry than frustrated? Maybe share a little bit more with the class?"

Although I could've said a lot about the anger I was feeling toward Gretchen just then, I refrained from causing a scene by making some insightful-sounding BS comments on restoring my mental health. The class then bounced around the same theories I'd run by Josh last night. To my disappointment, no one was strongly convinced of any suspect's guilt.

Sensible Julie piped in. "The point is, first of all, you've gotten yourself caught up in this situation with the parents, and you simply have to extricate yourself and end their disillusionment ASAP. Like you said last week, you feel sorry for them, and you've become a victim of your own empathy. But now it's time to wind things up there."

244

I actually agreed with Julie and promised the class and myself that I'd phone Sheryl and Phil and straighten things out.

She continued. "Second, you should be careful trying to name the murderer. That's not your job, and you may tick off the wrong person," Julie warned. Students nodded in agreement.

I carried a cell phone, I assured everyone, as though the miracle of wireless communication would keep me safe from a knife-wielding killer. *Don't slice me open yet! Not until I make a quick call to 911!* But I did promise to be careful.

In spite of finding my classmates somewhat intrusive and pushy, I was somehow relieved to know that I had a group of supportive peers to check in with once a week. In fact, I left the class with a surprising feeling of being cared for. During my next class, however, I was so busy fantasizing about Josh that I barely took in the professor's lecture on the social worker's responsibility to collaborate with multiple agencies when assisting families in crisis.

When I got home that afternoon, there was a voice mail from Josh saying he would pick me up at seven for dinner. My wounds from the hair-removal fiasco were healing nicely. A good omen!

Still, at five o'clock as I was looking through my closet, I decided not to doll up too much for dinner. Except on the morning we'd gone to the deli, I'd been primped and polished every time Josh had seen me, and I thought it was time for him to get used to the real me. On the other hand, Essence wasn't just anywhere, so I had to wear something nice. Furthermore, I couldn't very well get all dressed up and leave my hair in a ponytail. So, cursing my mane of curls, I caved in and blew out my hair. Puffs of smoke leaped off my head as I kept the dryer on high heat and worked to beat the clock. When my hair was finally smooth, it was still too puffy for my taste. Not knowing what else to do, I leaped onto the bed, lay down, and tried to flatten out my hair against the pillow. Cosmetic remedies having failed, I willed my hair to behave itself. *Please decompress. I apologize for burning you. If you stay nice and straight, I will not blow dry you for an entire week!*

Thank God, Josh was ten minutes late. He looked completely handsome in a pale blue button-down shirt. As he drove us to Essence, I could barely keep my hands off him. When we got to the restaurant, we were immediately welcomed by Joelle, the motherly hostess.

"Josh!" she smiled happily. "What are you doing here? Don't tell me you actually have a night off?"

"Amazingly, yes. I wanted to come in and see how Tim's doing—with everything that's been going on. Have you met Chloe?"

Joelle checked me out with a mixture of curiosity and confusion. The last time she'd seen me, I'd been here with Eric, and I now felt as if my mother had caught me doing something morally questionable.

Joelle said, "You went out with Mr. Rafferty, right?

246

You were here with him the night he was killed. How do you know Josh?"

"I was on a blind date with Eric that night. I met Josh after." I refrained from revealing that I'd picked Josh up at Eric's funeral.

"Chloe just had the bad luck to be here with him when he was killed," Josh said before changing the subject. "So how's business been?"

"Crappy. For the most part. Tim had to fire a couple of the waitstaff. And you won't believe the menu." Joelle rolled her eyes. I wondered exactly what she meant. "At least we're not totally empty. We've still got a few loyal customers, and some of the people here are just curious to see a crime scene. I mean, come on! There's nothing to see. They took the body away, for Christ's sake! The bathroom's been cleaned. That's it. Get over it. If one more customer asks me about that night, I'm going to chuck them out the front door."

When we'd been seated at a corner table, Josh practically yelped with surprise when he saw the menu, which was nothing like the lengthy one I'd seen here before. Dinner was prix fixe, with two choices of appetizer, two choices of entrée, two choices of dessert . . . and that was it.

"Wow," Josh said, dumbfounded. "Tim must be hurting to do this. I don't even know what to say."

"Is this saving him a ton of money?"

"Well, think of everything they don't have to buy. Certainly controls the food cost."

"Yeah, but aren't they going to lose people who actually want a choice?"

Josh nodded. "Yup. Usually you do a set menu for special nights, like Valentine's Day or Mother's Day, when you're going to be swamped all day and you need to have a limited number of dishes you're making. It doesn't make sense to do something like this now." He shook his head and tossed the menu down. "I don't know what's going on. It looks like Essence might be on the verge of closing."

Cassie came to our table. Although she was the same waitress I'd had when I'd been here with Eric and the one who'd sat with me after he'd been killed, she showed none of Joelle's confusion or discomfort. "Hey, guys! What's up, Josh?" She was as perky and adorable as I remembered. I glanced at Josh to see his reaction as she leaned in for a hug.

Josh hugged her back. "Hey, kiddo! How you been?" Good. I sensed more of a brother-sister friendship here than anything flirtatious.

"Well, I'm still working, so that's good. Ian and I are the only full-time waitstaff left. Katrina works part time. Actually, she's here tonight. You'll have to say hello." Cassie turned around and called over to yet another beautiful woman, who immediately came to our table. Katrina was tall, with long, thick hair that fell down her back in a cascade of unfrizzed curls. Was I the only woman in the world who couldn't get her hair to be either straight *or* curly and not some mess in between? I stared at her scalp in search of extensions, which were the only plausible excuse for having such phenomenal hair. Nope, hers looked real.

Katrina and Cassie sat down with us at the table and traded restaurant gossip with Josh for a few minutes. "They both used to work at Magellan," Josh explained, "and they came over here with Tim when he opened this place up. Ian, too."

Katrina snorted, "I don't know why Tim wanted *him*. Ian's a dirtbag." She pointed at me. "Does Chloe know about him?"

Oh, I loved gossip! "No, what about him?" Eager for juicy details, I looked to Josh.

He sighed. "See, while Tim was in the process of opening Essence, Madeline figured out that Ian was scamming Magellan out of money. Instead of just firing him, she sent him over to Tim's place without warning him."

The two servers nodded in agreement. "Yeah," Cassie said. "Ian was making good money from it, too."

"How did he do it?" I was totally ignorant of how cash registers and credit card machines worked.

"Well, in a couple of ways." Katrina leaned in with excitement. "Ian would run the customer's tab through on their credit card and then have them add their tip and sign for it. The check stays open on the computer until the end of the night. Ian is the head-waiter, so he's one of the only people who can void out items on the register. He'd just go back and void out an item or two, run the check through with the same total, and pocket the extra money for a bigger tip. Forging a signature isn't that difficult. When the customer gets their credit card statement, everything looks right—except that the restaurant got a smaller percentage of the money they paid, and they've inadvertently left Ian a bigger tip. Same thing if the person pays in cash. After the customer leaves, Ian can void out their old check entirely, as though that table was never there, or ring up a new charge with a smaller total, and pocket the difference in cash."

"Yeah," Cassie explained. "See, some people totally go over their check with a fine-tooth comb, and others just sign whatever you put in front of them. Lots of people don't ever look at their credit card statements. Ian just had to be able to read his tables well and figure out if he could pull it off. And most of the time he got away with it."

"So how did he get caught?" I asked. "I mean, when you ring stuff up at the cash register, you're alone, right? There's nobody there watching you every time." As someone who could barely jaywalk without guilt, I was amazed that someone else could engage in felonious activity on a regular basis without having a nervous breakdown.

"You're right," Katrina nodded. "Nobody's watching you at the register. But I think Ian got a little sloppy. And greedy about how much extra cash he could take home. And some of the diners caught mistakes in their checks. I guess Ian sometimes added extra items to checks, miscellaneous items or extra drinks, so that the customer would pay for a higher amount. Once in a while, Ian would have trouble with a table, or the customer would ask to speak to a manager, which would've been Ian himself. Or Madeline. Sometimes he could just explain it away as a mistake on his part and not bring Maddie into it, but after a couple of times, she figured him out and fired him."

"And let him work for Tim?" I said in disbelief.

"Right," Josh said. "I think it was her little dig at Tim for filing for divorce. Mostly they both handled it politely, but that was her underhanded way of sticking it to Tim. She probably figured Tim would figure out what Ian was up to sooner or later, and he wouldn't lose that much money in the process. And on the other hand, she did let Tim have Cassie and Katrina, and I know they were her top servers at Magellan."

"Listen, I have to get back to my tables," Katrina apologized. "We should all hang out sometime, okay? Good to meet you, Chloe."

"Since I'm your official waitress," Cassie said, "can I get you two something to drink? Or have you already figured out what to order off the vast menu?" she said sarcastically.

We asked for bottled water and then ordered different menu items for each of the three courses so we could try everything.

"Garrett must be miserable with this new menu," Josh said. "He's not the best chef, but he's better than this. Honestly, I can't believe—"

"Josh, listen," I cut him off. "That happened the

251

night I was here with Eric. The check thing with Ian. He was working a table near ours, and the couple complained to him about their bill. But what was odd is that Eric jumped in and took care of it. And then he gave Ian some kind of warning, something about remembering what they'd talked about. At the time, I guess I thought Eric had taken it upon himself to scold Ian for screwing up the check and being a bad waiter. But now I bet Eric knew what Ian was doing."

"And," Josh added, "Eric might've been getting a piece of the profits for keeping quiet about it. I mean, on a good week and with the high-end clientele, Ian could've been taking home an extra seven or eight hundred dollars. Fifteen, twenty dollars from, say, five tables a day? More from the bigger parties that come in and drink a lot and don't pay attention to what they're spending? That's good money. Split that in half, and Eric still would've been getting money that he apparently needed badly."

Josh and I stared at each other.

"Until," I said, "Eric threatened to tell Timothy unless he got more money from Ian. Or until Ian just got sick of sharing his profits with Eric and he killed him." We'd caught the murderer! I was sure it must be Ian.

"But," Josh pointed out, "for someone who owed as much as Eric did, he wasn't going to make *that* much money off of Ian. Although it might have been enough to pay minimum balances on everything he owed."

I dug my cell phone out of my purse. "I'm calling

Detective Hurley and telling him what we figured out."

Josh reached over and put his hand over my phone. "I'd rather you didn't do that. It's just going to upset Tim and piss him off that everybody knew about Ian and didn't tell him. Besides, I'm still a free man. If I get hauled off to the slammer, you can tell Hurley, okay?" He smiled.

I agreed to wait to pass the information on to the detective, but I did ask Josh why no one had informed Tim about Ian's nefarious check practices. In particular, why hadn't he told Tim?

"Look, Chloe," Josh sighed. "I've told you how tough this business is to be in. I just try to keep to myself. I do my job and let Maddie deal with everything else. I try not to rock the boat with anything, and I've got to pick my battles. Most people are out for themselves here, me included. And I'm not about to do anything to piss off Maddie and get myself fired. She pays me more than most restaurants pay their chefs, and I can't go ratting her and Ian out to Tim. Same thing for Cassie and Katrina. They need their jobs, and who knows what Ian might think of to say to Tim about them. And I don't think they care. They do their job, they get good tips, and they know they'll be the last to be let go if the restaurant fails. Why mess with that?" Josh took my hands in his. "I told you, I'm not perfect. But you might do the same thing if you were in my shoes."

I had to agree. In the scheme of the world, maybe

what Ian was doing wasn't that big a deal. Unless it implicated him in Eric's murder—and cleared Josh.

Josh continued to hold my hands, and we talked until our appetizers arrived. I'd just finished telling him about the awful paper I had to write for school when Cassie placed plates in front of us.

"Okay, here's a salad with pears, candied walnuts, and blue cheese for you, Chloe. And the butternut squash soup for you, Josh."

The salad was pretty good. Nothing out of this world, but good enough. I watched Josh and was mesmerized by how serious he looked tasting his dish. And by how wonderfully his blue shirt enhanced the blue of his eyes. And by the thought of ripping that blue shirt off his body, popping buttons across the restaurant, and ravishing him in between courses.

"So what do you think?" he asked.

"Oh, fantastic!" I practically pounced on him.

"Really? Mine has too much salt and doesn't taste like much else." Oops. He meant our food. "Garrett is always afraid of underseasoning things. Sometimes he goes overboard in the other direction."

"Right. I mean, mine is okay. It's good. It's just not amazing, and it's not something I would've ordered if there'd been other choices. This salad has been done plenty of times before at other restaurants."

"This sucks. I have to talk to Tim about this." Josh looked touchingly disappointed for his old boss.

Having resolved to take my social work studies seriously, I'd been pondering my Group Therapy class's focus on expressing feelings and now decided to practice my skills on Josh. "So, how are you *feeling* about everything that's going on?" I asked nonchalantly. "How is it at Magellan? I know Madeline doesn't think you're a murderer, but is it uncomfortable over there at all?"

"Surprisingly, it's not that bad. I've known everyone over there for a while, so no one's treating me any differently. We're all just waiting for this to blow over. I think we're just all on edge. It's such a freaky thing to have happen to someone we all knew. And at Tim's place, for God's sake. And only a few blocks away. The biggest problem we've had recently is all the accidents in the kitchen. Brian burned the crap out of his arm the other day when he walked too close to a burner. And I cut my hand on one of my knives."

"Is it bad? How did you do it?" I grabbed his hand and realized I'd been so distracted by my love goggles that I'd failed to notice the big bandage across Josh's palm. "I can't believe I didn't even see this!"

"I'm fine. Someone must've put one of my knives into the drawer where I keep other kitchen utensils. I reached in for something and got a good gash. Ever since I met you, I keep misplacing things and losing track of what I'm doing at work . . . but I don't mind. You're worth it. Chefs get burns and cuts all the time. My hands are covered with old burn scars, but I've got leather hands, so it doesn't bother me too much. I can just stick my finger in a hot saucepan and not feel it." He grinned proudly.

"You're insane, and I love it!" I grinned.

"I'm worried about Brian, though," Josh admitted. "He's still trying to get it together. We all have accidents, but Brian has more than most. Did I tell you about the fire the other night?" I shook my head in alarm. "Oh God. I didn't tell you about this? Something on the grill caught fire, which isn't that unusual, but for some stupid reason, Brian grabbed the hose from the sink and sprayed the flames. Idiot," Josh spat out.

Confused, I asked, "And that didn't work?"

"Chloe, you *never* hit a grease fire with water," he told me sternly. "It basically causes an explosion. I was standing right next to the grill. I was trying to grab the baking soda, which is what you're supposed to throw on a grease fire, and I couldn't stop Brian in time. He just panicked and went for the water, but he *knows* not to do that. Everyone who works in a kitchen knows that. He felt terrible about it and apologized a million times for being so dumb. He singed his hair and coughed for a couple of hours afterward, and I barely got out of the way in time. At least we weren't hurt badly."

"You shouldn't be worried about Brian, you should be furious with him! Josh, you could have been horribly burned!"

Josh paused for a moment. "Oh, I'm definitely angry with him. There's no question about that. And disappointed. He's been coming up with all these dishes he wants me to put on the menu, but they all

256

suck. Everything he thinks of has been done before—nothing original. And I know he's got it in him. Or at least I think he does. I want him to."

Josh looked miserable about Brian's failures. I wondered how angry Brian was with Josh for pushing him so hard and rejecting all of his ideas.

I had a suggestion. "Josh, why don't you run a few of Brian's dishes as specials, even if they're not great. It might boost his confidence and let him know you believe in him. He must look up to you so much, I'm sure it would mean a lot to him to get your approval."

"I can't do that, Chloe. It doesn't work that way. I'm not doing his dishes if they aren't up to snuff. No one gave me any breaks, and it made me better," Josh said heatedly. "Do you know, when I had my first job in a kitchen, I used to have a guy pace behind me while I cooked. He'd jab a steak knife into the back of my thigh if I wasn't moving fast enough. I'd stand on the goddamn line with blood dripping down my leg, cooking and sweating and working my ass off with this guy watching every move I made. So, no," he shook his head. "I'm not cutting Brian any slack."

Josh was riled up now, and I couldn't blame him. "Did you report the guy to your boss? That's sadistic! Sticking you with a knife!"

He laughed. "Chloe, he *was* my boss. And you don't leave one of the top restaurants in Boston because you don't like it. You suck it up and get through your training and put it on your résumé."

I was about ready to beat Josh's old boss to a bloody

pulp for knifing my beau, but I'd probably be kicked out of school for acting in an unprofessional manner. That stupid Social Work Code of Ethics and I were already beginning to clash. Cassie's arrival with our entrées temporarily cooled off our discussion, but I still wasn't done with the topic.

"Just because you had some asshole treating you like you were going through a fraternity hazing doesn't make it right. And it doesn't mean you have to treat Brian the same way. I mean, I know you don't stick him with a knife while he's cooking, but maybe you should ease up on him a bit. Positive feedback is a good motivator, too, don't you think?"

My chef smiled at me. "I see your point. You and I are different, I guess. You'd do the right thing."

"You know more about running a kitchen than I do, obviously. And as I've learned in my Diversity class readings, different groups have their own rules of behavior and their own cultural norms, and to thrive in a subculture, one must abide by those social laws." I better get an A on my midterm.

We worked our way through two more courses of pleasant but not outstanding food. Josh, however, grew more and more disgruntled with every bite. "This food is ridiculous," he complained. "Now is the time that they should be putting everything they have into the menu. Serving this crap isn't going to keep them afloat." Josh excused himself to talk to Garrett and quickly returned with more bad news. "Garrett is thinking about leaving."

"Really?"

"Yup. That's probably the main reason the menu sucks—Garrett doesn't care anymore. This place is about to crash and burn in a few weeks. If he leaves, I can't imagine Tim could stay open much longer. It'd be hard to find a chef to come into this place now, especially with the financial constraints Tim is obviously dealing with. Speaking of which, I wonder why he's not here now?"

"Maybe he doesn't want to sit around and see how slow it is," I suggested. "It's got to be upsetting."

Cassie appeared at the table in time to hear our last exchange. "Actually, he's out with Madeline right now coming up with schemes to bring some life back into this place. No pun intended. I don't know what she thinks she can come up with that Tim isn't doing on his own. So, listen, food is on the house, of course. You two want any coffee or anything?"

Essence was starting to depress me, so I shook my head at Josh, and we got ready to leave. Josh left a twenty-five-dollar tip for Cassie, who tried to push his money away. He wouldn't take it back. "With business the way it is," he insisted, "you need it."

Josh and I settled into his Xterra. He sighed. "You know what? I'd rather have good competition than have Essence doing so badly."

It was just what Madeline had said on her TV interview: that Magellan needed worthy competition to show how truly great it was.

Josh took me home and dropped me off. Dinner at

Essence had left us both in foul moods.

"Babe, I'm sorry," Josh apologized as he hugged me good-bye. "I'm grumpy, and I just need to go home."

"Sure. I understand," I assured him.

The food business was losing the aura of glamour I'd envisioned while watching the Food Network, poring over issues of *Gourmet*, and scouring ethnic stores for exotic ingredients. Before meeting Josh, I'd pictured restaurant professionals in a constant state of culinary enthusiasm as they brainstormed fantastic recipes and wooed elite diners with gorgeous decor and tantalizing menus. The restaurant world was rougher and meaner than I'd imagined or hoped. I hated to think where my disillusionment might lead. The aura around Josh still glowed brightly. Was he, too, rougher and meaner than I wanted to believe?

SEVENTEEN

My sister Heather was pleased with the unromantic aftermath of my dinner with Josh at the gloomy Essence. She'd kept calling to warn me that I was rushing things even more than usual and would scare Josh off. Furthermore, she was convinced that I'd better not sleep with Josh until he was no longer a murder suspect.

On the upside, when Heather and I talked on Thursday, she invited me to go to an upscale Boston spa with her on Sunday. Her husband, Ben, was going to watch Walker and Lucy for the day so that Heather could go pamper herself. As far as I was concerned, Heather had it pretty good: big, fancy house in Brookline, adoring husband, two beautiful kids. Meanwhile, the way things were going, Josh and I were apparently doomed to wait until our wedding night to consummate the marriage. I was beginning to feel like a guy: thinking about sex and not much else. Josh was working constantly for the next few days and wouldn't be off again until Monday. I'd had a few quick calls from him, but with Magellan doing such great business, he had hardly any time to talk. I was planning to go to Magellan after the dinner rush on Saturday night to hang around until he got off work. Then I'd drag him back to my place to do things that would send Naomi into cardiac arrest.

Schoolwork was beginning to pile up, and I forced myself to do some serious studying. The amount of reading and research was staggering. I couldn't believe how many papers I had due all at the same time. Although school had just begun, my professors were already hounding us about starting our midterm papers and preparing for exams.

Julie from Group Therapy snagged me on campus to complain about the work and to ask whether I wanted to meet up with her the following week to study. Despite my resistance to spending time on campus, I agreed.

"Oh, I'm hosting a toy party tomorrow night, if you want to come. Since you and your chef are getting so close, I figured you might be interested." Julie smiled

261

and handed me an invitation with her address on it. I doubted that Josh and I were going to make babies any time soon, but I thought I might pick out some things for my niece and nephew.

These Tupperware-style parties had gotten totally out of hand in the past few years. I'd been invited to everything from candle parties to organic-household-cleaning-product parties. A shelf in my closet was full of crap I'd bought out of a sense of obligation while attending these events. The salespeople at these gatherings were usually woman trying to make extra money, and I always felt I should do my part to support the poor victims who'd gotten roped into what were probably pyramid schemes, possibly illegal ones. Oh, well, what was one more? And I was making a new friend. At social work school, of all places!

By the time I got to Julie's on Friday night, she and her friends were already loaded on dirty martinis and were passing around edible massage oils. How could I have been so stupid? This was not the kind of toy party where there'd be anything suitable for Walker or Lucy. The salesperson, a woman in her forties, was expounding on the benefits of supplementing your sex life with artificial devices. She had a table set up with a variety of items for sale, and her presentation came complete with a real-life male model clad only in a G-string. I downed a drink and tried to make polite conversation with some of Julie's friends, but they had no interest in talking to me once the model began his demonstration of "stripping for your partner." His dance routine was surprisingly good. Still, as progressive as I thought I was, when the ring toss began, I made my exit. Julie seemed disappointed that I was leaving, but she handed me a goodie bag, thanked me for coming, and apologized if she'd offended me.

I set the alarm clock to wake me at eight on Saturday morning. With an early start, I'd get through so much work that in the evening, when I went to Magellan, I'd be wonderfully relaxed and even more wonderfully ready to lure Josh home. When the alarm went off, I rolled over, slammed my hand on the snooze button, and saw the toy party goodie bag, which was right where I'd dropped it, in the middle of the floor. An hour later, after breakfast and coffee, I was in the middle of deciding which would be a less boring Social Policy paper topic: the failure of Bill Clinton's health-care reform plan or the bleak future of the United States Social Security system. Inspired by the toy party and the early morning sight of Julie's parting gift, I'd just concluded that writing anything about Clinton would make the research bearable by giving me an excuse to review the Monica scandal, when the phone rang.

I mindlessly picked up without checking caller ID and was punished for my brainlessness by the sound of Phil Rafferty's voice. "Chloe, Sheryl and I are getting ready to move soon, and we wanted to see you so we could say our good-byes. Are you free to stop over later today?"

All right. The time had come to clear up the misunderstanding, and if I chickened out, Julie or Gretchen or one of my other classmates would eventually get me to confess to my cowardice and take me to task for failing to get closure on the episode. I compromised by telling Phil that I'd stop in at around six but would be able to stay only a short time.

I spent three hours at the computer Googling Clinton and printed out a bunch of articles on his health-care reform plan, plus a few on Monica and cigars, before taking a break to watch reruns of *Buffy the Vampire Slayer*. After that, I resumed my research. When late afternoon finally arrived, I regretted my promise to Phil Rafferty but knew that I'd be rewarded for enduring the visit by getting to go to Magellan later that evening. And I had the spa to look forward to tomorrow.

I arrived at the Raffertys' house at precisely six with a great deal of knowledge about Clinton, health-care reform, and Monica Lewinsky and not a single idea about how to tell the Raffertys that their late son and I had practically been strangers or how to explain why I'd let them go on believing that Eric and I had been madly in love. And how was I going to broach the subject of the family's finances? I couldn't just blurt out, "And so, how much money do you two actually have?"

Phil answered the door. "Chloe," he slurred. Damn. Drunk again. "Come in. Come in and sit down." As he stumbled to the couch in the living room, it occurred to me that inebriation was his version of Monica and that Sheryl Rafferty probably felt the same way about liquor bottles that Hillary Clinton did about cigars.

I sat down next to Eric's father and noticed on the coffee table in front of us a bowl of ice, two large crystal tumblers, and a bottle of whiskey, which seemed to be Phil's drink of choice.

I scooted to the far end of the couch. "So, um, where is Mrs. Rafferty?" It was a surprise to discover an occasion on which I'd be outright eager to see Sheryl.

Phil waved his hand carelessly. "Had to go out. She'll be back later."

Lovely. Much as I hated being stuck there alone with the drunken Phil, I decided that his intoxication was practically an invitation to practice my new interviewing skills to elicit information about Rafferty finances.

"Well, so you're moving soon? That's exciting, right?" I sounded more weak than professional, probably because I was trying to figure out how to confess my falsehoods to this grieving, if repulsive, father.

Phil poured drinks for both of us. I thanked him as he handed me a full glass with only two ice cubes. He belched loudly before taking a large swig of his drink.

"Look, Mr. Rafferty," I said, moving swiftly ahead with my agenda, "I know about Eric."

Phil laughed loudly. "You know what?"

"I know he was broke and that he owed tons of money."

"And you didn't leave him, huh? What a doll. Not

like that stupid bitch Veronica. She dropped him 'cause of it. But not you." Without warning, Phil lunged unsteadily at me and, to my horror, buried his head in my neck.

For a second, I was paralyzed with disgust and fear, but the feel of his wet tongue on my skin roused me to action, and I succeeded in shoving him forcefully away. "Oh my God! What are you thinking, you big freak?" I sprang off the couch and backed away from Phil Rafferty, who was now slumped in his corner of the couch. What a sicko! With anger ripping through me, I practically barked at Phil. "I was never involved with Eric! I had one blind date with him! One! The night he was killed. I didn't even know him. I didn't tell you because I felt sorry for you and Mrs. Rafferty. Your wife, by the way? Remember her?"

Phil stared at me in drunken surprise. "You two weren't . . . ? You didn't *know* Eric?"

Phil's revolting assault had destroyed my patience and sympathy. With no explanation, I said, "I'm trying to figure out what happened that night. Why he was killed. Now tell me," I demanded fiercely, "he was broke, right? Were you paying his bills for him?"

Eric's father nodded dejectedly and rested his chin on his hands. "Yeah, I was paying off everything. Sheryl didn't like it. She said we should let him bail himself out of his own mess. But I had to do it."

"So you knew about his financial problems before he died."

"Yes, yes. Just come sit back down with me." He

patted the spot next to him on the couch.

Fat chance, Phil. I didn't care what grief had done to him. Never again was I getting anywhere near him.

"I'm going now," I told Phil. "Don't call me. Ever. If you ever do anything to remind me of your existence, I'll call the police."

I bolted out of the house. My hands were shaking as I started the ignition. Thank God I hadn't touched that whiskey. Cold sober, I was in no condition to drive. Only a few blocks away from the Raffertys', I pulled over and called Adrianna, who picked up her cell right away. I told her about Phil's horrendous attempt at seduction.

"Oh my God, Chloe! Are you okay? I hope you told that bastard off," she yelled angrily. "Hold your head still, or you're going to be lopsided," I heard her say. "Sorry, I'm pinning up someone's hair right now. Some girl is having her eighteenth birthday party tonight, and her mother hired me to do everyone's hair. Okay, so you beat that Phil to a bloody pulp, right?"

"Yeah, right. I just told him to stay away from me or I'd call the police. But I did find out that he and Sheryl have been paying off all the money Eric owed," I said, pleased to have taken advantage of Phil's drunken pass to extract the information. "That's what he said. And I believe him."

"Chloe, I told you those people were bad news. How gross is that? Hitting on your dead son's girlfriend?"

"Well, I did clear up the confusion about my being Eric's girlfriend."

"Whatever. Have you told Josh about this yet? I bet he's going to have a fit. Maybe he'll do something dramatic like run over there and defend your honor! Wouldn't that be awesome?"

"No, it would not be awesome. I don't even know if I want to tell Josh about it. It's making me want to puke just telling you. Anyhow, I'm going home to make something to eat and then I'm going down to see Josh at the restaurant. You want to meet me there?"

"Sorry, I can't. I'm going to be working all night. The mother is paying me to stick around in case anyone needs their hair touched up. Talk about spoiled. I mean, special, right? Just kidding," Ade said for the obvious benefit of her clients. "This must be so fun for you girls, huh?" she cooed sweetly. "I gotta go, Chloe. I'll talk to you tomorrow."

I'd calmed down enough to be safe behind the wheel, but my lousy mood persisted all the way home. Once there, I decided to tidy up in hopeful anticipation of returning home later that night with Josh. There was nothing romantic about making love amidst a pile of dirty laundry, so I grabbed a load and headed outside, down the back steps, and into the basement of the house. Doing laundry in the winter meant teetering down icy steps with a basket of clothes while praying for survival. On this occasion, the steps were safe, but there was a nasty surprise awaiting me when I opened the door to the laundry room. Sitting on top of the dryer reading *US Weekly* was Veronica, the Peroxide Queen.

"Hi." She beamed at me. "Chloe, right? Noah said it'd be okay if I did my laundry here. My machine isn't working. He went to Chicago for the weekend, though, so I'm alone tonight. What're you doin'?"

"Laundry," I said.

Her shorts were shorter than short. The weather wasn't that hot, for Christ's sake. Well, unless you were sitting on a clothes dryer relishing the vibrations of the wrinkle-free cycle. Although the last person I wanted to be stuck in a laundry room with was Veronica, she seemed chatty enough, and I wondered what she could tell me about Eric. At a guess, she knew nothing about my history with Noah. That, or she didn't care.

With all the false friendliness I could muster, I smiled at her as I slowly started loading whites into the washing machine. "So, you and Noah, huh? That's great."

"Oh, yeah. He's the best. Better than my ex, Eric, that's for sure," she scoffed as she flipped a page in her magazine. "Oh God. Sorry. I heard through the grapevine at Magellan that you were going out with him. And you found his body? How totally gross!" she squealed. "But I hear you're with Josh now. Much better choice. I should know."

In dignified tones, I said, "I had a blind date with Eric the night he died, so I barely knew him. *You* must be upset, though. I mean, I know you two had broken up, but still . . . he *was* murdered."

"You know what? I'm not upset in the least. He was a big liar, and I don't give a crap that he's gone. I wasted enough time on him for nothing," she spat out. "Because he was broke?"

Without a hint of embarrassment, she nodded and said, "Yeah, you found out about that, too? I dumped his ass the minute I figured it out. What a moron he was. I mean, come on, who spends money like that when you don't have it? I'm a freaking bookkeeper, for cryin' out loud! Why he thought I'd put up with that is beyond me. After months of driving me around in his slick car, I find out he's worth nothing? I don't think so. Not for me. Broke up with him right after. Noah has tons more money than Eric did," she confided. "He's made really good investments."

It was hard to believe that someone so superficial had a brain with the depth to handle numbers. "So why did Eric pretend he was going to invest in Tim's restaurant? Obviously he couldn't afford to, so what was the point of making Tim think he could?"

"Oh, Eric was such a jackass. He was so obsessed with that restaurant gang. It was actually pathetic how much he wanted to fit in with Tim and Maddie and everyone who worked there. It's a tight group of people, and Eric was like some loser high-school kid trying to worm his way into the popular crowd. Nobody there particularly liked him, but he used to go into Magellan and throw money around—money, it turns out, he shouldn't have been spending. He latched onto the staff when they went out to the bars after work and tried to pretend he was, you know, the leader of the pack. People mostly just ignored him and hoped he'd go away." Veronica tossed her hair. I was pleased to see that she desperately needed a foil. "So anyway," she continued, "when Tim opened up Essence, Eric just barreled ahead and tried to jump on board and become part of the new restaurant by claiming he wanted to invest a huge amount of money. So he was just angling to hang out there, get free food, and feel wealthy and important."

"So," I asked casually, "did you tell everyone at work why you broke up with Eric?"

"No way. I mean, at the time I was totally mortified. I would've looked like a complete idiot dating someone as fiscally irresponsible as Eric. I was furious at him for fooling me and making me think he was loaded, and I didn't want *anyone* to know that I'd been tricked by a moron like Eric. So, between that and his awful parents, I was done with him."

I had to nod in agreement. "Yeah, I've met them. They're both pretty out there." I paused. "Especially the father." I glanced at Veronica, who was still perched on the dryer.

"He's an asshole. Do you know, he frickin' hit on me once?"

"No!" I replied in mock disbelief.

"Yeah, at a dinner party Eric's parents had. Phil had downed, like, an entire bottle of scotch, and he grabbed my ass in the kitchen. He tried to grab something else, but Eric walked in."

"That must've been a nice scene. Did Sheryl find out?"

271

"No. But then when I found out about Eric's money mess, Eric said he'd make his father pay it all off. Eric told his father that if he didn't fix all of his financial problems, he'd tell Sheryl that Phil had hit on me."

"And Phil agreed," I finished for her.

"You bet your ass he agreed. Would you want to piss off that woman?"

I shook my head.

"Eric thought he could get me back if he got Phil to pay off all his debt. At that point I didn't care. I'd had enough of his lying and his drunk father trying to grope me."

Was Phil so desperate to avoid paying off all the money Eric owed that he killed him? Was he trying to stop Eric from ratting on him to Sheryl?

"Did Detective Hurley talk to you?" I asked.

"Yeah, I told him what a prick I thought Eric was. Can you believe he actually suspected me of killing Eric? Because I was so mad at him for being such a jerk? Hardly. I was off the hook after about half a second because I was with Noah that night, if you know what I mean." She might as well have wink-winked at me. But Noah had implied as much in saying that he'd had company, as he'd phrased it, on the night of the murder. "Noah said something about all of his women reporting him to the police, which I didn't understand, since it wasn't my fault they went to talk to him after me. He was my alibi, so what was I supposed to do? He's a little nuts sometimes."

Since Veronica and Noah alibied each other, it was

possible that they'd acted together to murder Eric. Although Veronica's ego had taken a blow at Eric's deception, she didn't seem to have cared enough about Eric to bother killing him.

I asked, "Veronica, do you know why Eric went around telling people he was dating someone? After you broke up with him. His parents and everyone at Essence kept saying they'd heard so much about me and that Eric had been talking about me for weeks, which is impossible, since I'd just met him that night."

"Oh, easy. To see if he could make me jealous enough to go back to him. He was trying to spread rumors that he was hot and heavy with someone, hoping I'd hear about it and beg him to take me back. Yeah, right. I figured it was a bunch of bullshit, though. Sounds like he pawned you off as the mystery woman he'd been bragging about."

I was mildly insulted but recovered in about thirty seconds.

Veronica pulled out a nail file and started sharpening her talons. The dryer turned off. "Oh, that was toasty!" she chirped as she hopped off her seat to unload her dry clothes. "Well, I'm off. Nice talkin' to you, Chloe. Tell Josh I said hello and maybe I'll see you guys at Magellan. Hey, you two and Noah and I should double some night!"

Practically gagging at the suggestion, I raised my eyebrows and nodded. "Yeah, why don't you run that by Noah."

"See ya!" Veronica waved and walked out of the basement.

As much as I loathed Veronica, who would forever be the skanky blonde I'd caught leaving Noah's apartment, I had learned a few things from her. For example, tonight wasn't the first time Phil Rafferty had tried to grope his son's girlfriend or, in my case, alleged girlfriend. What would my classmates make of that revolting habit? Would they see it as some bizarre Oedipal twist?

I went back up to my condo. It was still too early to descend on Josh. But I was starving. I opened the fridge but found nothing of interest. Ordinary food had begun to pale by comparison with Josh's cooking; I was rapidly getting spoiled. I decided to settle for boring cheese and crackers. Josh had left one of his small knives in my kitchen, and I used it to slice some cheddar. *Ow!* I sliced a mean cut into the top of my left forefinger. Dammit, that hurt! Rinsing my hand under water, I winced at the sting. With a dishcloth wrapped around my hand, I went to the bathroom in search of a bandage. I probably needed stitches but was in no mood to waste five hours in a Boston ER on a Saturday night. It was hard to believe that a small knife had inflicted such a bad cut. My thoughts turned to the damage a large knife could do, a large, curved knife like cimiter used to kill Eric. One quick slice across the neck and . . . a wave of nausea rushed through me. I held onto the sink with one hand and bent over to send blood back into my head.

I needed chocolate.

My cabinets yielded the ingredients for chocolate chip cookies. I preferred to buy Tollhouse cookie dough, but with Josh in my life, I now felt obliged to cook from scratch. Besides, the wholesome activity of baking cookies might lift my spirits. As it turned out, what actually cheered me up was eating most of the batter. While the cookies baked, I changed into Josh-seducing clothes. With luck, my cookie-bloated stomach would shrink by the time he saw me naked, but for now I had to avoid anything too fitted. Also, I didn't want to look too obvious.

Clad in a white V neck and casual pants, I fixed my makeup and touched up my hair. I grabbed a handful of hot cookies for the car ride, none of which I was going to give to Josh, since I knew better than to try to impress a chef with my cooking. I hoped I never had to make *him* dinner.

EIGHTEEN

It was almost ten when I walked into Magellan, which was packed. Madeline stood by the bar talking to one of the waitstaff. I wasn't comfortable enough to charge back into the kitchen and claim my man, so I headed in her direction in the hope that she'd shove me into Josh's arms and tell us both to get out of the restaurant and enjoy some quality time together.

Madeline's greeting surprised me. "Chloe, thank God you're here!" Although she was, as always, beautifully dressed, a few wisps of hair had come loose from her sleek bun. I wondered what was going on.

"Hi, Madeline. I thought I'd just sit at the bar until Josh gets off, if that's okay."

"Of course. Maybe you can help calm Josh down. He's in a horrible mood tonight," she informed me, shaking her head.

Pleased that I was now considered to have influence with her chef, I nodded. "Sure. I'll try. What happened?"

She tossed her hands up. In an undertone, she said, "The damn health inspector showed up today for a surprise visit and found some things he didn't like. It's not a big deal. Every restaurant usually has a couple of violations, but it's never happened here. Josh Driscoll keeps a *very* clean kitchen, and he's out of his mind about this. He won't even talk to me about it."

"What did they find?" I asked.

Madeline sighed. "Oh, a few dead mice downstairs, incorrect temperature settings on some of the coolers, a couple of other things. Some expired meat that should have been thrown out." She looked at my disgusted face. "Yeah, I know. Mice are gross, but the truth is, every restaurant has them now and then. It's almost impossible not to. It's just not a big deal. The main problem is, someone must've called the health inspector and complained about something. We just had an inspection last month, and everything was fine, so there was no reason for them to come back."

"So it's not that bad, really? Right?"

"The mice aren't actually a big deal. But the temperature problems and the expired food are considered 'critical' violations. The only reason we're still open is that the inspector who came by knows Josh and knows that he wouldn't typically have a kitchen with these kinds of problems. Anyhow, Josh is taking care of everything, but he's completely pissed off right now. Do you think you could talk to him? I've tried to reassure him, but it hasn't worked."

So much for seeing Josh when he was relaxed and happy. I was definitely not going to tell him about the Phil incident or my talk with Veronica.

Madeline turned to the bartender behind her. "Jim, can you bring Chloe a glass of white, please? She might need it. Oh, and show Josh this. Maybe it'll help." Madeline handed me a folded printout from her pocket. "It's a review from the *Boston Globe*." She smiled at me and went off in search of her angry chef.

I sipped my wine and read the article, a laudatory review of Magellan that emphasized the elegance of many of Josh's dishes. The reviewer even referred to Josh as "one of Boston's hot new chefs." I smiled to myself. This ought to cheer him up.

A few moments later, Josh sidled up beside me. "Hi, sweetie! What are you doing here?" he said, kissing me on the cheek.

"I missed you, so I thought I'd just come in and hang around."

His chef's coat was unbuttoned at the top, he was sweaty from cooking, and his hair was messed up.

Yum. And he didn't seem to be in a rotten mood.

"Excellent. I'm glad you're here." Josh rubbed my back and kissed me again, this time on the mouth. Yum, again.

"I heard you had a rough day," I offered.

"Yeah," Josh answered, his face changing. "I don't know what the hell happened. I keep a goddamn spotless kitchen. I cannot figure out why the temps were off or why there was old food in the walk-in. I clean it out every day, and I always check the food temperature. Brian's been cleaning and recleaning the kitchen all day trying to do something to make me feel better."

"How could this have happened?"

"I'm not sure. Brian's been interrogating the other kitchen guys. He thinks one of them is fed up with working twelve-hour days for crappy pay and is trying to get back at us because we're salaried. It's a good crew back there, though, so I can't picture one of them tossing dead mice around. But that's the least of my problems."

"Why? What else?"

Josh sat down next to me on an empty barstool and took a drink from my glass. "I overheard Maddie talking to Brian." He cleared his throat and looked at me. "She told him the executive chef job would eventually be his."

"What?" I said in disbelief. "You've got to be kidding me. Look around. With a full restaurant like this, she couldn't possibly be thinking of firing you."

"That's what I thought. She'd pretty much told me this job was mine as long as I wanted." Although Josh stayed pretty calm, I could tell he was furious. And I couldn't blame him.

"Josh, you must've misunderstood her. Just wait until tomorrow and talk to Madeline then. There's no way she'd give Brian your job. Look," I said holding out the rave review. "She wanted me to show you this."

Josh scanned the paper. "Well, it doesn't seem to matter, does it," he said sourly.

"Have you asked Brian about it?"

"No, but it would explain why he's in such a good mood. I guess all his flirting paid off. And she wouldn't have to pay him my salary, so he'd cost her less money. Not that I make that much, but I'm making better money here than I have before. I can't even be mad at Brian. It's not his fault. You do what you have to to get ahead. But I'm glad he's off tomorrow. I don't want to see him." Josh shrugged and took another drink of my wine. "Look, I'm beat, and I can't wait to get out of here, but I have to finish up in the kitchen first. If Brian is going to steal my job, he might as well close up tonight. I want to go downstairs and clean up and recheck the coolers. Can you wait another hour or so?"

"Of course. Just don't try to talk to Madeline tonight, okay?"

Josh nodded. "I know, I know. I'd probably kill her if I tried. Oh, crap, I didn't mean that. Probably not something I should go around saying." Josh ran his hands through his hair and took a deep breath. "Why

279

don't you come sit over by the kitchen. I'll make you something to eat, and then you can talk to Brian while I finish up, okay? I've got a great mussel risotto tonight I ran as a special. Sound good?"

I nodded a definite yes and followed him to the counter by the beautiful open kitchen.

Brian was in the middle of plating Josh's fabulous egg rolls. Josh had trained him well: Brian took great care in decorating the dish with sauces from squirt bottles.

"Brian, Chloe's going to sit up here while I finish up downstairs, okay?" Josh said flatly.

"You bet. Good to see you again," Brian said, smiling as he looked up from the plate. "You hungry?"

"I'm getting her some risotto," Josh answered for me.

"You'll love it," Brian assured me.

A few minutes later, I was spooning up the creamy rice dish, which was, of course, phenomenal. The dinner rush was finally dying down, and Brian moved near me as he wiped down the counters.

"Josh is in a pissy mood tonight, huh? You're probably the best thing for him right now."

"Yeah, I heard about the health inspector."

"You should have seen Josh earlier. After the inspector left, Josh was screaming and swearing in the back. Good thing it was before we opened, or the customers would've heard him. He threw a bunch of pans across the room, and he was having a fit until Maddie walked in and told him to cut it out." Brian laughed. "She was so angry because she'd just bought a bunch of new cookware for the kitchen, and she was afraid he was going to break all of it."

This didn't sound like the Josh I'd known for the past few weeks. But he was a chef dedicated to his kitchen—I knew that much.

Brian kept on wiping the counter. "I was just glad she didn't fire him for acting like such an ass. I mean, Josh was lucky enough to get this job. I didn't want him to blow it." Lucky?

"What do you mean he was lucky to get this job?" I asked Brian.

"Well," Brian said as he leaned closer to me, "you probably know about Josh getting fired from the Langley Hotel? And from Spoons?"

I had no idea what Brian was talking about. Josh had said that he'd hopped around a bit before settling down at Magellan, but he never said he'd been fired. Twice.

Brian took my silence as ignorance and informed me that while working as a sous chef at the posh Langley Hotel restaurant, Josh had walked through the dining room shouting obscenities about the incompetent waitstaff and had promptly been terminated. Spoons, another well-known Boston eatery, had fired Josh for smashing a bunch of plates while cussing out the dishwashers for doing a terrible job.

All news to me. My risotto was beginning to lose its flavor, but I nonetheless finished off half of the huge portion Josh had made for me.

"He used to have a pretty mean temper," Brian continued. "But he's been totally great to me. Of course, he got angry today about the fridge and the mice and stuff, but usually he's great. You just don't want to piss him off, that's for sure. If you ask me, all chefs are pretty volatile, but Josh is up there. Love him like a brother, though."

I watched Brian as he finished cleaning the counters, wrapped up meat to be stored, and sharpened the knives that had been used that evening. I'd had no idea about Josh's history of losing his cool, and I didn't know what to think. He took tremendous pride in his cooking and his kitchen; anything that threatened the quality of his work would certainly anger him. Josh's temper must have been what Detective Hurley had been referring to when he'd said that I didn't know Josh that well and had warned me to stay away from him. But Brian must be exaggerating. The restaurant business was so gossipy. The tales of Josh's behavior must have blown up over time. At least I hoped so.

As I watched Brian, I wondered whether Madeline would really replace Josh with someone so inexperienced. He grabbed Josh's sharpening steel and began the chef's ritual of honing the kitchen knives against the rod. Although I was almost mesmerized as he stroked the blades against the steel, I couldn't help thinking how dangerous it was to repeatedly pull the blade toward himself. And he didn't look half as cute as Josh did when he sharpened his knives.

Josh finally finished work, and we stepped out of the restaurant and into the cool, dry evening air of mid-

September. Since he had his car with him, we drove separately back to my place. Josh took a shower and changed into sweatpants. As attractive as he looked with his chest bare, I was remarkably uninterested in leaping under the covers with him. My head was swimming with information I'd acquired that evening, and I didn't know what to make of any of it. We got into bed and lay there a foot apart. For the first time, something felt awkward between us.

Josh looked at me. "I'm so tired. Do you mind if we just go to sleep?" I knew he had to get up before eight and go in to Magellan. The restaurant was closed tomorrow, but an upscale client was having a wedding reception for fifty people at five, and Josh needed to prep for it all day.

He continued. "I've got so much to do for the party tomorrow, and for some stupid reason, I gave Brian the day off. Some of it's prepped, and I've got a couple of the line cooks with me, but still . . ."

"Sure. You need some sleep," I said.

I needed sleep, too; there was no point in staying up half the night trying to make sense of everything. Besides, I'd see Heather tomorrow at the spa, and she'd help me to think things out.

I awoke at three in the morning with horrendous stomach cramps. I rolled over on my side in search of relief. *I must be getting my period,* I thought. But when I'd crawled to the bathroom on my hands and knees, I realized that the pain had nothing to do with my menstrual cycle—and everything to do with food poisoning.

I spent two hours in the bathroom ridding my body of what I kept telling myself was some freakish parasite. Doubled over, all I could think was, *The mussels. The goddamn mussels.* My mind was racing. *Oh my God! Josh gave me the mussels. He did this to me. That's why he kept telling me not to call Detective Hurley,* I thought miserably. *He killed Eric, and now he's murdering me with tainted mussels.*

Wait a minute. That didn't make any sense. Although I *was* a little delirious from dehydration, I was able to understand that food poisoning was an unreliable murder method. Of course, I'd been sick for only a few hours. Maybe the illness would progress until I died right here on my ugly tile floor. While Josh slept peacefully in the other room. Or maybe the food poisoning was a warning? No! The health code violations: the mussels had made me sick because they'd been stored at too warm a temperature. And Josh had served them as a special that night at the restaurant!

I limped to the couch and pulled a blanket over my shivering body. At least Josh hadn't awakened to find me slumped over the toilet. Maybe I should have listened to Heather and to Detective Hurley. It was true that I hardly knew Josh. I hadn't known anything about his outbursts at his previous jobs; the angry side of Josh was one I'd never seen. Realistically, I had no idea who he was.

I heard the clock radio alarm go off in the bedroom at seven forty-five. Prince was hollering that he wanted to be someone's lover. I was still half asleep when Josh walked in and found me in the living room. I tumbled off the couch in dehydrated shambles.

"Hey, what're you doing out here? Oh God, was I snoring or something?"

"I'm sick. I was up all night throwing up," I barked before going to the kitchen for water.

"Oh, honey. Are you okay?" he asked, concerned.

"No. I'm not okay. All I could taste was mussels. Which I will never eat again."

"Oh my God. You must have a stomach bug or something," he called back sympathetically.

I stood in the doorway to the kitchen, angrily clutching my glass of water. "That or the risotto made me sick." I glared at him.

"Wait, you think I gave you bad seafood?" He went to the bedroom and pulled on a shirt.

"All I know is that you gave me dinner, and I puked it up for three hours," I shot back.

"Are you kidding me? You think I'd make you sick on purpose? There was nothing wrong with the food. I just got those mussels in yesterday. They couldn't have been fresher!"

"Fine, then I'm just sick, okay? And, by the way, why didn't you tell me you'd been fired, twice, for throwing raging fits?" I knew I was being unreasonable, but I couldn't stop myself from yelling at him.

Josh was angry now, too. "Who the hell told you that?" he demanded.

"It doesn't matter. I just know, okay?" I was starting to cry. There was barely enough fluid left in my body to produce tears.

"Oh, okay. I get it. So now you think I killed Eric, too, huh? You think I poisoned you because you've been trying to figure out who the murderer is? I'm outta here." Josh threw on his shoes. "Call me when you catch the real murderer, Chloe," Josh snapped as he walked out my back door.

I didn't stop him from leaving.

NINETEEN

"Heather, this is not a spa," I informed my sister. I peeked out of my mummylike wrappings and glared at my monster of a sibling. "We belong in one of the Egyptian rooms at the Museum of Fine Arts."

"Chloe, this is very trendy right now. Try to embrace this experience, and you might actually benefit from it."

Heather had lied to me. *Spa* meant pedicures, facials, relaxing massages. This place, called Wrap It Out, was some bullshit fake of a spa where clients paid *actual money* to be entirely wrapped up in stretchy bandage material, doused with smelly liquid—embalming fluid?—and have supposed toxins extracted from their bodies. I was lying on a padded table, totally immobilized, and stuck there until the spa warden returned to unwrap me.

"Especially," she continued, "after your food poisoning experience. This is the perfect way to completely remove foreign substances from your skin. You won't believe how refreshed you feel after. It's wonderful," she proclaimed, sighing with contentment.

I rolled my head to the left and stuck my tongue out at her. I turned to the right and looked at Adrianna. Heather had surprised me by inviting Ade along for the torture.

"Could we talk about something else, please? Anything to make time go faster?" Ade pleaded from her cocoon.

"Fine," Heather said. "Chloe, keep telling us about Josh and how he tried to murder you last night."

"He did not try to murder me. At least, well, he just couldn't have."

"The point is, you just told us that Josh has a history of unstable behavior and is a definite suspect. I told you you were rushing it," Heather said.

"No, that is not the point at all," I shot back. "Josh is totally pissed off at me because I accused him of assaulting me with bad risotto."

"Look," Adrianna began, spitting a loose bandage off her mouth, "nobody's perfect, but that doesn't mean he had anything to do with Eric's murder or your food poisoning. So what if Josh has been fired? Life is not neat and orderly with everyone behaving in exemplary fashion at all times. Christ, Owen has been fired from zillions of jobs. Before he got the blimp job, he was the personal assistant to a comedian, then he cleaned the shark tank at the Aquarium, and then he was the golf ball marshal at that country club."

"A golf ball marshal?" Heather shrieked. "What kind of job is that?"

"He was very important. Who do you think picks up all the stray golf balls off the course? But the manager found him swimming in the lily pond and asked him not to come back. See? So, Owen got fired from all those jobs, and he's perfectly normal." Ade paused. "Okay, he may be a little *unusual,* but it's just taken him a while to settle in to something. Same thing for Josh. He had to work out some issues at those other restaurants, but he's doing great at Magellan, right? And who cares if he freaks out once in a while? He's *passionate* about his work, which is probably one of the reasons the restaurant is doing so well."

"I guess," I said.

"He sounds dangerous," Heather warned.

"Heather, Josh is no more dangerous than you or I," Adrianna said. "Seriously, do you think I'd let Chloe go out with someone I thought had even the slightest chance of being a killer? Really. I met him, and he's totally into your sister and totally harmless. I know she rushes into every relationship, but that's because she's passionate, just like Josh. Which is why they're such a good match."

"And I think passionate is great. I do. But she also needs to display some sense of caution, guarded optimism, self-control, or whatever you want to call it," Heather elaborated.

"Hi. I'm still here. I'd wave, but I can't move. I know you can't see me behind the wraps, but I can hear you." I felt as if I were in my Group Therapy class again. How had I become everyone's favorite subject of analysis? "Josh did not set out to poison me, okay? And now he's never going to talk to me again."

"Okay, well, if Josh didn't kill Eric Rafferty, who did?" asked Heather.

"I don't know, and I don't care."

When we'd finally been released from our "spa" treatments, I had to admit I did feel pretty good. I said good-bye to Heather and Adrianna and headed to Home Depot. Instead of taking responsibility for my own behavior in the manner advocated at social work school, I'd begun to suspect that it was the unfinished and crooked stripe of paint in my bedroom that was the reason Josh and I hadn't slept together and were now fighting. Who wanted to have sex in that horrid environment? Just to prove how dedicated I was to reforming my unlucky bedroom, I was going to pay *full price* for Ralph Lauren paint. Choosing a color would be easy; my friend Ralph, as I thought of him, limited himself to attractive hues.

I kept the car windows down as I drove; the putrid liquid the evil spa-keepers had poured on my wrappings to detoxify my body was making me queasy. Also, my stomach was empty. I was sorry I'd eaten all of the cookies I'd taken with me last night.

The cookie batter! Made from scratch: with flour, butter, sugar, chocolate chips . . . and fresh eggs. Fresh *raw* eggs.

I was a complete idiot. Josh hadn't poisoned me; I had poisoned myself. Frantic, I yanked my cell phone out of my purse. Josh didn't pick up his cell, and I couldn't blame him. Like an obsessed stalker, I tried back six times in a row but didn't leave any messages. I didn't know what to say or how to apologize for being such a jerk; I just hoped I could make it up to him.

I took a break from my desperate calling to run into Home Depot. It was crowded, as it always was on Sundays, and to get to the paint aisle, I had to fight my way past a crowd inspecting leaf blowers. I'd almost made it to Ralph's paint chip display when the Oops paint cart loomed before me, and I succumbed to my usual sympathetic sense of obligation. I was putting a gallon of what I hoped was a sexy blue with aphrodisiac powers into my cart when someone started loading even more cans of rejected paint onto the shelf. I looked up to see Brian standing before me. He was now clad in an orange store apron instead of the white coat he wore at Magellan.

"Hey, Brian. I didn't know you worked here," I said, completely caught off guard. It was like seeing your math teacher at the mall: teachers existed only on school grounds and had no business materializing in places where they had no reality. Similarly, Josh's sous chef had corporeal form only at Magellan and could have appeared at Home Depot only because of some sort of cosmic accident.

"Chloe," Brian said with surprise. "Hey, what're you doing here?"

"I come here all the time. I have so many cans of Oops paint at home you wouldn't believe it." I paused.

It felt uncanny to talk to Brian outside Magellan. "I can't believe you have the time to work here, too."

"Well, I just work a couple days a week to make a little extra money. This is my section, the paint department. Being a sous chef pays the bills and not much else, so . . ." As his voice trailed off, he shifted from side to side, clearly uncomfortable talking to his chef's girlfriend except at the restaurant. He looked down at my can of paint. "So, um, I gotta go. I have a couple more hours here, and then I might go in to the restaurant to help Josh. I'll see you later, Chloe."

I watched him walk away, staring dumbly at Josh's protégé as he made his way awkwardly to the back of the store. I flinched with embarrassment for him as he tripped over his own feet and bumped into a woman pulling rollers off a shelf.

I pushed my cart with its gallon of paint to the front of the store. Skipping the self-checkout, I went to a human cashier to pay. I was disconcerted and confused and couldn't shake the feeling that there was something off about Brian. He certainly was clumsy; no wonder he'd had so many accidents in the kitchen. I handed over a five-dollar bill, took my receipt, and picked up the can—the can with the neon orange splotch of paint on its lid.

The can marked with the same color as the traces of paint found on Eric's body.

In all that Josh had said about Brian, he'd never mentioned a second job. I wondered whether the police knew about it. And Josh. Did Josh know?

Clutching the gallon of paint, I ran to my car, got in, and tried Josh's cell phone, which he still refused to answer. Damn! Smelly or not, I had to see Josh.

Next I dialed Detective Hurley's number. As I listened to the ring, something else hit me. Last night at Magellan, after Brian had told me about Josh's fits of temper and the jobs he'd lost, Brian had been sharpening the kitchen knives. I now realized that Brian's technique had been the reverse of Josh's. When Josh sharpened a knife, he held it with the blade facing away from him. Brian had done the opposite: instead of safely drawing the sharp blade away from his body, he'd drawn it toward himself. For any chef, even a young sous chef like Brian, it was second nature to sharpen knives all the time. When Josh had made that wonderful dinner for me at my house, he'd brought his own sharp knives, but before using them, what had he done? He'd sharpened them. The practice was ingrained in any chef. If Brian had used Josh's cimiter, there was good chance that he'd sharpened it, not in the men's room at Essence, of course, but at Magellan, when he'd first picked it up. The police had the cimiter, which had undoubtedly undergone close forensic examination. A forensics expert would certainly be able to determine whether the blade had been honed by someone who pulled it toward him along a sharpening steel, as Brian did, or by someone who moved the blade away from his body, as Josh did. But had the experts looked *for* that difference? What did forensics experts and police detectives know about *chefs?* And about chefs' all-but-instinctive habit of putting razor edges on the blades of all the knives they touched?

I finally got the detective's voice mail and, speaking more quickly than clearly, said that I was on my way to Magellan, that Brian worked in the paint department at Home Depot, that chefs sharpen knives all the time without even thinking about it, and that different chefs sharpen their knives differently! I hung up only to have Detective Hurley call me right back.

"I couldn't understand anything you said on the message," he said with annoying calm.

I explained my theory as best I could while peeling around corners and beeping at cars to get out of my way. I simply *had* to warn Josh about his murderous colleague! I told Detective Hurley about the orange paint used to mark Oops paint cans and informed him that Brian worked in the department that sold Oops paint. I asked the detective to find out whether or not the murder weapon had been examined for evidence about how it had been sharpened and who had sharpened it. Maybe differences in sharpening techniques even revealed themselves in wounds? I was willing to bet that the medical examiner could examine photographs taken during the autopsy and confirm that Josh's sharpening style was inconsistent with Eric's neck wound. But that Brian's style was a perfect match.

"Chloe, I appreciate your desire to help, but you need to go home. You're done for the day," Hurley barked at me.

"Okay, okay. I'm just going to Magellan to find Josh, and then I'll disappear."

"Go home now."

"I'm turning the car around as we speak," I lied before saying good-bye. In fact, I'd pulled into a residents-only spot around the corner from Magellan. I raced out of the car and to the front of the restaurant. Magellan was closed, as I knew it would be, but I tried the locked door anyway. Josh must be hard at work in the kitchen preparing food for the wedding party. I pounded on the door but got no response. Peeking through the window, I saw no one. The lights in the dining area were off, but the kitchen lights were on. Josh had to be around somewhere. Sprawled on the floor with a neck wound identical to Eric's? Or with a knife sticking out of his chest?

There had to be another entrance to the restaurant, a delivery entrance at the back. I rushed around the corner and past my car, and came to an alley that ran behind Magellan. My heart was pounding as I entered the alley and tried to determine which door was the restaurant's. As it turned out, the correct door was easy to identify because someone else was also trying to get into Magellan: Timothy Rock.

"Chloe! What are you doing here?" he asked. "Oh, that's right. I heard that you and Josh are an item. That's great news." Although Tim smiled at me, he looked harried, probably because Essence was failing. I couldn't blame its owner for having left a button undone on his flannel shirt or for having missed a patch of whiskers when he'd shaved.

"I'm looking for Josh. The front door is locked, though, so I thought I'd come around the back." I banged on the door.

"Me, too. I tried my old keys in the front, but they didn't work. I can't believe Maddie changed the locks. Why would she do that to me?" Tim looked hurt and pitiful.

"It might have nothing to do with you, Tim," I tried to reassure him. "Maybe she fired someone who had keys or someone lost the keys or something." Worried about Josh, I rapped on the door with my knuckles until they hurt.

"Speaking of firing people," Tim turned to me. "The reason I'm here is that I've been trying to reach Maddie all morning, but she isn't answering the phone. Home, work, cell. But I've got to warn her about one of my waiters. This guy used to work for us at Magellan, and Maddie sent him over to me because she knew I needed someone strong to lead the waitstaff. Turns out, though, he's been stealing money from me, and he was probably stealing from Magellan, too. I fired him last night, and I want to make sure Maddie doesn't take him back."

"I'm pretty sure she won't."

Tim looked puzzled.

I mustered all the social worker sensitivity I could. "I hate to tell you this, but Madeline knew about Ian's scams. That's why she let him go."

Tim stared blankly at me.

"Josh!" I bellowed. "Josh, open the door!" After again banging it, I said to Tim, "About Madeline and the waiter. I'm so sorry. I'm not sure why she did it. Damn it! Josh! Josh, open up!"

"No," Tim said, "you're wrong. I don't know how you *think* you know that, Chloe, but you don't know Madeline. She would *never* have knowingly sent me a crook. She was great throughout our divorce, and she's done nothing but try to help me with Essence. You've got your story mixed up on this."

"It's Ian, right? The waiter you're talking about?"

Tim nodded in surprise. "Yes," he started slowly. "But you're still wrong. And since you seem to know all the restaurant gossip, you probably know that Maddie kept Veronica on as her bookkeeper. So you can see, there were no hard feelings there," he announced triumphantly.

Tim and Veronica? He had to be kidding. "Look," I said, "I have to talk to Josh." Inspiration struck. "Do you have a key to this door? Maybe she just changed the front locks."

"Got it," Tim said, working his key into the lock. His satisfied look said, *See? I told you so.* He swung the door open.

Ahead of us was a dimly lit hall with a flight of stairs running down on the left and, on the right, a corridor that led to Magellan's lovely open kitchen. This corridor, unlike the corresponding one at Essence, was obviously for employees only; the floor was covered in linoleum, a clipboard with loose papers hung from a nail, and the overall appearance was slightly shabby. I wondered whether it had been Madeline who'd advised Tim to locate Essence's restrooms almost next to an exit that provided a convenient means of escape for patrons skipping out on their bills—and had allowed Eric's murderer to vanish, too, of course. As I'd seen when I'd peered in from the main entrance, the kitchen lights were on. It immediately became apparent that Josh was here at Magellan, not in the open kitchen, but somewhere down the flight of stairs. Josh's voice echoed through the hallway and stairway, as did loud crashes. I followed Tim downstairs to the lower level of Magellan.

"Josh is in a mood, I guess," Tim whispered to me. "He can get a little wild sometimes." Tim grabbed my elbow and stopped me. "Chloe, you need to know something. Josh is a great guy and a great chef."

"But?" I prodded.

Tim let out a big sigh. "He's got a mean temper. And you can't expect him to be in a great mood these days. After all, the knife used to kill Eric Rafferty was Josh's. And he knows how to use it. He has no alibi for the night of the murder." He paused. "You should think about whether or not this is the kind of person you want to be involved with."

"Get out of here, you little bitch!" Josh shouted. There followed a loud clatter of metal.

Then Madeline's voice. "Stop it! Get away from me!"

My heart was pumping ferociously. Josh was

attacking Madeline! Tim pushed past me and flung open the door to what proved to be a storage area and lower kitchen with stacks of boxes, a gigantic stainless-steel sink, long counters, a zillion-burner gas range, a walk-in refrigerator, and big pots and pans suspended from hooks.

Josh stood a few feet away from Madeline, his forehead covered in sweat, a large cast-iron sauté pan raised above his head. Madeline was backed into a corner of the room. She look petrified.

"What the hell is going on here?" Tim demanded.

TWENTY

My heart broke as I stared at Josh, who stood poised with the heavy cast-iron pan, ready to attack the terrified Madeline. I'd been wrong about Brian. It was Josh who had killed Eric.

"Josh," Tim ordered, "drop the pan and move away from Maddie. Now!"

Frozen with a look of utter confusion on his face, Josh stared numbly at Tim and me. "Hey, guys. What are you two doing here?"

With no warning, Tim lunged at Josh and, with a mock-Samurai howl, collided with him so fiercely that he and Josh crashed to the floor.

"Tim, what in God's name are you doing? Have you lost your mind?" Madeline rushed over to her ex-husband and her chef, who were now tangled in a heap. "Good Lord, get off him!" She pulled Tim's shoulders and managed to haul him off Josh.

Bewildered and relieved, I had no idea what was going on but realized that Madeline had not been the intended victim of an assault. I went over to a stunned Josh and helped him to sit up. "Are you okay?"

"Yeah, I'm fine. Pissed off"—he glared at Tim—"but fine."

The ex-spouses were now facing off. Madeline went first. "Could you please explain what the hell you were doing hurling yourself at my chef?"

"Protecting you! I walk in here, and he's about to bash you over the head with that pan." Tim defended himself.

Madeline rolled her eyes and snorted in disgust. "Rats. We have rats."

"Oh," Tim said sheepishly.

"You know how I hate those filthy creatures! And I just saw two of them running toward me when you walked in here and jumped on Josh like some sort of kung fu asshole." She bent over, grabbed the pan that had fallen to the floor, and waved it at Tim. "He just happened to have this sauté pan in his hand, and he started yelling at the little vermin. What the hell is wrong with you!"

"Well, what about the mess in here?" Tim asked.

I hadn't noticed when we'd first walked in, but there were pans everywhere, stainless-steel bowls on the floor, cooking utensils scattered around. I looked at Josh, who admitted, "It's my fault. I was pissed off about the health code violations we were cited for and everything else going on, and I just started throwing crap around. That must've been what scared the rats out from hiding. I was ready to fling a pan at one of them when you walked in." He shrugged his shoulders. "Probably not the best way to exterminate, but I was going to give it a shot," he said grumpily.

So, the stories about Josh's bad temper were more than unfounded gossip.

"Josh," Madeline said firmly, "I told you that the problems in the kitchen are not your fault. You have got to calm down. I hate rats more than anyone, but I'm not blaming you. You are a phenomenal chef, okay? So relax."

"If I'm such a phenomenal chef, why did you tell Brian he was getting my job? Can you explain that to me?"

I had no idea why Josh had picked this moment to make good on his promise to me to have an open and honest talk with Madeline. His timing was dreadful; everyone was too heated to have a rational discussion about anything.

Maddie looked taken aback by Josh's words, but I couldn't tell whether she was surprised at his knowledge of her plan or shocked at the lunacy of such a possibility.

But Tim wasn't done with his ex. "Speaking of explanations, why did you send Ian over to Essence? I just found out that you knew he'd been stealing from us at Magellan. And you recommended him to me anyway. What have I ever done to deserve this kind of

300

treatment from you?" Poor Tim looked sad and confused.

More interested in Josh's question, I spoke up. "Madeline, what about what Josh just asked you? Are you really going to make Brian the executive chef?" As a good clinician should, I was trying to refocus the discussion on the relevant issues and help the group make sense of a convoluted situation. Mainly, I was on Josh's side and didn't want him to get fired.

Maddie looked directly at Josh. "Why would I ever fire you, Josh? You're one of the best chefs in Boston. I'm not about to lose you. Why would you even think that?"

From the doorway came a new voice, a loud and angry one. "Because that's what you told me."

Josh, Madeline, Tim, and I all turned to see an enraged Brian facing us. In cold, menacing tones, he said, "You told me the job was mine."

Madeline took a few steps toward Brian and spoke vehemently, "Brian, I don't know what's going on here, but I'm beginning to think that *you're* the cause of all the accidents and the health code violations here. You left those dead mice. And all the rest. Is that right?"

"This is Josh's kitchen," said Brian, sounding like one child blaming another, "and anything that happens here is because of him. But you know what? It's time for things to change. You told me you were going to get rid of Josh and make me the executive chef."

"Josh, you can come work for me!" Tim sounded

overjoyed at what he probably saw as the salvation of Essence.

Maddie spun around and glowered at Tim. "So now you're going to steal my chef, too? First you leave me, then you open Essence, which is almost an *exact duplicate* of Magellan, and now you want my chef, too?" Seething, Madeline walked slowly toward Tim and spoke deliberately. "You want the best chef in the city? Too bad. You had him. And you gave him up and left, all because of your little blonde whore." She snickered. "And you wonder why I sent you Ian? You are so stupid! You didn't begin to guess."

Tim backed into a corner and practically shriveled up.

Brian, however, was still preoccupied with his boss's false promises. His face showed shock, but his voice revealed rage. "The best chef in the city? What about *me?*" Brian screamed. "What about *ME!*"

"Brian," I said gently, "I think Madeline lied to you."

Brian looked at me for the first time. "Did you follow me here, Chloe?" he demanded furiously.

I took a step back to position myself close to Josh. "No, I didn't follow you, Brian. I came here to warn Josh about you."

"Warn me about Brian?" Josh asked, confused. "What do you mean?"

"He works at Home Depot. In the paint section. Where he uses neon orange spray paint to label cans of paint. Probably the same paint found near Eric's body," I stammered out. I started to shake. "And the knife," I continued, "the two of you sharpen your knives differently, and—"

"Shut up, Chloe!" Brian shouted. "Shut up! You don't know what you're talking about! Everything that's gone wrong is Madeline's fault!" He turned back to Madeline, his eyes full of tears and fury. "You bitch! I did everything you asked me to. Everything! You promised me!" With speed and agility surprising in someone so clumsy, Brian reached to his right and grabbed a lethal-looking knife from the counter. It was six or eight inches long and had a thin, narrow blade. I had a vague recollection that it was meant for skinning or perhaps for boning fish. "You promised me!" He held the knife out in front of him, his hand surprisingly steady.

Uninterested in heroism, I backed up yet more and bumped into something. Turning my head, I saw that I was resting against the rim of the gigantic stainless-steel restaurant sink, which had mammoth draining racks and an oversized sprayer. When I looked forward, Brian was moving in on Madeline, his arm raised, the knife heading toward her throat.

Then, with no warning, Josh rushed at Brian.

In terror, I turned rapidly around, grabbed the industrial-strength water sprayer from the sink, aimed, and squeezed its trigger. Before Josh could take another step toward the shining blade in his sous chef's hand, a massive, powerful jet of water caught him in the back of the head, knocked him off balance, and saved him from the knife-wielding Brian. Soaked in cold water, Josh yelped in surprise.

With superb presence of mind, Madeline, who'd continued to hold the cast-iron pan in both hands, raised it high in the air, moved toward Brian, took an audible breath, and smashed the pan down hard on the crown of Brian's head. Twice. He fell to the floor, and Madeline raised the pan yet again and was about to deliver a final blow when Tim grabbed her by the waist and pulled her away.

"Jesus Christ. Okay, Maddie. He's down. It's over."

Josh got up and rushed over to Brian, who was curled up on the floor and clutching his head in agony. It was hard to believe that he was still conscious.

"Oh my God. Brian." Josh leaned over him.

Brian managed to open his eyes and to speak softly and hoarsely. "I'm so sorry, Josh." Brian began sobbing. "You know I didn't take your knife, right? I know better. No one touches your knives, like you always say. I wouldn't do that, Josh. I'd never do that if you said not to."

With gruff affection, Josh replied, "I know you wouldn't. So who did?"

"Maddie. She gave it to me."

"No!" screamed Maddie, who was still in Tim's grip. "I didn't do anything. It was Brian! He did it! He killed Eric!"

Brian shook his head a little. I had to strain to hear him. "She said she'd make me executive chef. She said she'd give me your job. That's all I wanted, Josh. I just wanted to be like you. I didn't mean to get you in trouble, Josh. With the health code stuff, you know? But I figured you'd be okay, right? And I didn't mean for you to get hurt by the fire or the knife I put in the drawer. I just wanted to get you out of the kitchen for a while so I could have my chance." He looked up at me. "Chloe, you're right about everything. About the paint, about . . . She said she had to destroy Essence."

I had to ask. "Did you sharpen the knife before you killed Eric?"

"Yeah," Brian nodded. "And then, that night, when Maddie told me to, I just snuck over to Essence. No one even paid any attention to me. Ever. No one ever even noticed me." Brian passed out.

Josh pulled his cell phone out of his pocket. I saw him dial 911.

"Josh," I said, "remember you told me Maddie kept calling Tim that night to check on how things were going with Eric? She was waiting to see if there was an opportunity to send Brian over to kill Eric."

Madeline began ranting. Brian was delusional, she claimed. He had a concussion and was delirious. He was imagining things! Who could believe—

"Madeline, shut up!" Josh snapped before telling the 911 operator to send an ambulance and the police to Magellan and giving the restaurant's address.

I guessed that it would take the paramedics and police at least ten minutes to show up. I was wrong. In no time, Detective Hurley came bursting in through the back door. "Chloe, I told you to go home. You're not on the payroll, you know," he huffed. Looming over the unconscious Brian, he said, "Forensics is running a check on the knife as we speak. What happened here?"

I sighed. "Brian isn't the only person in major trouble here."

The detective looked to Josh.

"No," I said, "not Josh. Madeline." I gestured behind me. "She convinced Brian to murder Eric. She promised to make him her executive chef. Her divorce from Tim wasn't the amicable parting of ways everyone thought. She hated Tim. She wanted to see him suffer. She wanted Essence to fail. Getting Brian to murder Eric guaranteed that he wouldn't put money into the restaurant, and at the same time, it tarnished Essence's reputation. Brian admitted it before he passed out."

"Where'd she go?" he asked.

I looked toward the spot where Tim and Maddie had been standing. They had disappeared.

TWENTY ONE

At eleven o'clock the next morning, I snuggled up to Josh and kissed him awake. "Hi, sleepy," I murmured.

"Hey, babe." Josh gave a stretch and growl of contentment. "Finally," he sighed.

"I know. I was starting to doubt whether we'd ever—"

"Oh, but we did," he cut in. "And it was *goood!*" He laughed. To prove his point, he moved on top of me.

306

When we finally emerged from the bedroom, I went to the kitchen and opened the new coffeemaker Josh had bought for me. When Detective Hurley had finally finished questioning us on the previous day, we'd left Magellan and both gotten into Josh's Xterra. I'd been too shaky to drive and had yet again left my car illegally parked.

"We're going to get you a new coffeepot," Josh had announced. "And then I'm taking you home, making love to you all night, and waking up to—what will it be? An improved cup of coffee. Among other things."

In fact, we decided to spend the entire day making coffee. So to speak. And other things. I called in sick to my field placement. I'd eventually have to return to Naomi and her miniature office, where I'd be drowned in syrupy hugs and forced to participate in hand-holding that I couldn't face yet. As it turned out, Josh, on the other hand, didn't even have a job to go to.

Here's why. When Tim and Madeline disappeared from Magellan, they didn't flee to some exotic country or do anything else juicy and dramatic. Rather, the police found them together at Essence. In spite of everything Tim had just seen and heard, he refused to believe that Madeline had participated in arranging Eric's murder. As Josh and I learned when Tim called on Wednesday, he was so outraged at the accusation against dear Maddie that he had hired the best criminal defense lawyer in Boston to represent her. Tim's loyalty to his ex-wife failed, however, to stop him from begging Josh to come to work for him at Essence. On Thursday, when he again called to try to steal Madeline's chef, we learned just how good the lawyer was: Madeline wasn't even in custody. As Tim pointed out, it was Brian's word against hers. Despite Brian's injuries, he actually was capable of speech, or so Tim reported. Unlike Madeline, he was, however, in no financial position to hire a lawyer and was consequently in the hands of a court-appointed defense attorney. What's more, the evidence against him was and remains strong. He'll probably go to prison and, specifically, to a prison kitchen. At least he'll have a chance to keep cooking, and the other inmates will no doubt notice a remarkable improvement in the food.

On Friday, Tim quit trying to lure Josh to work at Essence, which he had finally decided to close. To my astonishment, he informed us that he was rejoining Madeline at Magellan. I assume that Madeline was taking back her ex as a ploy to convince everyone of her innocence. In any case, the newly reunited couple, angry at Josh's continued insistence on Madeline's guilt, immediately fired Josh.

Madeline, with her usual spin-doctor charm, used all of her media contacts to play the story in her favor. She skillfully presented herself as a superlative restaurant owner who gave a troubled young sous chef a chance to work in a top restaurant. Unfortunately, the young man was more disturbed than she'd known and had gone to extreme lengths to climb the culinary ladder. In her version of the story, Brian was furious at her for not promoting him and killed Eric in an attempt to frame her. Oh, please. Tim was welcome to her. When asked why her executive chef was leaving, Madeline insisted that it was a mutual parting of ways and that she wished Josh Driscoll the best. Bitch. As it turns out, Madeline was far from the generous, giving, supportive ex-wife everyone thought she was. So much for my personality assessment skills. I'd have to read up on pathological lying, among other things. God, wait until I got back to Group Therapy; my classmates would have a field day with me.

That weekend, as Josh was cooking another phenomenal dinner for me, I asked him what would happen to all the staff from Essence. Cassie and Katrina? Joelle? Garrett and his kitchen staff?

"See? That's why you're in social work school. God, I haven't even thought about those guys." Josh shook a hot skillet full of squash, mushrooms, and red peppers. "I'm not sure. They're all great. Some of them might go back to Magellan, but I definitely know that Garrett's out of a job. Tim's blaming him, among other people, for Essence doing so badly. I'm sure I'll run into some of them again. Boston is not that big a town. Every time I go out to eat I see someone I know working there. Anywhere." He smiled at me. "They'll be okay, don't worry."

"And what about you? Do you have any leads on another job yet?" I knew Josh was miserable about losing the best cooking gig he'd ever had. And for having had so much faith in Madeline.

"No. I've got some calls in to friends around town,

but there aren't that many good chef jobs out there. There's some crappy stuff, you know, working in corporate cafeterias, universities, all that stuff. Those have good benefits, at least."

Oh, no. The thought of Josh's talent going to waste in a college dining hall made me sick to my stomach. "No, Josh. You are not taking a job like that. There's got to be something else."

"We'll see," he said with obvious doubt in his voice. "I've got a headhunter to call, too. He might have something."

"I'm sure he will. Anyone would be lucky to have you." I stood behind him and wrapped my arms around his chest. "Oh, hey. I've been meaning to ask you. Did you know that Tim and Veronica had a thing together? He told me that before we went into Magellan."

"I didn't know about that one until Maddie called her a blonde whore. But I'm sure Veronica's downstairs right now with Noah, if you want to go ask her about it. Half those people have slept with the other half, but I had no idea about Tim and Veronica. I always tried to keep out of the gossip since I could never keep up with it anyway."

"Are you telling me you weren't *ever* part of that gossip?" I teased.

"Of course not. I was all innocent and sweet until you corrupted me." He pretended to wipe a tear from his eye. "And, truthfully, I'm feeling a little vulnerable right now."

"I intend to take full advantage of that. Right after you finish cooking." I hugged Josh tighter. "Oh, and what about Ian? I can't imagine Tim would give him a reference!"

"Not likely, but he'll get another job somewhere, no problem."

I guess the Ians of the world are everywhere. Perfect chefs, of course, are not. But I got lucky. I found mine.

RECIPES

You don't have to be a professional chef to make the romantic dinner that Josh served to Chloe. Here are the recipes for all three courses. Notice that many steps in the preparation may be completed well ahead of time. *Bon appétit!*

Bibb and Radicchio Salad
with Three-Tomato Vinaigrette

1 head Bibb lettuce
1 head radicchio
2 ounces goat cheese, dry enough to crumble

Remove the stems from the Bibb and radicchio, and wash and dry the leaves very carefully. Layer the leaves, alternating colors, on individual serving plates. Use four or five leaves of each. Drizzle with the tomato vinaigrette and then crumble the goat cheese around the leaves.

Three-Tomato Vinaigrette

1 red tomato
1 green tomato
1 yellow tomato
1 tbsp. minced garlic
2 tbsp. red onion, diced

2 tbsp. fresh oregano or ½ tbsp. dried
2 tbsp. fresh marjoram or ½ tbsp. dried
½ tbsp. honey
¼ cup white balsamic vinegar or champagne
 vinegar
½ cup extra virgin olive oil
Salt and pepper, to taste

Cut the tomatoes in half and scoop out and discard the seeds and liquid. Dice up enough tomato to make one cup, and place in a bowl with the garlic, onion, and herbs. (If you are using fresh herbs, remove the leaves from the stems and add whole to the dressing.) Mix in honey, vinegar, and oil, and season to taste with salt and pepper. Let the dressing stand for at least an hour before serving, or make the day before and store in the refrigerator.

Spiced Tuna

2 tsp. minced garlic
2 tsp. minced fresh ginger
2 tsp. ground cumin
2 tsp. ground coriander
4 tbsp. olive oil
2 fresh tuna steaks, approximately 7 ounces each,
 preferably 3 inches thick
½ tsp. salt
½ tsp. pepper
1 tsp. sugar

Mix the garlic, ginger, cumin, and coriander with the oil. Rub both sides of the tuna steaks with this mixture and let them sit for approximately 30 minutes. Heat a large pan on medium-high heat. While waiting for the pan to get perfectly hot, sprinkle tuna with the salt, pepper, and sugar. Sear tuna on both sides for 1½ minutes per side. The tuna should be very rare inside, with a beautiful seared crust on the outside. Serve with the cardamom sweet rice and bok choy slaw. If you'd like, you can drizzle the plate with a little sweet soy to enhance the flavors.

Baby Bok Choy Slaw

2 heads of baby bok choy
1 tbsp. honey
¼ cup rice wine vinegar
½ cup salad oil
1 tsp. ground coriander
2 tsp. salt
1 tsp. pepper
1 red pepper, julienne
1 yellow pepper, julienne
¼ cup cilantro, whole leaves

Cut off the stem from the bok choy and julienne (thinly slice) the entire head.

To make the dressing, mix together the honey, vinegar, oil, coriander, and salt and pepper. Let the dressing sit out at room temperature to have the flavors meld together.

Mix the peppers and bok choy together and gently toss with the dressing. You may serve the slaw cold, or you may heat it for a minute or two in a hot skillet. Don't actually cook the slaw, but heat it up just enough for the bok choy leaves to begin to wilt. Garnish with fresh cilantro.

Cardamom Sweet Rice

1 cup sushi rice
¼ cup sweet soy sauce
1 bunch chopped scallions
1½ tsp. cardamom
1 tsp. ground coriander
1½ tsp. sesame oil
½ tsp. salt

If you have a rice cooker, cook the sushi rice in it with 2 cups of water. If not, you may cook the rice on the stove top, following directions on the brand you use. Simply mix the rest of the ingredients with the hot rice and serve.

Warm Chocolate Cake

*5½ ounces dark chocolate (not baking
   chocolate), preferably Valrhona
5½ ounces butter
3 eggs
3 egg yolks
¾ cup sugar
⅓ cup all purpose flour
fresh berries or other seasonal fruit
ice cream*

Preheat oven to 400°.

Melt the dark chocolate and butter together over low heat and set aside. Using a whisk or an electric mixer, whip the eggs and the yolks together with the sugar until the mixture turns pale yellow and almost doubles in volume. Using a spatula, gently fold in the chocolate mixture and then the flour. Let the batter sit for about an hour or until it is somewhat firm. Fill small brioche molds (or other individual-size oven-safe nonstick dishes) about three-fourths of the way up with the batter. Bang the dishes on the counter to make sure the batter fills up all of the crevices. Place the molds on a cookie sheet and bake for 4 to 7 minutes. The edges should feel set, but the center (about a quarter-size area) should still be jiggly.

Do not overbake the cake, or you will lose the delicious, gooey center. Unmold cakes and serve with ice cream and fresh fruit.

If you use very high-quality chocolate, extra batter may be kept in the refrigerator for later use.